FROM MOURNING TO DANCING

HEATHER CAMACHO

RENEWED HEARTS | BOOK TWO

FROM MOURNING TO DANCING

HEATHER CAMACHO

FOR MY YOUNGER SELF — *I'm sorry I ever doubted you.*

FOR MY MOMMY — *Thank you for <u>never</u> doubting me.*

JARED

1

Two hundred and thirty pounds of muscle, determination, and gear sought me out through the masses, then barreled toward me. The trick play was in motion. The real hand-off had been made to me, and although only one of the opposition had picked up on it, he was ready to pounce.

"Two o'clock!" I shouted to Dan, who moved up for a right tackle. After four years of playing together, Daniel Schellers and I had teamwork down to a science. Over time, we became an unstoppable force. It was no wonder he'd also become my best friend in the process. We played together and partied together, and that's how it always was.

A chill ran the length of my spine, one I had to shake off quickly. *Keep your focus, Tomlin. Fifty-six is heading right for you.* Shaking loose any errant thoughts before they took hold, I redirected myself to the task at hand—the ball in my grasp. It was the final game of the season. Scouts from two universities were there to watch. This was my opportunity. I had only one goal.

Get that ball down the field, Jared! Dead or not, Dad is watching.

Letting fifty-six come at me, I continued my diagonal trajectory. At the last second, I juked to the left, rushing infield, taking the path my linemen created. My opening was there; the play was working. Sliding through the throngs like butter, I lengthened my stride, opening up and gunning it for a twelve-yard touchdown. Not my career best, but certainly something inspiring for the scouts to witness.

The band leaped into their victory song, and everyone in the stands stood to their feet, clapping. Color guard ran across the sidelines, proudly displaying our school colors and mascot. The cheerleaders jumped into their celebratory cheer and dance number, and when it was over, they threw goodie bags into the crowd, where eager hands received them, fueling the excitement.

In the beginning of the final quarter, we'd managed to lose our lead. For most of the evening, the score had been much too close. With a glance at the scoreboard, I released a pent-up breath. We only had two minutes and forty-five seconds left to gain extra ground and recover the game.

Then came the grand finale in the form of my winning touchdown. Mine. I did that for us, for the team, and for my family. What an incredible finish to my final high school season. By the satisfied look on Coach Haworth's face as he ran onto the field, arms out, smiling wildly as he celebrated with us, he agreed.

"And that's a wrap for the Corpus Christi Titans, with a sensational final victory," hailed the commentator, his voice crackling over the speaker with the thrill of our win. The roaring in my ears drowned out the rest of his acclamation.

Coach gathered us in the locker room, and we filled up the benches, some of us sitting right on the floor.

"Congratulations, fellas," Coach began. "What a marvelous finish to our season! You should all feel very proud of yourselves. Especially you, seniors. Stand back up, please." Coach Haworth led the locker room in our own round of applause. Alongside the seven others who just played our last game, Dan and I stood, exhausted, sweaty, and, if I'm being honest, a little misty in the eyes.

"Everyone did their best tonight, and it really counted. We haven't had to push that hard in a long time. Portland really hoped to show us up. Good thing they did because you all came through in a big way. The scouts out there got one heck of a show, and these boys right here were given the send-off of a lifetime. Some of you younger ones may forget this game, but these nine won't. Congratulations, Titans!" Coach threw his fist up with gusto, and it riled everyone all over again. Voices rose with increased vigor and palms slammed against the benches. He was right. I'd never forget this game.

After showering and dressing, I emptied my locker. It was modestly packed and lacked decorations, save for the picture of me and Dad when I was little, so it didn't take long. Closing it for the last time, a strange mixture of emotions hit me. Sadness, because my dad wasn't there. Excitement, because the scouts were. Leaving football for the rest of the year would be hard, but I reminded myself it wasn't forever, just for now.

A heavy hand came down on my shoulder. "Crazy, isn't it?"

I turned to see Coach. "Yeah, it really is. All of that, all those years, and now it's just done."

"You'll feel that way about high school, too. Graduation will be here before you know it. And after that, maybe a bit of conditioning to keep you in shape before college starts." His voice edged around the news I had been waiting for all season long.

"Did an offer come in?"

"Officially, I can't say. Unofficially, make sure you stay fit, and keep your nose clean when you go off and celebrate tonight. You know what I'm saying?"

Party less. Train more. "Got it. Thank you, Coach. I really needed this."

"You're welcome, Jared. You have talent, but even if they hadn't picked you, you would still have value. True fulfillment isn't found in worldly achievements, even though they feel great, don't they?" He smiled. "Football isn't all you are. When you take off to college to play next fall, you try to remember that."

There was nothing to remember. If I had a spot on the university team, then I was golden. I needed this for so many reasons, namely, the two who were waiting for me out in the stadium. If not for them, then for my dad. I wanted him to be proud of me, too.

"Thanks, Coach."

"Have a good night. Be safe."

Dan was emptying his locker, too. As I approached, he withdrew a flask. "You ready to celebrate, superstar?" he asked, taking a swig.

I grabbed it when he handed it to me. "Sure am," I said between swallows as Coach Haworth's warning rang in my mind. With a new scholarship on the line, I'd have to take it easy. It wasn't worth getting smashed and risking botching a meeting if the scout called one. But a couple of drinks couldn't hurt. We'd earned it.

"Excellent. I'll meet you in the parking lot once you shake your par— er, mom..." He flicked a quick glance to see if I'd noticed, and I did my best not to let on. It'd been a year and a half since my dad died, and sometimes even I forgot. I wouldn't hold it against him for the slip-up.

"Sounds good," I said, letting him off the hook.

Making my way out of the locker room, pushing past people who wanted to congratulate me, I finally reached my mom and brother. "It's about time, hotshot," Jeremy said.

Mom threw her arms around me. I could tell she had been crying, and my heart constricted. She made me feel so cringy sometimes. "That was an amazing game, Jared." She squeezed thoroughly and then withdrew. Putting her hands on my shoulders, she took a good look at me. "Your dad would be so proud. *So* proud."

"Thanks, Mom."

"And I'm so proud, too," she said. "This is going to change things for us all, Jared. You're going places." What she didn't have to mention were all the perks and benefits that would come with a recruited placement in college ball. "If only your dad were here to see you."

Yeah, if only he were.

SAMMY

2

THE SUN BEAT down on the six of us as the game raged on, growing more intense by the minute. Jenna had her arms spread out, ready to throw her weight into darting in whichever direction was necessary. I assumed my crouched position, wiggling my toes against the sand, taking a firm foothold. No distraction could penetrate my extreme focus and get in the way of my victory, not even the alluring crashing of Padre Island's waves beside us nor the squawking gulls above. When that ball came my way, I would be prepared to spring into action, with intent to destroy, spiking it fast into Jared and Dan's faces. They wouldn't know what hit them.

"Hurry up and decide on your next move, boys. Though it won't make a difference. You're going to lose," I helpfully informed them. It wouldn't matter which of them served or where they aimed. Jenna and I had this game in the bag.

"She's right. Might as well give it up, boys," Sarah called from the confines of her tent, drawing our gazes to her small, unzipped window. She'd retreated to her solitude a while ago, and I wasn't aware she was paying attention to us. She still seemed pretty preoccupied with why her boyfriend Kevin wasn't among us. As much as I wanted to dig deeper into whatever was going on, I had to let it go for the time being. We were all there to relax and enjoy the night, not to grill each other.

"The game isn't over until it's over," Dan barked.

Jared laughed off our threats, finding humor in his eventual humiliation, while Dan was busy deciding on their next play. He rolled the ball in a stationary spin between his hands with a determined look of concentration on his beach-pinked face. Beside him, Jared's tropical button-up billowed, exposing and covering his torso over and over again. *That* was only the slightest bit distracting.

Bolting upright, Jenna had grown weary of her prepared stance since her boyfriend was taking too long to put the ball into play. "Seriously, Daniel. I'm pretty sure I feel grey hairs growing in."

"Yeah, and I'm pretty sure I can see them!"

From her perfectly manicured lounge area on the sidelines, Birdie Jo hooded her hand over her eyes, pretending to squint in Jenna's direction. Birdie wore a neon pink bucket hat, under which her golden curls spilled out with flawless curation. Her entire towel spread was covered expertly by a six-foot wide umbrella, anchored deeply into the sand, protecting her delicate, creamy white skin from the power of the sun. Our Birdie Jo was all parts beauty queen, save for the conceit and conspiracies.

"That's not funny," Jenna fired back, but I turned away and snickered, giving Birdie a wink of solidarity.

Light-heartedness was the best way we all knew how to deal

with Jenna's eccentrics. The girl was barely eighteen and freak-ishly vain. While she and Birdie shared the desire for hair perfec-tion, Birdie came at it from a place of joy. Caring for her appearance made her happy, whereas Jenna used her bad hair days as an excuse to complain.

"Chill, woman. The men are ready to serve now."

The girls and I snickered, rolling our eyes almost one after the other. Dan and Jared exchanged glances, and after a decisive nod, the ball was hot.

"Oh, please," came Jenna's reprimanding tone as she watched the ball soar way too far overhead. I could only laugh because these boys knew they always lost to us. No amount of big talk would change that, but it sure was entertaining to watch them try. If anything, today would be a testament to the legacy I was leaving behind. For my own sense of worth, it was essential I played a good game here.

When the ball came to our side, it was hectic and easily handled. Dan could put a lot of force into a hit, but his form was sloppy; therefore, his attempts were aimless. Nearly every time they served the ball, it was out of bounds. He and his cohort really made dominating them too easy. It almost wasn't fun.

Almost. Winning, in general, was always fun.

My final season of high school volleyball was already over (and we ended with a winning streak. You're welcome), but it took a lot longer for the season to leave me than it did for me to want to leave the season. Letting go was a work in progress. Even when school was finally out, and there wasn't a net, ball, or timer in sight, I was sure I would still miss it all. The best I could do was make every game I played now count, even if it was only a handful of friends running around the beach for fun.

Del Mar, the local community college I'd considered attending, didn't have competitive sports teams, so, assuming that's where I end up, beach games with friends could be all the volleyball I had left.

That was okay with me though. I had a great run as Sammy "The Bull" Ballard, six years strong. It was time to hang up my horns and move on to the adult things in life, like English 101 and Texas History. But that was for Fall Sammy to worry about. Spring Sammy was still on break and out for proverbial blood.

The game didn't last long, though some tension remained. We beat them fairly quickly, but the game wasn't truly over until Sarah, who had retreated into her tent a while ago, finally decided to take off on her own. Nobody's mind was on playing anymore. All eyes watched her go, curious about her vague excuse to take a walk. I was sure we all had the same major question in our heads: What more was there to the story about Kevin that she had told us earlier?

After succumbing to Jenna, Birdie, and my last-minute urging, Sarah agreed to join us all on an overnighter at Bob Hall Pier, our usual go-to spot. It was spring break, after all, and we'd hardly spent any time together. Sarah and Kevin were newly coupled after an awkward beginning as reluctant lab partners, and things were going great for them. Or, at least, we all thought that was why she'd been absent from our circle a lot lately, and understandably so. Nobody was upset with her for getting a boyfriend, though we were thrilled she'd said yes to this sleepover.

But at the beach that day, her inclusion seemed a bit different than I expected. She didn't seem to want to be there, and we weren't sure how much we should push. The sun was setting, anyway. The warmth of the day was drowned out by the sunless chill of the night air, so it was time to light up the fire.

Without Sarah, the girls and I huddled together under Birdie's umbrella, wrapping ourselves in towels. We had to sit on the edges to keep them from flapping and letting out our meager warmth.

Behind us, in the tent, Sarah's phone went off. Not once, but twice. "Oh, that's Sarah's," came our mutual recognition, though Jenna said it first. "Do you think that's Kevin?"

"Probably," I answered. It was the most likely guess.

"Maybe it's her parents. Should we get it?" asked Birdie.

"No, I'm sure it's fine." Her parents would've been calling us all by then if there was a problem.

Dan slapped his hands together to shake off the sand. "Jared, grab me the matches?" Dan got no response and looked around, drawing our attention. Jared was gone, and Dan shook his head, going for the matchbox in the back of his car himself. "He's so whipped."

"What do you mean by that?" I asked, put off by the idea.

"Where do you think he went? Obviously, he's chasing Sarah down for a sunset stroll."

Giving Jared the benefit of the doubt, I said, "I'm sure Jared knows better."

"Just like he knew better about the tablets at my party?"

At the mention of that dreaded night, I caught a chill.

Early last month, Jenna fixed Sarah up with Jared, who at the time was only an occasional acquaintance of the rest of ours. We didn't know it then, but Sarah was already head over heels for Kevin, even though the guy was being stubborn. While preparing Sarah a drink, Jared had mistaken one of those *tablets* for food coloring, which had inadvertently caused her a terrible reaction. That, coupled with a bad night of tending to the needs of her type 1 diabetes, had landed her in the hospital. That night, Kevin snuck back into the hospital after we'd all left, finally confessed his feelings, and they made their relationship official. They'd been inseparable ever since.

So, whatever was going on today must have been something big if it was keeping them apart after all they'd already endured.

"I just hope Sarah is okay," I said, contemplating everything.

Dan crouched, flicking an extended match and dropping it in just so. The wind snuffed it out before the wood had time to catch. I set my jaw to keep it from chattering. "I'm sure she'll be fine. She's smart. Jared is my boy, but *he's* an idiot."

"Daniel Fitzwilliam Schellers, some best friend you are," admonished Birdie Jo. Her future kids were in for a *real* Southern upbringing.

"Whatever, we all love him, but y'all know it's true."

My next thought was interrupted by a chorus of shouting coming from down the beach. We all froze and listened before looking at each other.

"See? I told you," Dan said firmly before abandoning his efforts with the fire and starting off. Jenna jumped up before Birdie or I could, and we both got a fresh dusting of sand in our faces. We sputtered but stood, linking arms and walking down the beach, suddenly unaware of how cold we were.

The *three* of them came into view like a movie. The sun had set, and the only light available was a tall utility light across the driving path along the beach, a ways away. Still, it was more than enough to make out the scene in front of us. Jared and Sarah were there, just as Dan had predicted, but so was Kevin. And he was fuming. I might've seen actual smoke leave his nostrils.

And they call me *The Bull.*

Their back and forth raged on until, at last, it looked like Jared was doing the smart thing and leaving them alone. We stayed silent and out of the fray, but no one could walk away. Just as Dan threw his arm over Jared's defeated shoulders, Jared shrugged him away, along with the idea of giving up, and went back for more.

Okay, maybe calling him an idiot was more or less a fair assessment, but still. Dan's statement live on display had me feeling grumpy. I really wanted to root for Jared but not with Sarah. Even if Kevin hadn't been in the picture, and for a long time he wasn't, Sarah was never into Jared.

Even if he was rather attractive.

Suddenly, Kevin had Jared laid out flat. Blood shot out of his mouth as they had their final words before Kevin did what they both should've done sooner and walked away. Sarah chased after him, but Kevin would not be held up; he was bound and determined to go.

"You okay, man?" Dan held out his hand only for it to be batted away as Jared came to a wobbly stand.

"I'm fine."

"Totally. You're not bleeding all over the beach or anything."

"Whatever," Jared retorted, and they started back to camp.

Sarah was on her way as well, tears pooling in her eyes, her sadness right on par with her anger. She opened her mouth to speak but only managed to shrug. The three of us swooped in and grabbed her in a group hug until her threatening tears dried up. Then we all waddled back to the camp, arm over arm.

In my head, I was hurting for my best friend, but another part of me hurt for Jared. That, in and of itself, created such confusion in me. I didn't know what to make of it.

JARED

3

MARCH—SPRING BREAK, SENIOR YEAR OF HIGH SCHOOL. THEN.

TRUDGING BACK TO CAMP A LOSER, my thoughts bristled harder than the swelling skin on my face. By morning, it would match my ego—bruised and battered—and all I did was try to apologize to Sarah. From the moment she showed up, I was overwhelmed with a stark desire to clear the air once and for all. Something inside me needed to hear her accept my apology, even if she couldn't mean it. I would have understood that, but I needed one opportunity to be bold and just tell her I was sorry. When she took off down the shore, I knew that was it.

So, while I gave her a little while to be alone, I hyped myself up, garnering all the courage it would take to get the weight of my stupidity off my chest. I could hurdle myself into a pile of giant offensive linemen, but I grew weak from the idea of this confrontation, necessary though I knew it was. Talking it out was the only way I'd ever feel relief. I was counting on it.

Later, by the end of our brief conversation, through her

graciousness, Sarah forgave me honestly and completely. No doubts remained in my mind that she meant her words, which meant I should've had the absolution I craved. An actual weight lifted off my shoulders when she spoke; I could tell that much, and yet, wrongdoing was still buried deep inside me.

I thought her forgiveness would be the right tonic for my ailment, but the longer I lived with my shame, the more it festered. Perhaps I waited too long to initiate my apology, and retaining guilt was my penance. Sooner or later, everyone had to pay their debts, right? I guess I had accrued more interest than I first realized.

"Do you want a drink or something?" Dan offered as we arrived back at our spot.

"No, thanks." What I wanted was to wash off my face and cool down. Kevin was gone, and the air was cold, but I was still heated.

Earlier, for half a second, I felt brave enough to speak my mind against Kevin. Even though I knew there would never be anything more than friendship between Sarah and me, I still couldn't stand to see Kevin be the one to get her.

What exactly had he done to earn all her affection? What did he have that I didn't? A criminal record? He sure seemed like the type. What would a girl like Sarah want with a guy like that?

So, in my blind, dumb ambition, I didn't want to walk away. I turned around, ran my mouth, and my mouth got put in its place real quick. There was no point in retaliating for long because, even though I wanted to do the right thing for Sarah, and a part of me still hoped she would choose differently, I still felt less than. In the end, I was fighting for nothing. He hated me because of what I did to her—albeit accidentally, however stupid it was—

and she didn't pick me. It was never a matter of Kevin versus me, anyway. I was intelligent enough to figure that out.

My mind still hadn't moved by the time I saw the girls' dark wall of a figure finally on their way back from consoling Sarah.

I turned to Dan. "Was Sarah ever actually into me? When you guys set me up with her, did I ever even have a chance?"

"You really want to hear this? Now?"

"Yes, and make it quick before they get here."

"No, man. Not from what I heard. Jenna said it was a hard sell to get her to go out with you at all."

"Because of Kevin?"

"Yep."

"Cool. That's that, then."

Sarah might not be able to see the trouble she had in store if she stayed with Kevin, but I could. He was going to hurt her, and at least I knew I didn't just sit idly by and let it happen. If I cared about her at all, which I really did, staying silent just wasn't an option.

Not all brave moments were heroic ones, apparently. But I tried.

Yanking free of my shirt, I tossed it toward my tent, not caring where it landed. If I hadn't already committed to dousing myself in the cleansing water, I would've backed out the second my feet hit the surf. It wasn't quite North Pole cold yet, but the wetness combined with the unforgiving whips of the wind would have me feeling like the Arctic in no time. My poor body was in for it, but it was the quickest way to rid myself of the humiliating blood, and the heat responsible for putting it there.

When the rest of my body reached the waters, I realized there had to be worse things than being punched in the face by the guy

I lost the girl to. And once I figured those things out, maybe my beat-up body and rejected heart wouldn't hurt as much anymore.

LATER, in my tent, after everyone had gone to bed, my phone vibrated.

SAMMY

Hey, slugger. How's your pretty face?

JARED

It's fine. Nothing a little frozen T-bone wouldn't have fixed.

You think I'm pretty?

I sat up to look out the mesh window toward Sammy and Jenna's tent. Birdie and Sarah's was the next one over. To make up a secure perimeter, I was on one end of the girls, and Dan was on the other. The tents themselves were anchored to the backs of our vehicles, well-protected against the elements and passing traffic.

I could see Sammy through her own tent's little window. The light from her phone was casting on her face. She was smiling.

SAMMY

Oh, yeah. You should consider modeling as a back-up career if your football prospects fall through. That blond hair, those blue eyes—so wasted underneath that bulky helmet. smh

I laughed out loud, disrupting the peace. Rustling sounds came from around me, and I instinctively hunkered down inside my sleeping bag.

SAMMY

Way to go. Wake up the whole beach, why don't you?

JARED

My bad.

SAMMY

I'm only teasing. Don't worry about it. It's a public beach, so you're prolly not gonna be the loudest thing around tonight.

But seriously, are you doing okay?

JARED

I mean, yeah. I'll live. I had it coming, anyway.

SAMMY

Do you really believe that?

JARED

Pretty much.

SAMMY

Well, I think you're both crazy. Y'all need to let this thing go. Sarah has.

JARED

That's what she told me.

I won't be picking any more fights, so hopefully he got kicking my butt out of his system.

SAMMY

Only time will tell.

JARED

Yeah. Agreed.

SAMMY

Don't forget you have friends here. Eventually, Kevin will get over it and probably come around, too. If not, who cares? His loss.

JARED

Thanks.

Sammy had a point, which was the same one Sarah was trying to make earlier. She had forgiven me already, and it was my turn to forgive myself and let things go. Kevin and I would never be friends, that much I knew for sure, but I didn't have to go through life hating him. Whether or not he hated me was his problem. This group of people accepted me, even if he didn't.

I rolled over, intent on rest, and let the coming and going of the tide serenade me to sleep.

SAMMY

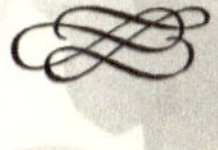

4

MAY—AFTERNOON OF GRADUATION. NOW.

MY LIVING ROOM was standing room only as I waded through my immediate and extended family, all gathered together to watch me graduate high school. As if it were all that interesting, but in a family as big and proud as mine, you could get congratulated for sneezing with your eyes open. I'm pretty sure my uncle Demetrius did that once, and there was a party thrown in his honor.

On my way to the door, I collected my keys from the bamboo bowl on the entry table. "Okay, Mama. I'm heading out now," I said over my shoulder.

"Wait, wait!" she called back as the seas parted to let her through. "Are you sure you want to do this? At least six other people in this house have offered to pick your grandparents up from the airport instead."

"I know, but I volunteered because I want to do it."

"Yeah, but this is your day. You're graduating this evening. Do you really think it's a good idea for you to leave?"

"I've made the drive to the airport plenty of times, and it will be the only one-on-one time I get with them. It'll be fine. Besides, I don't want to take anyone away from what they're doing. They already came from out of town for the ceremony. They don't have to do us favors, too."

Mom's expression was understanding. "Just be sure to call us if you need anything."

"I won't need anything. I know what I'm doing."

Things were going to change soon, anyway. I wanted to experience and remember things exactly the way they were right now, *before* my 18th birthday. Before I finally heard the truth about who my birth parents were. That nugget of information had been long awaited, with varying levels of patience, since before I could remember.

A feeling of dread formed in the pit of my stomach, and I shoved the thoughts away.

Mom unknowingly helped cut into my rumination. "I know, I know. You're so smart and perfect and amazing."

"Naturally," I preened, happy to feel the quick shift in my mood. Besides volleyball, deflecting was what I did best. For now, I had nothing to worry about. For *now*, my parents were my *only* parents, everyone in my house was a cherished member of my family, and nothing else mattered but picking up my grandparents and graduating. Best just to let it stay that way for as long as possible.

With a glistening smile, the first of many I would see today, no doubt, Mom nodded, placing her hand on my shoulder. "How did I get so lucky with you?"

"Trial and error, I'd say." I glanced over to where my two older brothers, Caleb and Ronnie, were sitting on the edge of the coffee table my parents were given as a wedding gift twenty-eight years ago. They were currently engaged in a video game, completely absorbed despite the mass of people rustling around them. Ronnie reached for Caleb's controller, but he saw it coming and yanked it skyward just in time. After so long, they had no more tricks to play. Ronnie may be the oldest at twenty-three, but you put those two in front of a gaming console, and all bets were off.

At any moment, I wondered if one or both of them would rip their T-shirts and start arm-wrestling each other. Neither had ever fought fairly with the other, but when it came to me, the baby sister, best believe things were different. There's nothing they wouldn't do for me, and that included letting me win.

It didn't matter to them or anyone else in the family that I wasn't actually blood-related. Most of the time, everyone, including myself, simply forgot that detail. To all of us, family was family. Having been adopted as a newborn was never something that bothered me. It was just the news I would get next week that had gotten under my skin. The more I thought about it, I was no longer sure I still wanted to know.

"Well, if you're going, then you'd better go. Your grandparents land in less than an hour. You still have enough time not to rush, but hopefully you don't run into traffic."

"It's a Saturday in Corpus Christi, Mama. Of course, there will be traffic."

"All the more reason to hurry off! But be sure to only hurry safely. You know the drill, sweet pea." She brought me in for a hug strong enough to resurrect a dead man. It was probably the 108th time that morning. "I'm so proud of you, Sammy-Girl. And we're all so excited for this evening and everything that comes after." She watched me with a faraway look before giving me another squeeze.

I could tell we had the same thing on our minds, and both chose to ignore it.

I patted her on the back. "Thanks, Mom. I know."

Graduating high school didn't seem all that special to me. In a few short months, I'd be a student somewhere else, so what did it really matter? Oceanside Community College would have me for the next two years, but maybe after *that* graduation, I would feel a smidgen of what my mom was feeling. If I ever decided to finish my application…

Whatever happened, hopefully, it would hurt my chest a lot less.

"Mom, you're going to crack a rib," I protested, assuaging the pain when she finally let me pull away.

"Oh, please. You're a lot tougher than that. A little love won't break you. But really, now, go. We can't be leaving my parents stranded at the airport." She kissed me on the cheek and, following a lingering pat that brought fresh mist to her eyes, scuttled away into the crowd.

Truth be told, I had been dragging my feet when applying to school. What did a girl who only excelled at volleyball do at a community college with no sports teams? Particularly if she had botched half of her university applications and had been rejected by the rest of them. Having reached graduation day while still feeling like a supreme failure felt a little odd, but it was par for the course for me.

Hopping into Roxy, my boxy red gal, I flipped to the Air1 station and put the air conditioner on high. A concerning sound burst out of my air vents accompanied by small dark puffs, and I hastily shut it off and closed them up, having remembered too late that my AC was a little bit on the fritz. The last time I used the cold air, my entire car shut off. It took a while to start back up after that.

Apparently, I was also dragging my feet on calling my dad's mechanic.

"Sorry, Roxy," I said sheepishly, rubbing the top of the dash affectionately. Manufactured around the turn of the century, she was my mom's Kia Sportage until my dad got her a newer one, and Roxy became mine. As much as I loved my car, she'd endured a lot over her faithful years of service.

Windows down it was, then. So what if it was already 92 degrees with 96% humidity before noon? Neat hair and a dry back weren't requirements for a stop at the airport. Roxy and I had been through worse together. Besides, I had time to shower and tame my unruly waves again before go-time. That's what straighteners were for.

Hopefully, Grandpa Gary and Grandma Maro don't mind a bit of sweat.

I was cruising along confidently until I rounded the corner of the airport exit, and my car started to make a familiar and unwelcome sound. It was a combination of somebody dropping a giant wrench through a hole in my engine, metal scraping against metal, and tires on gravel. Or something. However it was described, I knew it meant no good.

Please, God, no. Oh, no, no, no.

I had the luxury of a wide shoulder to my right, so I quickly signaled to merge and flipped my hazards on. But as soon as I shut off the ignition and heard the unfortunate way it died, I knew I wouldn't be going anywhere fast. Between the misty-eyed look of my mother and my visual of my grandparents lost and wandering the Corpus Christi International Airport alone, my heart began to race. Oh, and the multitude of cars zipping past me at 80 mph was also somewhat disconcerting.

Picking up my phone, my shaky fingers pressed until I was calling Sarah. She answered on the first ring. "What's wrong?" she asked in her mother-hen tone.

"So much. How did you know?"

"You never call. You're a prolific texter."

She had a point. "Girl, Roxy broke down on the side of the highway. She barely made it off the ramp to 358."

"Oh no. So, you went through with picking up your grandparents?"

"I'm trying to!"

"Did you not have your car looked at last week?"

"No… Not exactly…"

"Meaning?"

"Instead of physically taking it in, I Googled what it could be, and everything I read said that if I just don't engage the cooling system, it should definitely probably be fine. But when I got in the car a bit ago, I forgot and cranked it up. Why should the AC affect my engine anyway?" I yelled in frustration.

"I don't know. I wish I could ask Kevin to look at it for you." Her deep inhale and exhale could have been heard four lanes over. But she couldn't ask. Kevin was gone, and my poor friend was still hurting.

"Me too. I'm sure he would be able to get it fixed right up."

It hadn't been very long ago that Sarah's boyfriend, Kevin Sloan, had gotten involved in some illegal stuff over at the auto shop where he'd worked. Long story short, Kevin ended up in jail, where he was currently serving the remaining five months of his six-month sentence. Sarah was doing her best to cope without him, but her best wasn't always enough.

"Maybe you need to write him a letter or something. Get how you feel off your chest."

"I'm really not ready to talk to him at all, Sammy. I don't feel confident enough to say anything."

"It'll come to you. These things always do," I assured her, but couldn't say whether or not it helped.

There was a short time of silence, followed by some muffled sniffling. "Anyway, I wish I could do something to help, but I can't get away right now. I'm so sorry," Sarah said. "But we need to get you off the side of the road."

I worked against the growing anxiety in my gut by changing my tune—my primary maneuver. "Oh, it's okay. I just needed to whine more than anything. I know I'll get something figured out." *Right, God? I'm not just going to be stuck here, am I?*

"You can just call your parents, you know. That's what they're there for."

"Hold that thought. I have an idea," I bluffed, sparing her my worry. "I'll text you."

"Oh, okay, you better. Be careful. Love you, and keep me posted!"

"Love you, too, and I will."

Sarah always meant well, but she didn't understand the relationship I had with my parents. They were not around to bail me out of my problems, especially when I caused them myself. They would help me if I needed it, but I couldn't stand to ask. It might only be a volleyball moniker, but calling me The Bull was seriously befitting.

Guilt rose quickly. I volunteered for this; nobody put it on me. My mom hadn't even wanted me to do it, but I'd insisted, unaware I was about to let them all down. They would all be so disappointed. I had *one* job.

I released a deep breath of frustration. No, I wouldn't be calling them.

A wayward thought crept its way into my head, and suddenly, I knew exactly who to call, and I couldn't believe I didn't think of him sooner.

SAMMY

5

JARED AND I WERE JUST TEXTING ABOUT GRADUATION A COUPLE OF nights ago. He didn't have extended family or any pre-ceremony plans, so my confidence was quickly restored.

And he just so happened to have a white horse to save the day with.

"Hey, hey," he answered. "What you doin', Ballard?"

"I need a huge upon huge favor. Please, I'll do anything."

"Oh, boy. What's up?"

"What are you doing like right this second?"

"Not a lot. Was just trying to meet up with Dan to hang for a bit, but he's busy. Too much family stuff going on."

"Yeah, funny you should say that. So, here's the deal straight up. I need to get to the airport to pick up my grandparents. Is there any way you could possibly, maybe, hopefully, come help me get my car started?"

"Your car isn't starting? Where are you?"

"Oh, you know, just hanging out on the side of the highway."

His baritone laughter tickled my ear. "Wait. You serious?"

"Unfortunately. I'll share my location…"

"You know we graduate soon, right?"

"Exactly. And my grandparents are flying in right now to see it, so you see my extreme predicament."

"Well, I'm no mechanic, but I do have jumper cables, an air pump, and a screwdriver. We can give it a try. If nothing else, I'll take you myself."

I pumped the air with my fist in silent celebration. "You don't know how you've just saved my butt. Thank you."

"I'm more worried about your grandparents' butts. We can't be leaving them hanging at the airport. That would be cruel."

Bubbling with laughter, I was made harshly aware of my situation by the loud passing of an 18-wheeler beside me. It rumbled so jarringly that I could only brace myself against the wheel and rock back and forth as my car wobbled. "Thanks again, dude, seriously. But, um, can you hurry, please? It's getting kinda scary over here."

"I'm already on the road. You'll be all right. Sit tight, keep your flashers on, and don't get out. I'll be there in a bit. Got it?"

After thanking Jared again, we hung up the phone. I texted Sarah.

SAMMY

Jared is coming to the rescue.

She replied back with a lone smiley face. I swear I could feel her depression seeping through the symbol on my screen.

SAMMY

We're going to talk about everything soon, you know that, right?

SARAH

Yes, I know. Thanks, girl. Let me know how
everything goes.

SAMMY

That goes without saying.

I told my best friend everything. Sarah had good instincts about people. Once upon a time, Jared Tomlin was quite the meat-headed jock and somehow unknowingly drugged her on their first—and only—date. He helped make it right and put in true, remorseful effort, making it all a thing of the past.

Sarah told everyone that Jared was one of us now, one of the group, and I'd done my best to treat him as such. For the most part, we all had, if for no other reason than we felt bad for him.

While waiting, I lost myself in worship music on my phone, ensuring I wouldn't panic on the side of the freeway. Jeremy Camp instructed me how not to have an "Anxious Heart." With my eyes closed and the music filling more than just my ears, I forgot about my circumstances.

Then, at last, I saw familiar headlights in my rearview.

My knight and his white stallion had arrived!

After parking his Ford Bronco, Jared sauntered over and leaned his forearms over my lowered passenger-side window. The warm wind carried his scent of citrus and musk into my car. It was so very reminiscent of Jared-Jock-head, but it didn't bother me.

"You are my hero!"

He looked to his feet and chuckled in reply. His bashful laugh was kinda cute.

"So, can you give me a jump?"

"First, try to start the engine and let me listen real quick."

"Okay, but it won't be pretty." I turned the key, giving him the demonstration he asked for.

He winced, waving for me to turn it off. "Pop the hood. Maybe your battery could use a reboot. I'll grab my cables and see what we can do about getting you the rest of the way."

"Thank you so much, seriously."

"I'll do my best, Samantha."

Obviously, Jared didn't yet consider himself one of us if he was calling me by my full name. In the next second, I decided I would help change that. It's the least I could do. "Call me Sammy."

He gave a quick nod and grinned, taking off to his car. After a moment of digging in the back, Jared came around with a large portable battery jumper. I followed his instructions, and eventually, the battery fired up just like it should and sounded as good as new...ish. Having my AC dials securely turned off, I was confident everything would go smoothly from there.

A phone call to the mechanic would still be required.

After closing my hood, Jared draped himself over the window once more. "It sounds good to me, but are you comfortable going the rest of the way after all this? If you want to leave your car here, I will take you. We can call for a tow."

"Oh, no, that's okay. It sounds brand new again. As long as I keep my AC off, I don't think I'll trigger another shutdown. I'll get it looked at as soon as possible."

"You sure?"

"Positive. Thank you so much, Jared. I owe you big time."

"It's all good, but do you mind keeping me updated? Let me know when you get your grandparents and when you get back home?"

"I absolutely will."

Watching Jared return to his car, I had the impression that he'd walked out of it one person, and now he was another—at least in my eyes. Sarah said Jared was one of us now, and I was no longer going along with it because I felt bad for him. I wholeheartedly agreed.

6

Mom had her hands on her hips when I returned home. "Where did you run off to? Kind of bad timing, don't you think?" She was in one of her moods, as she always was when important milestones came around. It made me groan on the inside.

"Sorry, my friends can't really choose when their cars break down."

She stood with a blank expression. "You didn't tell me that. Who broke down? It wasn't Dan, was it?"

"Sammy Ballard."

"I don't remember a Sammy."

"She's one of Dan's girlfriend's best friends."

"Just like that other one, what was her name? Sarah? She nearly got you into a lot of trouble."

Now, I groaned on the outside, too. "You have that wrong. I've explained it so many times. Just stop talking about it already, please. It's over and done with, and they're all my friends. Period."

"Fine, let's stop talking and ignore it. That's what we always do, but fine. I'd rather not argue, anyway. It's supposed to be a joyous day."

Joyous. It looked like she nearly choked on the word. There was no way she could feel anything close to joy when she could barely speak the word out loud. We all had our own ways of coping, and hers was to not.

She turned and waved her hand as she stalked down the hallway. "Just go get ready then. I want to leave early. You know how the traffic gets downtown."

I did know. It was made painfully more obvious every time she had to do the things that Dad used to do. Mom was a nervous driver and took back roads everywhere she went if she could. One day, when we had to go somewhere, and she was in one of her moods, I dutifully—pitifully—offered to drive us. She'd been so offended I hadn't dared do it a second time.

When Dad died, I threw myself into football like never before. I made varsity as a freshman and barely slowed down to take a breath since. I lived the sport, and the only thing keeping me going was the scholarship waiting for me. Come August, I would have a new team to play for at a new school in a new town where the failures and depressions of yesterday would stop holding me back. I was ready to go. If my mom wanted to live in the past, dead set against the present, she could do it without me.

I only wished my little brother had the same option, but he still had four years before he got to leave for college. Without me at home, she would drag him down, too. It was only a matter of time. Laura Josephine Tomlin was the living embodiment of the expression *'misery loves company,'* which was a subconscious fulfillment she took very seriously.

But she was still my mother. And even though she had stuff she hadn't worked through, I hoped someday she would. Most of the time, she was perfectly capable... or she passed for it, at least. Maybe not considerably happy, but still sane. But, at times like these, her façade didn't just crack; it deteriorated. I couldn't imagine how losing a husband was worse than losing a father, but whatever. I wasn't her, and she wasn't me.

All I knew was that losing my dad and spending the following years trying to pretend my mom was legitimately stable sucked.

With a deep, cleansing sigh, I endeavored to let it all go. Mom said today was supposed to be joyous, so I would let it be, even if it was only that way to her. In the back of my mind, I knew better. Fake was fake.

Jeremy came around the same corner Mom had just disappeared from. "What's her deal?"

"Nothing. She's fine. Today is a joyous day, didn't you hear?"

"Oh yeah? What's so great about a bunch of you eggheads walking across a stage?"

"Probably the adoring looks on the faces of our family and friends in the audience."

He sneered, sticking his tongue out. "So, who's Sammy?"

"No one." I attempted to walk away, but he stepped to the side and blocked my way.

"A new girlfriend?" he taunted.

"No, not a girlfriend. Just a friend-friend."

"She think you're ugly, too?"

"Exactly. She says I look too much like you."

"Yeah, right." He was hiding a smirk, along with something brown, leathery, and oblong behind his back.

Who was he kidding?

"Think fast!" Jeremy cried, throwing a football across the room with all his strength. He had good power but no control. It flew over the couch and wobbled in the air, losing its forward thrust. I followed it and reached, letting it slam into the palm of my hand, then clamped it down against my chest, cradling it with both hands. Almost losing my balance completely at the awkward catch, I stumbled into the end table. The lamp on top nearly came to a crashing fall, but I dropped the ball and caught it. The whole ordeal had been louder than either of us would've hoped.

When Mom stomped back into the living room, she was not happy. Half her shoulder length blonde hair was perched atop her head, held haphazardly by a large clip. "What in the world was that?"

"Nothing. I just knocked into the table and almost dropped the lamp. I saved it, don't worry."

"You guys sound like circus elephants jumping around out here. Try to be more careful, okay?"

"Sure, Mom."

"We're always careful," Jeremy ruefully added.

"I'll pretend that's true," she guffawed and retreated to her preparations.

Jeremy trained an indignant stare on me. "Way to go, loser. You almost dropped that lamp and barely caught my throw. Some wide receiver you are."

"I'm a running back, and you're the one who throws like a blindfolded donkey on roller skates. You're lucky I caught that and saved your rotten behind. You owe me."

He rolled his eyes and puffed up his chest. "You wanna go, Oh Great One? I'll take you right now."

I laughed, the hearty rumble reverberating through me. "Oh yeah?" I eyed him and waited. The longer I stared him down, the weaker he grew. He began to crumble, and, at last, I knew I had him.

I darted forward, and without missing a beat, he spun around and bolted to the back door. Hot on his heels, I heard Mom shout something again, but neither of us was listening. We were already in the back yard, grappling and wrestling on the ground. Fresh-cut clippings got everywhere, but we didn't care.

We laughed and wrestled around, which was mostly me letting him think he stood a chance until I pinned him with his face in the grass with his arms crossed behind his back, straddling his flailing legs. I slapped the ground ten times to prove myself the victor.

Just like Dad used to do to us.

I hopped up, smugly crossing my arms over my chest. "What was that you said, donkey boy?"

"Yeah, whatever." He waved his hand at me as he stood to his full height. "I let you win because it's your day."

Laughing again, I yanked him in for a side hug and ruffled his hair. He hated it when I did that. "I know you did. Thanks, man."

Jeremy stood just a tiny bit taller as we made our way back inside. "You're welcome."

Now, it was really time to clean up. Jeremy took off to get ready, and I had just gotten to my room to start prepping my clothes when my phone pinged. It was an airport pickup selfie of Sammy and her grandparents. She was squished between them, arm extended for the photo, with entertaining grins on their faces.

SAMMY

Safe and sound. Thanks, Jared. I mean it. I owe you one.

JARED

You're welcome.

Though that silly picture was thanks enough, I was glad to see at least someone around me was experiencing real joy. Not the fake kind, like those in my house. It was enough to make me smile, and for that, I was grateful.

SAMMY

7

GGRADUATION WENT OFF WITHOUT A HITCH, AND AFTERWARD, WE all poured out of the American Bank Center in droves. Photos galore were taken, and when I finally found a second, I slipped away.

Jared tipped his graduation cap at me as I spotted him and walked over. He was leaning back against a palm tree facing the water with the Blue Ghost, Corpus Christi's floating WWII museum, appearing to the left of him. The crash of the waves and the blast of the wind drowned out the murmurs of those around us.

He greeted me with a lenient smile. "Can you believe we did it?"

"Sorta. I just can't believe it's over. Like, I know we just accomplished this big important thing, but I feel like we still have school on Monday."

"I know what you mean."

Something about him seemed down, but I wasn't sure I should draw attention to it. This was supposed to be a happy occasion. We were going to keep things light. I had to for my own sanity. "Hey, you got a football scholarship to Corpus Christi University, right? When does practice start up for you?"

"Pretty quickly here, actually. There's a bunch of preseason training programs. They really don't want anyone becoming unfit or not having time to get the hang of conditioning before first kick-off. I'm excited to get going."

"Right. It sounds like it'll be amazing. Good for you, Jared. You'll have to remember to write when you're big and famous. Just because you will become a major football stud, that's no reason to forget the little people. Oh, and we'll all want season box seats!"

He chuckled and shook his head in his boyishly adorable way. "There isn't an incredibly high chance of that. It's just college ball."

I shrugged. "High chances, low chances, who cares? Any chance is a chance if you take it. Besides, we've all seen you play. You're good."

"Well, thank you, Sammy. Hopefully, my time at college will impress the right people, and that big and famous thing will be more than just a possibility."

"And those season tickets?"

Again, he chuckled. "And the season tickets, sure."

This guy made me smile. I couldn't help it. What a good friend he had turned out to be, a stark difference to how things had begun a few months ago. I would feel eternally grateful for his coming out to help me with my car earlier. "Too bad you're leaving right when we're all getting to know you so well. You're actually really cool."

"I know. But not as cool as you."

"Certainly not," I confirmed, as though his statement was as plain and simple as the crashing ocean. "So, what are you doing over here by yourself? Are you tired of taking family photos, too?"

He rolled his shoulder. "Something like that."

Over toward the parking lot, I saw my parents beckoning me back with waving arms. Sarah and the others were with them. "Well, looks like I'm being summoned for more," I laughed, and he only pretended to. "You okay?"

"Yep, just waiting for Dan to finish up with whatever he's doing so we can head out."

"Going anywhere fun to celebrate?"

"Just going home. He's giving me a ride. My mom cut out early to avoid the rush."

I nodded, debating if I should invite him to join me—in what, I didn't know—but deciding against it. "Alrighty. I'll catch you later, Stud."

At that, he did laugh. "Later, Sammy-Jammy."

I gave him a humorous glare before walking away. That nickname better not stick, but I could let it slide this time. Why give him a hard time about something so trivial when he was clearly in his feels about something?

Weaving through people and vehicles, I crossed the street and caught up to my crowd. My family kept walking, making their way to the car, while Sarah and the girls waited for me under the palms on the sidewalk. Even though we'd just done it ten minutes ago, squealing hugs abounded.

My eyes stung with the unwelcome thought of how things would be when summer was over, and we all went our separate ways. Or rather, they did. I wasn't going anywhere.

Jenna picked up her bag and began searching through it.

"Who is up for more photos? My mom gave me her Nikon and said we should fill the rest of the memory card for her. Maybe a few near the marina, with a pitstop at Whataburger for milkshakes? Or maybe the shaved ice guy has his truck out by the sea wall." Jenna appeared to salivate at the idea. Considering how hot it was, I agreed. An ice-cold sweet snack sounded like perfection, but I wasn't sure what my family had planned at home.

"I can already feel the sun giving me a headache, but that sounds like fun!" Birdie encouraged. "We have dinner plans with my dad and his family tonight, but I'm totally free until then. Is my makeup holding together? Better question: how's my hair?" She looked to us to be her mirror and inform her how great her hair-sprayed blonde curls were looking since the last time she asked.

"It's perfect," Sarah laughed.

Jenna rolled her impatient eyes. "It's always perfect, and so are you. Stop worrying. You look better than the rest of us combined."

"That's not true at all." Though Birdie beamed at the compliment as pink marred her darling cheeks. "Sorry, y'all know how evil the humidity is. Frizz is not a good look for me."

Sarah checked the time on her phone, then sent a text to her parents, wherever they had gone off to. "Looks like I can spare an hour, but I'll have to go after that."

"Do your parents have plans?" I inquired.

"Yeah, but nothing big. I'm just getting really tired really fast. It's been a long day."

"Hm." This reaction was about Kevin, I could tell.

Ever since Kevin was arrested last month, Sarah kept a tight lip around the details. That was her prerogative, but the fact that she kept getting progressively worse worried me. I couldn't help my friend when I had no idea what the problem was. But more and more, her pretenses were slipping.

"An hour sounds better than nothing. What about you, Sammy?" Jenna asked, pulling my focus away from Sarah.

Photos. Girl time. Snackies. That's right. I'd gotten sidetracked.

We had a lot of family in town, and I wasn't sure what our plans were. Maybe they could afford to spare me one hour, too. "Let me run over and ask."

Turning around to face the parking lot, I jogged toward my parents' car. "Mom, wait," I called, slowing her down. "Can I ride home with Sarah and the girls? They want to head down to the water for a few more pictures and maybe swing by Whataburger. Just for about an hour and a half, tops."

"Aw, are you sure? I have dinner planned for us at home."

"You do? Who's cooking it?"

"The Crock-Pot." She laughed with her whole face, making me smile. "It will keep, though. If you're not hungry when you get home, you can have some tomorrow. We'll all spend time together with the family after you get back."

"Really?"

"Really. We can entertain them for an hour. Go with the girls, have fun! Just be safe, okay?"

"Always. Thanks, Mom!"

"For what?" Caleb asked as he and Ronnie leaned into our conversation. Dad was ahead, already in the car, letting the AC do its thing for everyone else, as he always did.

"I'm ditching your lame behinds," I told my brothers.

"Mom, did you hear what she said about your behind?" Caleb tattled, pulling on her dress sleeve.

Ronnie flanked her other side. "Yeah, she called you and your butt lame."

"Have mercy, you two. It's too hot for your shenanigans."

Ronnie put on his best angelic face. "No shenanigans, Mom. We're just looking out for you."

"Yeah, that's right," confirmed Caleb with an enthusiastic nod.

Mom lifted her purse, and the two of them shrank back, hissing as though they were vampires and her purse was a giant clove of garlic. Mom laughed louder than the rest of us, and when we reached the car, I gave everyone a final hug as they loaded into the SUV.

"See y'all later," I said, closing the door behind Caleb.

I moved to the front, and my dad opened the door and got out. He picked me up in a big squeeze, my toes hovering inches above the ground. "Have I told you yet how proud I am?"

"I think I might have forgotten by now if you and Mom hadn't been telling me every fifteen minutes since I woke up this morning," I spoke into his shoulder. I inhaled his spiced cologne and felt at home, praying that whatever news I got on my birthday didn't change how I felt about any of this.

He settled me back to my feet and looked at me. His eyes were wet. "I mean it. You don't know what a blessing you are to us— your mom and me. We love you so much, Sammy-Girl."

"I love you, too. Honest, I do. But can I go now?" There was no time for worries today. I wanted only to snack and take photos and hang out like old times, while they were still around, for the next hour.

Dad laughed, and I could hear Mom behind him doing the same. "Yes, go ahead. Get outta here."

"Thank you! See you guys later." I stepped back, stuck my

tongue out at my brothers, and let Dad get into the car before spinning on my heel.

"Love you!" Mom hollered.

"Love you, too," I threw over my shoulder as I trotted back to my friends.

AT THE END OF OUR GIRLS' evening, when it was just Sarah and I sitting in her car beside my driveway, I flipped off the radio. "Sarah, talk to me. How are you actually doing? Unload, tell me everything you're feeling."

She rested her head back with a sigh. "I can't even begin to explain everything I'm feeling, but what I'm trying to do is move on with my life. I'm trying to just be okay since I have no other choice."

"Move on? You guys broke up? Is that why you haven't gone to see him?"

"I don't..." Sarah sniffed and wiped her eyes. She went silent for a minute before heaving a big sigh. "You know what, I thought I was ready to talk about this, but I'm not. Can we just... try again another time?"

I would have protested, hugged it out of her or something, but my phone was already going off. My family could be heard from the road, getting lively in the house, waiting for me to join them. "I'm sorry, girl. I wish there were something I could do. I feel useless."

"Me too. I'll be okay eventually." She gave me a meager smile and hug that didn't pass for convincing. I hoped to be of more help to her but came up dry. "Oh, and don't forget about church tomorrow. You still coming with us? Pastor Brian will be talking about the upcoming mission trip. I am hoping I'll be able to go on it."

"You still picking me up?" Roxy hadn't been fixed yet, so I was driving her as little as possible.

She laughed. "Yep. I'll see you at nine."

"I'll be ready. Love you, girly."

"Love you, too."

JARED

8

On June 3ʳᵈ, a week after graduation, Sammy turned eighteen. With another reason to celebrate, we found ourselves back at the beach. Amidst the occasion, I got lost in my own head and turned toward the parking lot for the hundredth time that morning.

"Hey, Tomlin! Do you think you could stop staring over there and actually play?" Dan's voice cut through my distraction, but the ball spiked down right beside me before I could get my head in the game. I missed it completely, and the impact against the ground sent a waft of sand into my face. "Way to go, dude," Dan said sarcastically with a slap on my back. Then, he lowered his voice. "You're not waiting for Sarah, are you?"

I tore my gaze away from the road. "I'm not waiting for anyone."

"Do you think that since Kevin's locked up she's free game now? Because I kinda think he'd still manage to escape and kick your butt for even considering it."

"I'm not into Sarah anymore, dude."

"Yeah, sure. Keep telling yourself that."

"I'm being serious. I know she's with him, and I know that ship has sailed. That ship was barely in the water to begin with. But I do have a lot on my mind. Thank you for asking," I said sarcastically. My mom had given me grief for going out with everyone to the beach again, but nobody needed to hear that. "It's the first time we've all tried hanging out since the *last* time we were all at the beach."

"You mean since Kevin brutally knocked your—"

"Shut up already, man." I walked off the sandy court and sat down against the cooler, my back to the group.

Dan growled as he called for a time-out and followed me. "Come on, dude. Are you sure this isn't about Sarah? It's been months, you know."

"I'm. Not. Into. Sarah."

"Then what is the big deal?" Dan dragged out his question like a petulant child.

"I just don't want any issues with anyone. We don't have a lot of time left as a group before everyone starts leaving. Summer doesn't last forever, you know. I just want it to be fun and drama-free."

"Don't try to kill his girl again, and I think it'll be all good." Dan laughed, expecting me to find it funny, and sighed when I didn't. "It's gonna be fine, dude. Stop worrying. Some people got way bigger problems than that. I'm sure she's not even going to look at you twice." Dan outed himself by looking down the beach at Jenna. She was sitting alone in the surf, resting back on her palms while the edges of the tide washed up and down her legs. She watched the water out ahead like she'd been doing for most of the morning. There was trouble in paradise, and I hadn't realized.

"Yeah, I really don't know if you're trying to help or not, but you suck at this."

He laughed, and at last, so did I. Something in his eyes changed. "Sorry. There just always seems to be so much going—"

Reaching into the cooler behind us for a soda, Sammy interrupted what I anticipated was going to be the reason behind Dan's unusual aggression. Her stark brown hair draped over her left shoulder in a French braid, and sand dusted her skin, beautifully bronzed by nature rather than sunshine. "You girls about done gossiping so we can finish whooping you?"

Beyond Sammy, Birdie Jo stood beside the net with the volleyball on her hip, watching us from beneath the brim of her bucket hat. They both meant business, even Beauty Queen Birdie.

They were both going *down*.

"Don't think we'll go easy on you guys just because it's your birthday, Sammy."

"You would offend me to even consider it," she retorted, placing an incredulous hand over her heart, drawing my attention to her alluring brown skin.

"Let's go, MacLean, you can do it," called Nick Benavides, Birdie's date, from his seated position on the water side of the net. Birdie rushed over and bent down, fist-bumping him in thanks. Jenna was usually Sammy's volleyball partner, but she had opted out, and Birdie was obliged to fill the role. She was doing a fair job of it, too.

I pushed back to my feet, and the sand kicked up behind me. I willed my focus back to the game, as I was conditioned to do.

"Go ahead, *ladies*," Sammy hollered. "I believe it's your serve." With a smirk, she ducked under the net, assuming her outside hitter position, and waited for a return strike. She was average height for a girl, and Dan and I were tall, so compared to us, she had a handicap in the sand.

Not that it has ever given us much of an advantage in the past.

In fact, Sammy always played a good game. The girls on her old team nicknamed her The Bull for a reason; it's how intense she played. She always hit her mark like she was charging everything head-on.

Making my move, I struck, and the ball was in play again. We went back and forth for a minute, encouraged by the cheering of our benched friends, when, at the last moment, Sammy caught my spike with her forearm in a dive. A good save, but I was ready to return. Taking control of the play, Dan gave me a beautiful set, and I was mid-jump to spike it when I saw Sarah's little blue sedan pull up. Turning, I missed the freaking ball. Again.

Dan saw it unfolding and tried to save it with a valiant effort of a dive, but it was too late. The ball slammed on the ground, bouncing back up into his face in the process. As he came to his feet, exhibiting a bit of blood, I couldn't help but laugh.

"Oh man, that's my bad," I apologized.

"Thanks a lot, dude." Wiping the red from his dripping nostrils, he stomped over to the water. Jenna hopped up, and though the wind blew their voices away, I imagined she asked him what happened. He splashed his face over and over before plopping down in the surf beside her. I felt relieved for him when Jenna scooted closer and reached her arm around his shoulders. Maybe things weren't all that bad between them.

"Hey, guys!"

I turned around to see Sarah walking toward us, her blonde-red waves floating freely. She carried a large beach tote stuffed full of who knows what with a folding lawn chair under her arm.

My nerves fried at the sight of her, remembering our last encounter, but I smiled and waved as casually as I could muster. If I kept my feet rooted in place and my eyes indifferent, I couldn't possibly stir up any trouble.

"Hey, lovely lady!" Sammy exclaimed. "I missed that big smile on my girl's face."

After the girls all took their turns hugging, they helped her place her things. Birdie reached to take Sarah's bag, causing her to exclaim in surprise.

"Good grief, Birdie. Where did that come from?"

All eyes within hearing distance were drawn to Birdie's right forearm, which boasted a sizable purple and red bruise.

"Oh, that's from when Sammy and I dominated the boys just now."

Jenna jumped in, grabbing Birdie's arm for a better look. "Dang, it got that dark that fast?"

Sammy observed the arm herself. "Impressive, MacLean. You bruise even better than me."

"Y'all have no idea," Birdie laughed.

When Sarah was good and situated, she then turned to me and walked over for a shoulder hug. "It's nice to see you, too, Jared. Graduation feels like forever ago already, and it's only been a week." She laughed, but something about it fell flat. "How have you been?"

"Not too bad. Been doing a lot of conditioning and stuff, prepping for preseason. What about you?"

She sighed, looking as though her happiness could slip at any moment. "Decent."

I understood what that was about, and my teeth ground together to prevent me from saying something stupid. It sucked that she felt that way. She must be so lonely. Her boyfriend should be here on the beach with her, not tied up in legal trouble in the jailed arms of the county.

But whatever. Things would be fine, as I repeatedly told myself. I couldn't get invested in her like that again. Yes, I wanted better for her, but I was okay with being just friends. I would welcome literally anything but the tension.

Sitting down in our respective places amongst the group, everyone decided to start eating, so I reached into the cooler and grabbed something for myself, satisfied. The initial encounter was over, and it didn't go horribly. I didn't even feel the pain I had secretly anticipated when spending time with her again. Even her morose reactions about Kevin's absence only made me feel upset for her sake.

What a relief.

WHILE WE WERE SITTING around the fire munching on the cupcakes Birdie Jo had baked for the occasion, Sarah offered a proposal.

"In honor of our girl's birthday and to kick off another amazing summer together, let's all share what we're looking forward to in the fall."

"I bet I know what Jared's looking forward to," came Sammy's helpful prompting.

"And what would that be?" I inquired, knowing exactly what she would say.

"College football, of course."

"Of course," I repeated, matching her flippant tone.

At the mention of it, everyone clapped. Their cheerful looks didn't match my own lacking enthusiasm, which left me with a sense of confusion as the conversation moved on from me. Judging by their reactions, they were all a lot more excited about the summer ending than I was.

"What about you, Sarah?" I prompted.

"I'm excited about starting college, though I'm still not sure what I'll be studying just yet. I'm sure I'll figure it out soon enough." Despite the sadness in her eyes, Sarah smiled brightly. I thought I even saw a bit of something flicker across Sammy's face, but it was quickly replaced.

"And what about you, Sammy?" I wondered, curious about that flicker.

"I've decided I'm going to Mexico in September on a mission trip."

"You're doing it?" asked Sarah, taken by surprise. "Pastor Brian only just made the announcement."

"Yep, I know. I'll be starting the application process soon."

"Wow, I had no idea you were seriously thinking about going. Sammy, that's so great!" Sarah leaned in and hugged her friend. "You're going to have an amazing time. I didn't realize it would interfere with school. I wish I could go with you."

"Me too."

Jenna shot them both confused glares. "What did we miss? What's in Mexico?"

"Donkeys and tumbleweeds." Birdie's matter-of-fact response had us all barking with laughter.

"Good one," Nick said. "You're not wrong." He was the only one among us actually from Mexico, so he would know.

Jenna was curious through the laughs. "But what are *you* going for, Sammy?"

"Sarah's church is doing a mission trip to Mexico, and I'm going with them. You know, to do missionary stuff." The way

Sammy's confidence wavered ever so slightly had me even more curious.

"What about Oceanside?"

Sammy's face changed again, there and then gone so quickly. Nobody else seemed to notice. She waved her hand. "It'll still be there when I get back. This is more immediately important. People are in need."

"Since when are you this big on church stuff?"

"Since now," Sammy answered plainly. "And I can't wait to go."

"Oh, okay. I hope it's awesome." Jenna didn't seem overly optimistic it would be, but it was a visible effort nonetheless. "Who's going next?"

"I'll go." Nick un-slid his arm from around Birdie's shoulders. "I graduated high school with my associates, so I'm finishing my bachelor's degree in Marine Biology here at Texas A&M Corpus Christi. I'll be starting my internship at the aquarium next week, too," he beamed.

Birdie patted him on the shoulder with kindly pride, then leaned over and pecked him on the cheek. "I'm so excited for you, Nick."

"Thanks," he smiled. "I am, too."

And I believed he was. I craved that sort of sure-fire joy about my own plans.

"I'll be starting online classes in the fall, myself. I'm thinking about social work, but not sure yet," Birdie told us.

"All that school crap sounds boring," Dan suddenly announced. "We just got *out* of school, guys. I'm so excited not to be going back. I'm fixing to leave for Houston for my welding apprenticeship soon," he added with a bold flare. I smacked him supportively on the back. On his side, Jenna's shoulders rose and fell silently. Clearly, she wasn't as excited as he was about it.

Sarah turned to Jenna. "Your turn. What are you excited about?"

"Me? I'm *so* glad you asked," she said, flipping back her hair. "I'm excited for truth or dare!" she cried. "Who's up first?"

SAMMY

9

"Oh, great," I mused, though I was secretly grateful for the change of discussion. The last thing I wanted to think about was all the things to come. None of it was going to be any good for me. Even the idea of going to Mexico—which I literally decided on the spot—wasn't exciting enough to cover up the worry over everything else, including the news I was expecting later.

My friends were all moving on, most of them leaving—while I was staying.

Alone.

What Jenna asked me was true. I hadn't been this *'big on church stuff'* before, and I wasn't totally convinced I was now, but beggars couldn't be choosers. I hadn't gotten into any good schools, particularly not the ones I was too chicken to apply for, and I didn't want to admit community college was all I was capable of. Maybe doing some of God's work in the process would help me figure out what would come after that.

In any case, I had nothing better to do.

"This ought to be fun." Birdie Jo's tone was in agreement with mine. She wound her hand around Nick's and raised her eyebrows at him.

He looked around questioningly. "Y'all still play Truth or Dare? Isn't that a kid's game?"

"Not when we play it," Jenna told him, and not without a hint of annoyance. Nick was still new to the group. Newer than Jared even. With his dark hair and eyes and olive complexion, he reminded me a lot of Kevin. Everyone liked him well enough, but we all agreed he wasn't good enough for our Birdie Jo. Nobody ever would be—Marine Biologist or not.

Speaking of Nick, I should've started a pool on whether or not he would even play the game after witnessing a couple of rounds. He may have brains, but I wasn't sure he had the brawn to keep up with the ridiculousness.

Jared, however, spouted from out of nowhere, "Sounds entertaining. I'm in."

Maybe it was ignorant bravery, or maybe he was just being dumb, but it was obvious from the sounds around the fire that we had little confidence in Jared's valor. Jared had never been privy to one of Jenna's games of Truth or Dare, but he had to have heard about them. He could've been acting in the name of *YOLO* or whatever that stupid expression was, but I knew something for sure: After one round in the hot seat, his attitude would change.

"You say that now," I laughed. "You will soon learn."

Shrugging, he didn't appear worried. "I think I can handle a silly game."

Dan leaned and whispered, "Shouldn't have said that." I snickered when I heard it.

"Alright, guys. Jared just volunteered to go first," I announced with a conspiratorial grin.

Jenna, experiencing an instantaneous mood boost, bounced on her bent knees and clapped. "Fantastic! A new victim! I mean, player, of course." Light laughter resounded. Jared smiled, but he truly had no idea what he was getting into. We all had years of practice learning how to play Jenna's "silly" game. At this point, taking a game of Truth or Dare with a grain of salt and watching what you said was a fine, carefully honed skill.

The very cockiness that made Jared a jock-head was about to get him hazed hardcore. It probably wouldn't be all bad; most of the truths and dares were really fun, but somehow, this game still managed to prey on everyone's weaknesses.

Last year, Birdie was forced to let Dan style her hair and had to wear his design for the entire day. Another time, I was dared to run to the sidewalk and disco dance for ten minutes without music. It wouldn't have been so bad had it not been dusk on Halloween. I can't even recall how many Iron Men and Peppa Pigs walked by laughing hysterically at me.

Though some of them dropped candy for me like I was a sweet-toothed street performer, so, you know... Upside. There would be no candy this time, but we'd already had cake. And if laughter was the best medicine, I'd take all the goofy, embarrassing dares I could tonight. If I was laughing, then I wouldn't be thinking about the future.

"Truth or dare, Jared?" Jenna demanded, restoring my attention.

Dan nudged Jared's arm with a flask of something, nodding for him to take a drink. "Trust me."

Jared appeared incredulous but took the offer. When he handed it back, Dan gulped down the rest before stowing it away again.

Jenna watched the exchange with great scrutiny. "Well?" she probed.

"Let's try a truth."

Everyone murmured in entertainment. Rookie mistake. Truth did not guarantee anyone an easier time. Usually, she took it as a challenge and gave the person a harsher punishment. Because that's what the game was. Punishment. But somehow, it was still fun.

"Do you still have a crush on Sarah?" Jenna inquired ruthlessly.

Sarah's countenance dropped. She clearly suspected something like that. "Really, Jenna?"

"What? He picked truth, and I wanna know. I'm sure we all do."

"Jared, you don't have to answer that," Birdie said.

"Yeah, Jared. You can pick dare instead," I teased, but he didn't catch my tone.

"That's true," Birdie confirmed. "But the catch is, you can't refuse it if you do. It's either you tell the truth now or you have to do the dare later."

Jared looked like a lost golden retriever with his big blue eyes and blond hair shimmering in the firelight. For a second, I almost-kinda-sorta felt bad for him. But yeah, even I was curious about the answer to Jenna's question, even if it was a low blow to ask.

"Just give me the dare," is what he settled on.

Boo! Chicken.

The startled reactions around the fire caught on. Jenna seemed ever the more excited.

I wondered why he didn't just tell everyone he didn't have feelings for Sarah anymore. Make it easier on himself. Surely, those feelings had dissolved by now. It had been long enough, I would say, not that it mattered to me. But one glance at Sarah and my heart constricted. I was suddenly grateful he had dodged the topic. She didn't need that kind of attention, especially not while she was hurting the way she was.

"Let's get the birthday girl involved." Then Jenna blurted a new absurdity. "I dare you to kiss Sammy."

My brain scrambled to catch up with what was going on. "Who? Wait, what? Why?"

Wow, intelligent. You only forgot when and where, genius.

"You all heard me. You bypassed the truth, Jared, so now you have to do the dare or else."

"Or else what?"

"Or else, why are you playing?" Birdie presented to him. "You'd agreed to all on your own, after all."

"Those are the rules. You have to do the dare." Jenna's expression was all business, but he looked unimpressed by her threat.

"Actually, no, I don't. But I will."

I couldn't believe my eyes as Jared rose, brushed sand off his shorts, and came to stand in front of me. He extended his hand to help me up, and I was too stunned to think about refusing. Even once I was already standing, he didn't let my hand go.

This is... interesting.

"As long as you're willing," he added, piercing me with his lightning blues.

At full height, Jared towered over me. I wasn't a short girl by any means—5'7", thank you very much—but I could rest my forehead on his chin if I wanted to.

Not that I wanted to.

At some point, the hooting and hollering of the enablers around us reached my ears. They were excited to see Jared in a small act of defiance against Jenna, the Truth or Dare ringleader. He told her in such a calming tone, with so few words, that he wouldn't be following along just because she said so. He agreed to go through with the dare of his own accord, on his terms. He'd refused to let her stir up drama for Sarah, and for that, I wanted to applaud him, too.

But was that all? Was this one of those moments I wasn't supposed to read into? Because I totally was. I was reading a whole lot into it, and I couldn't do a thing except stand there, wondering what it meant that he had yet to release my hand. Maybe I was so confused because I'd never stood that close to Jared before. He'd never looked at me so intently.

And he was still awaiting my response. "Sammy?"

Let me see if I have this straight.

Jared only wanted to kiss me if I wanted him to. So, did that mean he wanted to kiss me? Or did he just want permission before fulfilling a stupid dare in front of our friends? He could absolutely have just been playing it extra cautious because of what happened with Sarah, but who knew for sure? Did it matter?

I hadn't kissed anyone in ages, not that there had been many kisses, period.

So, why not?

Steeling myself, I lifted my chin. "Whatever. Nobody can say I'm not a team player."

His almost indiscernible smile caught me off guard, and I forgot all about our hands, my heart pounding as his lips drew near.

What is wrong with me?

Going straight for the kill, Jared leaned down, his eyelids lowering on the way. My eyes about popped out of my head until fluttering to a close right at the moment of impact when his soft, full lips hit home against mine. It wasn't just a peck, either. He pressed in. His fingers tightened ever so slightly around mine. I inhaled, breathing him in. I leaned up, seeking more, when he broke away, causing me the tiniest stumble forward.

Wow. So, Jared Jock-head is a really good kisser. I did not expect that.

He pulled back with the sultriest smile; my weak knees nearly buckled. Jared returned to his spot as the cheering resumed, and trying to restore my composure, I smiled boldly and did a curtsy. "Thank you, thank you. You're all a wonderful audience."

"Well played, Tomlin, even though that was hardly a kiss," Jenna griped.

I beg to differ.

Before I allowed myself to look at him, Jared had already plopped himself back down on the sand, drew his knees up, and draped his arms over them. He was in good spirits, smiling, but he seemed completely nonchalant about it all, save for the smatter of pink on his cheeks. I could have chalked it up to the flames of the fire, but I questioned if that might not be all there was to it.

And when Jared met my gaze across the fire, he gave me a friendly wink. The flutter in my heart told me I was veering down a disastrous path. There was nothing to the kiss at all, and thinking otherwise would be stupid, but I had been stupid before.

The bottom line was that I did *not* have a crush on Jared Tomlin, so why did it feel like this game of Truth or Dare just got much more dangerous?

JARED

10

Jared, you idiot. Why did you do that?

Clearly, it was my fault for taunting Jenna about her little game. She'd thought she had me in a chokehold, but the idea of kissing Sammy hadn't seemed like much of a threat to me. All I intended to do was stick it to them how silly it all was. When I decided to kiss her, I had no idea I would enjoy it so much.

For the rest of the night, I was fixated on the feel of Sammy's touch and that kiss. I had never kissed Sarah, but I had surely imagined it a time or two. When I thought about it, I couldn't even remember the last kiss I had at all. Not being kissed much was a consequence of not being constantly on the prowl like many of my buddies were, which was fine with me. I'd always preferred to focus on football than girls. They were nothing but emotions and drama.

Not gonna lie… part of me only agreed to do the dare because I expected Sammy to reject the whole thing. I was surprised when she said yes, refusing me the out she hadn't known I'd hoped to gain in giving her the choice.

And then, we both went through with it. I kissed her, and

despite my empty expectations, she kissed me back. When I felt her pressing in, it became a strain to hold back and keep myself at a respectable distance. I wanted nothing more than to give over to the new feelings rushing through me, which were clearly the result of being single for so long.

When I broke away from Sammy earlier, I'd hoped she couldn't tell how much I struggled. I had no opportunity to consider the weight of my newfound feelings, but I didn't know that she and I had chemistry until it was very boldly, loudly clear we did. It took one kiss for me to realize what I hadn't noticed before.

Cliché, much?

So, what's a guy to do with a situation like that?

No wonder Dan and Jenna had sought to set me up in the first place. I must seem so pathetic to them, the golden couple who had made a relationship work since junior year.

With the group unaware of the mixture of my thoughts, the game raged on long enough for everyone to get their turn in the spotlight and then some. To my relief, there were no more questions about Sarah or myself and no more kissing. The craziest thing someone had to do was get buried for the rest of the game. *Well endured, Nick.* It seemed they would all agree to just about anything in order not to fail. I guess Nick and I fit right in.

What even happened if one "failed" to do a dare? The seriousness of this game was ridiculous to me, but when Jenna challenged me, I didn't like it at all. I have free will and authority over myself, so if I said no, I meant no, even if I did agree to play in the first place. But I didn't want to talk about Sarah, especially not in front of her. No, thanks. If it had to do with Sarah, I would keep it as respectful as possible. Crossed that bridge already. Not going over it again.

Truth or Dare hadn't ended the night. It merely kicked it off.

"Here." Dan offered me his flask again, which I could hear was fuller than it was before. Where was he getting his refills from?

"Nah, man. I'm good." It tasted like crap, and I needed to watch my caloric intake. Staying fit and away from junk like that over the summer wasn't just a recommendation; it was common sense if I wanted to keep my spot on the college team. Which I very much did.

"Since when? You quit drinking or something?"

"Pretty much. I need to stay in shape and pass all my screenings. It's not worth the risk."

What Dan didn't know was that I hadn't drunk at all since the party I went to with Sarah. That little sip earlier was the first thing I'd had in a while, and I really didn't miss it.

He gave me a hearty pat on the shoulder with a big, dopey, lazy-eyed grin on his face. "You're a good kid, you know that?"

"Thanks, Dad." The sarcastic remark hit me too late. It's an easily repeated phrase, such a casual thing to say that not many would notice it. It had been a good minute since I'd personally said it.

"Anytime," he said, as oblivious and happy as a clam.

The sound of girls' laughter had us both glancing up. From the corner of my eye, I saw his frown serving as a reminder that he had something to say earlier. Maybe now was a good time for him to divulge.

"Hey, man. Are you guys okay?"

He was still watching Jenna when he answered, his tone resigned. "I don't really know. We might not be. I've been trying to figure it out all week."

"What's going on?"

Turning to me, he hesitated before shaking his head. "A lot.

Not any one thing. We just never have an honest conversation about anything anymore. She always turns things into a joke or just blows it off. And that's when I can even get her to speak to me at all. She's ignored me almost all day."

"Sounds frustrating."

"To say the least."

"Maybe you guys need to spend some time alone together. Stick around here after everyone leaves and see if she'll open up. If things are that bad off, she must be pretty upset about it all, too. I can get a ride home with one of the others."

His shoulders slumped. "Won't make a difference."

"Why don't you go over there right now? Everyone's kinda doing their own thing at the moment. It's a good opportunity to try."

"I really don't think it'll work, but you're right. I certainly can try. Again."

"Good luck, man."

"Thanks," he said flatly.

I watched him go, concerned for my friend. While this wasn't the first time he'd had problems with Jenna, it seemed like the longest bout they'd had yet. Dan had a way of being able to soothe her, which was something nobody else could figure out how to do. For most of their relationship, they'd been great together.

They hardly ever fought, which I thought was a miracle in and of itself, considering how high-strung Jenna could get. She was a great friend, but there was no way I could put up with her high maintenance as a girlfriend. Dan was a warrior to do it and for so long.

There were a number of things I and everyone else knew about Jenna Rodriguez. She was loud and outgoing with classic

Latina looks, so basically, she was a beautiful handful. It took Dan a lot of work to keep up, but he was crazy about her and had been ever since they first met.

Whether or not Dan was making any progress with her now was up for debate. There was a lot of animated discussion going on, and I was concerned about the perturbed look on Dan's face after Jenna got up and walked off. She'd definitely been crying, and typically, that wasn't a good thing, but she did an okay job of playing it off. She simply wiped her face, stuck a smile on it, and joined the other girls.

By the end of the night, after there was no more birthday left in us, the vibe of the whole group was disjointed and sour, and everyone seemed ready to leave.

Jenna started packing up first, and the rest of us had no hesitancy in following suit. One by one, everybody left. Having brought the most stuff, Dan and I were the last ones remaining after an awkward goodbye with Jenna.

Dan joined me to help finish loading the volleyball equipment into the back of his truck.

"So, what was all that about? She at least talking to you now?"

"Oh, yeah, she's really talking. Won't shut up now." Dan slammed up the tailgate, bouncing the flat canopy bed-roof. He stormed off, leaving me behind to question everything.

Shaking my towel one final time to ensure it was free of sand for the ride home in Dan's new GMC, I laid it out beneath me and buckled in. On top of his troublesome attitude, my trunks were still damp, and I definitely hadn't gotten all the sand out of them.

It would be a *very* uncomfortable ride home.

We got out onto the paved road that led to the island highway, and Dan's behavior was getting more concerning by the second.

"You okay?"

He didn't immediately answer. Charging along the highway, he swerved three times, nearly swiping at least one car, and came to a screeching halt at a traffic light. "That was a bit too close, don't you think? I kinda feel like driving. Why don't you stop off at the gas station up ahead."

He ignored me, squeezing the gas the moment the light turned green. Dan took something silver from his pocket. My eyes followed the glinting reflections to his mouth, where he was chugging its contents. He swerved again.

"Dude, pull over."

Dan drained the flask and tossed it over his shoulder. He managed to stay in his lane over the island bridge, but he almost scraped the barrier wall. My insides were so bunched up with fear they could've cultivated a pearl.

This is bad.

Coming down on the other end of the bridge, Dan picked up speed, too much, and merged without looking into the slow lane. A car's horn and screeching rubber rang out around us. "What is wrong with you? Are you trying to kill us?" I yelled.

"Jenna finally told me what's wrong. Everything is ruined."

"Whatever it is, it'll be okay, I'm sure of it. You guys will figure everything out, but you can't do that if you're dead." I swallowed hard, flicking on Dan's hazard lights. "Just take the next exit, nice and easy, and trade me spots. I'll take you home. Things will look better in the morning."

Another horn blared around us. I couldn't tell where all the chaos was coming from anymore. My blood was pumping so hard that it just about snuffed out my hearing. Beside me, Dan visibly broke, tears falling freely from his eyes. If I could have offered any comfort I would have tried, but no words formed.

One minute, he was finally pulling to the right to get off the free-way, and the next, we were wrapped around the exit median.

With all the various sounds ringing in my ears and the strange fire surging through my limbs, the whole world faded to black until everything, even the sudden, piercing pain, disappeared completely.

SAMMY

My parents were waiting for me when I got home. There was no more avoiding it.

Possibly reading the trepidation on my face, my mom offered me a way out right away. "We could also wait until morning if you'd be more comfortable."

"No, I'd rather rip the Band-Aid off now. It's been eating me up for weeks. I'd get no sleep tonight if we waited. Though the beach did serve to distract me, better than anything else had in a while, I didn't have anything to do that for me now.

"I understand, baby. Come on in here then. We're ready." My mom waved for me to join them.

Walking over, I dropped my sandy backpack against the arched wall that separated the entryway from the family sitting room, the one that was too opulent for the family to actually sit in, except for on special occasions.

Technically, it was still my birthday, but did I want this moment to be a special occasion? Was this conversation family sitting room worthy? Was this information that I was truly ready for, legal adult or not? Did my age mean I would magically be able to handle knowing all there is to know about myself on a biological level?

As my nerves increased, so did my questions.

Settling onto the stiff imitation Victorian across from its mate, the one my parents sat on, I could do little to calm my nerves. My heartbeat raged inside my chest, and sweat tickled my neck.

Mom's comforting smile faded, and she sighed, uncharacteristically anxious. In her lap, her fingers kept twisting. Beside her, my dad reached his arm around and comfortingly anchored himself to her shoulders.

Before she could speak, my dad's soothing timbre secured us both. "I know this was never going to be an easy conversation, but don't be scared. Everything will be fine. Just remember that regardless of what we tell you, you and your brothers mean everything in the world to us. There's nothing about that we'd change, and nothing can change that. Understand?"

"Yes, sir," I said, as I always did when my father took on that tone of voice. He was not giving an order but rather instruction—wisdom, instead of berating. I could comply with that.

My mom sat up taller as her lungs slowly inflated. "When Caleb was about two, we knew we wanted just one more child. However, we'd decided a long time ago that our last would be an adoption. It was a mutual conviction we both had to provide love and life for someone special someday. Someone who needed us as much as we needed them. And lucky for us, that someone special turned out to be you. Praise God. You came to us as nothing short of a miracle when you were just three hours old. But you already know this part."

I certainly did. It was the same origin story I'd heard all my life.

Just get to the point!

"The part you don't know—the part we've committed to tell you now—is that your birth mom is my sister," said Dad. "Your Aunt Claudia."

Confusion swept over me, knocking my mental state to the ground. "Hurricane Claudia? *She's* my birth mother? The woman who cons the family out of every generosity? The walking, talking disaster that everyone talks crap about eleven months of the year?"

Even the Ballards take Jesus' birth month off in kindness.

"Really, Samantha, I wouldn't expect you to call her that," chastised Mom.

"Sorry, I'm just a little thrown for a loop here. I expected you to hand me a photograph of some woman across the country or even the ocean. I was nervous enough for *that*. But this is the craziest thing I've ever heard. I don't even know what to think."

Yes, I did, but it was nothing they'd want to hear. I didn't even want to be related to Claudia when she was just my crazy aunt. I sure as crap didn't want to be her *daughter*. If the Ballards had a black sheep, Claudia was a whole flock, all on her own. She didn't have her life together. She didn't have a husband or children. That's not necessarily a bad thing, but it was because she had zero stability. She couch-surfed at different family members' homes and pretended she had work when she really did—I didn't even want to know what—to earn money.

On and on, my thoughts rolled, banging against my brain like a shoe in a dryer. No wonder I look so much like Dad when I get angry. No wonder we all have the same attitude and the upturned Ballard nose.

I was still a Ballard. The biggest difference was my skin being a shade lighter, and my natural hair was more of a wave than a curl; that was it, and that could mean absolutely nothing. No wonder, in all my life, my relation to my family had never once been questioned, not even in a joking way.

But… Aunt Claudia? Really? Many times over the years, I thought long and hard about what I wouldn't give to be really and truly kin to my parents. To be their flesh and blood as well as their daughter. I never would've expected the truth that I actually was to be so disappointing.

My unstable emotions started to escape the chokehold I had hoped to keep them in. "If my birth mom has been around all this time, why did you guys bother waiting to tell me?

"We swore to tell you once you were an adult," Dad explained. "There was never going to be an easy way to say it or the perfect time to tell you. We made the best decision we could, and we stuck to it."

"And, of course, we are an open book, whatever you want to know."

It seemed a little too late for the truth to matter much now. How did one minute of honesty make up for eighteen years of lies? They shouldn't have kept this one to themselves.

Take a deep breath, Sammy. Deep breath in. Deep breath out.

Okay, I know they didn't *lie.* I always knew I would get the honest truth someday, but the end result still felt the same. I was pained by the truth and all that the truth made me realize. Instead of receiving the name of a person I would have to hunt down and introduce myself to, it was somebody I already knew. Worse, she already knew me.

My parents let that woman interact with me as though I was nothing more to her than an occasional niece when, in reality, she was my biological mother all along. My stomach felt sick over it.

I don't know if knowing sooner would've changed anything, but in my emotional craze, I only cared that they'd waited. Somehow, hearing it now felt like a big joke. It was bad enough just to be the daughter of that crazy woman, but to have seen her act foolish all this time and then be slapped with the knowledge? I couldn't think of anything worse.

Claudia was a joke. *And I'm her offspring.*

My bewilderment took a gradual turn to anger. "Are you guys even sorry?"

My mom looked wounded. "Sorry about what, honey?"

My throat constricted as my thoughts floundered. I didn't know what I wanted from them or what I expected them to say to such a stupid question, but I felt like retribution of some sort was needed.

"We chose you and loved you more than anyone ever could," she continued. "We spoke with numerous social workers and counselors and came to the conclusion a long time ago that we would tell you when you were an adult, and now we have. You're still our daughter, and we're still your parents in every way that counts."

Ready to bolt, I still had one more question. How much worse could things get? "So who's my father? One of the bums under the overpass?"

"My sister is a unique person, Sammy," began Dad. "She doesn't have the same morals we do. I think you realize that. When she showed up pregnant, nobody was surprised, but we didn't know she was seeing anyone. She used to come and go even more than she does now. At least now, she stays fairly local or with one of our sisters, if not us. Someone usually has tabs on her, which is as much comfort as we're able to get when it comes to Claudia. She's just always been that way. I suspect it has something to do with our father dying when we were younger, but who knows?"

Dad cleared his throat.

"What I'm trying to say is we don't know who your birth father is. She's remained tight-lipped about your entire conception since day one. Nothing we've ever tried has yielded any answers from her. I'm very sorry, Sammy-Girl. I wish I could give you more information about that." Reaching out, Dad patted my knee. "It's a lot to take in, we know. Do you have any more questions or anything else you would like to say so far?"

My mind stepped into the void, blackening. There may have been a hundred things I wanted to ask or say, but the only thing that emerged from the darkness of my mind was the compulsion to leave. "Can I go now?"

"Sure, you can. Whatever you need, we are here. Please, just never forget how much we love you."

"Perhaps after a nice shower and good night's rest, you'll want to talk some more," Mom said, making a feeble attempt.

"Thanks," I said with empty measure, shoving myself to a lightheaded stand.

My parents stood with me, each one taking it upon themselves to embrace me with too much force. Each hug lasted an eternity, one I could scarcely withstand. I stood there, hardly reciprocating. I mimicked the motions. I let them hug me, but I felt nothing. The usual warmth an embrace from my parents could give was gone.

SAMMY

12

As morning approached, I searched my waking mind, hoping to realize the previous night had been nothing but a bad dream. Coming to full awareness, of course, I realized it wasn't. By the time the dimness of dawn had completely disappeared, I had about a million questions, but the one that remained the most important was the one I couldn't get answered.

Who the heck was my birth *father?*

I shuddered to think and shoved the question away. One problematic parental issue at a time. Besides, the only way I would get anywhere near that information was to go to the source, and from what Dad said last night, the source was a dead end.

Downstairs at breakfast, everyone was already at the table. After I sat down, Ronnie and Caleb glanced at each other, barely looking in my direction, then took off.

My mom greeted me with her soft smile. "Good morning, baby."

"Good morning." Just twenty-four hours ago, those were the simplest words in the world. Today, they were anything but.

Simple conversation seemed to be a thing of the past between my parents and me.

Another horrifying thought registered as I watched their retreat. "Do Ronnie and Caleb know about you know who?"

"No, they don't," Dad answered.

"Why'd they just bail like that then?"

"They knew what the deal was and probably feel awkward about things. Your eighteenth birthday has been a long time coming for everyone."

I knew it. I'm on my way to becoming a pariah in my own family. So, there really was space for things to get worse. "Are you going to tell them?"

"Eventually."

"When is eventually?"

"That's up to you, more or less. We have to be reasonable. Everyone deserves the truth, but we want you to be up for it. You could even tell them yourself if you wish."

"What do you mean you want me to be up for it?"

Clearing his throat, Dad spoke again, "We want you to have time to ask questions and adjust before we bring their opinions into the mix. It might be hard for them to accept. You never know how someone will react."

"That's why you just prepare as best you can and then leave it up to God," Mom added.

I'll bet. "And God told you that eighteen was the magic number, huh? Wait until I was just adult enough to really under-stand how bad Claudia is before being cast as her daughter?"

Mom winced. "There is no magic anything, but yes, we felt that as an adult, you would be better equipped to deal with the truth."

"Samantha Olivia Ballard, don't you sass your mother. You're permitted certain allowances, but disrespect is not one of them. You were not raised that way."

"Sorry. I guess it would seem that my feelings and how I was raised are not getting along at the moment."

"And we completely understand that. We've had a long time to prepare ourselves, and you will need your own time to process. We're more than willing to give it to you."

"Can I take some now and be excused, please?"

My dad looked at me from above the rims of his small-framed glasses. "If you're sure you don't want to talk about anything else."

"I'm sure." And I proved it by noisily scooting my chair back and retreating to my room. Maybe if I got this off my chest, it wouldn't suck so much, but I wasn't ready to tell my brothers they were my cousins. I just couldn't do that right now.

I reached for my phone. With unsure fingers, I texted the girls' group chat.

SAMMY

I have to talk to you guys.

BIRDIE

What's goin' on?

SARAH

Are you okay?

Over and over, I typed my response, and over and over, I deleted it. The words just would not come out, even in text. Maybe text even made it worse. Once it was out there in the ether, revealed to those who didn't already know, I couldn't take it back. Some part of its existence would always live on.

Before I could decide between making up something lame or

trying to *"never mind"* my way out of what I'd started, Jenna dropped a bomb ahead of me.

JENNA

Dan and Jared got into an accident on the way home last night. I've been at the hospital for hours. I can't believe I forgot to say something sooner.

Guys, I'm so scared…

At nearly the same time, all three of us sent the same reply:

I'm on my way.

JARED

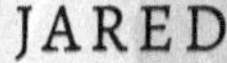

13

I WOKE UP IN THE HOSPITAL, PLAGUED BY THE NEWS THAT I HAD sustained an MCL tear in the crash.

"Is there any *good* news?" I asked bitterly.

"Of course. You survived a nasty car crash. Your friend did, too, in case you were wondering. And if you take the recovery process as seriously as you need to, you will bounce back from this injury. Without needing surgery." The doctor, I didn't even get his name, smiled. It was comforting, which only annoyed me more.

"Great."

"I know you're not thrilled, Jared, but you really got lucky here. Look at this scan… I can point out a dozen different ways a crash like this could have completely ruined your right knee. I'd definitely call your outcome good news."

"Just tell me when I can play football again."

"Well, the bulk of this kind of recovery depends solely on the patient's dedication and response to it. How seriously will you be taking your treatment plan?"

"Hold on. What about my scholarship?" I panicked, looking

from my mom to the doctor, hoping one of them would speak faster. My mom sat there silently, her face a crumpled, teary mess.

Not helping.

"I'm afraid we just don't know yet. I know you're a very athletic kid, so you'll have a tough road ahead, but be patient. We'll have to see how things go for a while before I can comfortably say anything more optimistic. Right now, it's just hope and see."

"What if I do a ton of physical therapy?"

"You're going to need a ton of physical therapy regardless, but we won't know how your injury heals until it heals. We'll keep a close eye on your progress, and I will refer you to an orthopedic clinic for follow-up in one month. I don't want you driving at least until then. We'll do a fresh scan and see where it's at. Hopefully, we're all very impressed with your progress. For right now, go easy on yourself and do only as instructed, okay?" He reached for a pair of crutches inside a long cabinet. "You're going to be using these, wearing one of those." He nodded toward the brace I already had on.

"You've gotta be kidding me," I grumbled. I focused all my attention on the doctor. "I have a scholarship," I bemoaned again. "I can't just not play. What if I don't heal in time?"

"If you want to heal, you have to work for it, and part of that requires allowing time for it to happen. It's the only way." As my heart sank, the doctor's face was sympathetic but resolute. I would've rather he'd been a jerk. "I'm sorry, Jared."

The doctor left, and it was just my mom and me. Avoiding eye contact with her, I shifted in my bed. The brace holding my maimed knee together made my movements slower and more uncomfortable, but I managed.

There was a chorus of sniffles. From the corner of my eye, I could see my mom's handful of tissues at work on her face. I prayed she wouldn't talk.

"You shouldn't have been in that car," she muttered, proving prayer didn't work. "Better yet, you shouldn't have been at the beach with them. I knew those new *friends* of yours were trouble. Remember what happened in February? Now look."

I would never understand her hatred toward them for something I did. The party incident with Sarah was my stupid fault, and that was that. I was the one who mixed our drinks using what I thought was just food dye. I was the idiot who accidentally sent her into shock. What did any of the others have to do with that? Where was their fault in it? Exactly. Nowhere.

"None of them were responsible for what happened in February, and I really wish you'd stop bringing it up just so you can blame them."

"You weren't the one who brought drugs to the party in the first place. You didn't know what they were. *That's* not your fault."

"Yeah, but the rest is. Nobody else at the party had trouble except me, and you don't consider the situation fairly. I've already beat myself up for it time and time again, and all you do is remind me how stupid I am. I don't want to talk about it anymore, Mom, *please*. You get meaner and meaner every time you bring it up."

How quickly her tears dried. Anger replaced her despair. "I'm so sorry if my concern is such a burden to you, but you are my son, are you not? If I see a red flag in those you spend time with, why wouldn't I point it out?" She scoffed, crossing one leg over the other in her chair. "Heaven forbid I do my job as your only parent. It must make me so terrible."

My only parent. That stung. "That's not what I mean. It's the way you constantly voice your opinion on it, like you want it to stay a problem. I'm over here trying to move on with my life, and you keep picking the scab raw again. In the end, nothing happened, and that's a good thing. There were no charges, Sarah is fine, and everyone—but *you*, it would seem—has forgiven me for it. It's like you wish I *had* gotten arrested so you could gloat about being right or something." Her face couldn't have gotten more red. I almost feared her silence. My tone softened. "It's okay to let it go, Mom. These are good people."

"Oh yeah, so good one of them ran you into a cement wall going sixty miles per hour. Great friend. And if I recall correctly, he was the very same one who hosted the party with your food coloring, too. You're right, Jared. Your friends are fantastic. I'm so glad I can trust your judgment. What was I thinking?" She pushed briskly to her feet. "I'm going to check on your brother."

With my mom out of the room, I looked around for my phone. I hadn't looked at it since before yesterday, and I still had no idea what was going on with Dan. All my mom had told me so far was that he was in another room, pretty beat up but not as bad as me.

I had dozens of missed calls and hundreds of missed texts, but none from Dan's phone. I looked next for Jenna's name, and sure enough…

With my gut in a giant twist, I clicked her conversation open. There were multiple texts over the course of the night.

JENNA

Dan isn't answering me. Are you guys still together?

Seriously, don't cover for him. Where is he?

> Hey, did he tell you anything?

> A CAR ACCIDENT?? DID YOU HAVE ANYTHING TO DO WITH THIS?? WHAT HAPPENED??

> JARED!!

> There's a criminal investigation because Dan was drunk. His parents aren't happy to see me. They think it's all my fault.

> Maybe it is.

> The cops won't let me in to see him!!

> I have no idea what's going on anymore!!

> OMG, they just took him from the hospital in handcuffs!! They took Dan away, and I didn't even get to say goodbye!!

Backing out to open my other unread messages, the knot in my gut enlarged. Sarah and Sammy were among those who had sent their fair share of texts—some asking after me more than others.

SAMMY

> Are you okay?? Jenna just said you and Dan were in a car accident. Please tell me you're okay...

> You better be in a coma. I hate being ignored. You know I hate being ignored. This must mean it's serious.

> Sorry, I'm just kidding, in case that wasn't obvious.

> I'm praying for you, Jared. We all are. Wake up and come back to us. <3

There were more unread texts, but I couldn't stand to open them. Their concern was incredible, but how could I face anything else right now? All that had transpired without my knowledge was too much to handle. Dan arrested for drunk driving? He and Jenna separated when they were dealing with whatever was going on between them? A car crash possibly wrecking my career before I'd even started it?

Yeah, much too much to handle.

I tossed my phone onto the end table—out of sight, out of mind. When I tried to roll onto my side, pain shot up from my knee. Bitter and fatigued, I slowly turned to face the window. It was bright and early, but the day meant nothing to me. The sun could try all it wanted; things would never be bright again.

My dad was dead. My mom had become so callous I didn't recognize her. My brother was painfully naïve. My best friend had been carted off in a police car. My other so-called friends were frustratingly absent when I could've really used their support.

And I didn't even want to draw my attention back to my knee and the implications that came with it, but the reality was, in a single night, my dream and the small pieces of my life that made things tolerable while I waited for it were all gone.

All those texts everyone sent, but not one person had come to see me? Not even Sammy? What good were her prayers if she and the others clearly blamed me for what happened to Dan? If nobody had been injured in the accident, maybe he wouldn't have been so severely punished. I wasn't sure if that's how it worked, but it might be how our friends felt. Or else, wouldn't at least one of them have shown up to visit?

Or maybe they were only visiting him because being arrested was a bigger deal than being on crutches.

I wish Dad were alive. I wish he were here.

Although I was glad he couldn't see me flounder and possibly lose the dream we'd built together. Football wasn't just about me; it was something we'd shared. A dream I couldn't have possibly built alone. He taught me how to throw a ball, how to understand plays, and what it meant to be a team player. Because of him, I have my great love of the sport. And now I could be losing it all. He would be so disappointed. But not half as disappointed as mom seemed to be.

And he would have encouraged me to pray about it. Were things different, were he still here, he would've taken my hands in his and done it for me, whether I wanted to or not.

His words still echoed in the deep corners of my mind: "Praying isn't about you or what you want or need. God already knows all that. You can't change His mind, anyway. What *He* wants is your *surrender*. Just open your mouth and talk to him, Jared. It's that simple."

In one last act of defiance, as one final way to stick it to the crappy situation I had woken up in, I clamped my mouth shut until I tasted blood. There was nothing left of me to surrender.

SAMMY

14

My bed never looked so good as I threw myself down on it. Coming home from the hospital was draining, and I wasn't even involved in the accident. My eyes were sore and stinging from the emotion of it all. I couldn't even imagine how Jared, Dan, and their families felt. If only Jared would text me back.

Not being allowed to see him had left me with a ton of unresolved feelings. It hit me in a weird way. Even though his mom had told us he would be okay, I didn't want to take her word for it. I wanted to see him for myself.

Dan was taken out in handcuffs right in front of us. The only thing we knew was that, at the time of the crash, he was way above the legal blood alcohol limit, under-aged, and was in for it. For what exactly, we didn't know and probably wouldn't for a while. Jenna was destroyed, and Dan's parents couldn't have cared less about her. They left as soon as he did, but not before pleading with her to take this as a sign to finally leave their son alone.

Harsh. Just harsh. And all Jenna could do was cry. I wanted to take a page from Kevin's book and lay them out for being so heartless and cruel, but of course, I didn't. I wouldn't. I wasn't necessarily a lover, but I wasn't that kind of fighter, either.

Poor Jenna. We all consoled her as best we could until finally deciding it was time to leave. We weren't going to see Jared, there was nothing to do about Dan, and we were all exhausted.

As I replayed the scenes of the evening in my mind, sneaking glances at my phone on my nightstand, hoping for a response from Jared, Mom opened my bedroom door and stepped inside.

"Sammy-Girl? I need to talk to you."

"The last time I heard that, it didn't go so well."

"You know, pain doesn't provide free rein to treat me with attitude. I don't appreciate your continued sarcasm. How many times can I tell you I love you, or how many ways can I show you it's the truth before you forgive me?"

I sat up with a sigh. Parents always used big words or complicated phrases that were great at causing guilt in a child, no matter how old they got. Apparently, being an adult didn't mean anything when your mother was upset with you. "It's not that. I don't doubt you love me. Just… what do you need to talk about?"

Her eyes told me she was still skeptical and a little hurt, but she put on a brave face and sat down on the edge of my bed. "Your… Aunt Claudia will be here for her visit next weekend."

"Oh. Is that all?" I asked, suppressing my real feelings and lying back down on my side, facing away from her.

"It would mean a lot to your dad and me if you tried to spend some time with her."

Rolling, I met her gaze. "Is that a joke?"

"No, baby. Not at all."

"Then is it a request or a demand? Because I don't want to."

"I know you don't, and I know you're still mad. I'm not going to tell you that doesn't hurt, but I understand. I'd prepared for it.

But now that you know, we want you to give Claudia a chance. You may be able to see her in a different light."

"What for? I can't believe you're pushing me toward her like this. Do you want me to start calling her Mom, too?"

A storm cascaded over her features, her dark eyes clouding with intensity, and she deeply inhaled and exhaled, her eyes taking on a glossy sheen. I had to look away from her again, unable to face the consequences of my words. "Just think about it, please. She'll only be here for a few days. You know how we feel about it, but you're an adult now. Ultimately, it's up to you." She lingered, watching, waiting, *hoping* for a response, but I couldn't give her one. After another long sigh, she squeezed my forearm and left.

Long after she'd gone, I remained trapped in my head by my stunted emotions, letting them fester until I felt completely rotten inside. I considered reaching out to my friends again, but the will to tell them about Claudia hadn't returned. I picked up my phone to feign a distraction, then while browsing my conversations, I was taken back to Jared.

I wish he would respond.

SAMMY

15

Birdie Jo, Sarah, and I stood in Jared's foyer. Jenna should've been there, too, but refused to leave her house. Her woe-is-me behavior was the first of many things that set my acidic mood into motion. She wasn't the only one affected by that terrible night. Besides, her boyfriend was the one at fault. Legally—and morally—Dan deserved the outcome he got. Nobody forced him to drink and drive. He was extremely lucky a totaled truck and Jared's torn knee were the worst things that happened.

Poor Jared, I thought. That kind of injury was rough on an athlete. I hoped he was okay. We'd been told very little, and I still hadn't heard from him.

Over a week had gone by since Jared's release from the hospital, and he refused to see us. Any of us. And for some reason, that stung. I wasn't sure how much more pain I could personally take in light of my revelations at home. Even though I was getting exceptionally okay at hiding it, today felt like the perfect day to snap.

With Aunt Claudia arriving tomorrow, I just might.

I pulled my phone out and composed yet another text to Jared.

SAMMY

> You've been home over a week. How long are you going to refuse to see us?

Read. But no response. Just like all the others.

Jared's mom looked us over as we stood there, probably appearing pitiful. I was surprised she let us inside, considering her tone every time she spoke.

Uncomfortable, Mrs. Tomlin turned to her other son. "Jeremy, go tell your brother he has guests here to see him."

"I don't want to. He's in a bad mood."

"Just go."

"Fine," he groaned, lazily spinning on his heel.

We watched him disappear through the hall. We heard something fly from the room, hitting the wall. There was a secondary sound as Jeremy shouted, "Ow!" then whatever object had been thrown out was promptly thrown back in. Their mother gathered her face into her hands before releasing a chest-rattling sigh.

Jeremy returned, red-faced and grimacing. "I told you."

"What did he say?" she asked him.

"His Majesty said he's trying to sleep. Can I go to my room now?"

She sent him off with a flick of her hand, unsatisfied, then kept her gaze cast down the hall.

"I'm sorry about Jared." She spoke so mournfully, as though to herself. "He's been holed up away from the world since we got back. I'm lucky if I get him out of bed to do his exercises. He's just devastated."

"We are, too," Sarah assured her, and Mrs. Tomlin turned toward us, seemingly remembering our presence.

Fighting the urge to roll my eyes over Jared's dramatics, I reached for my phone.

SAMMY

Are you seriously going to just ignore us

Read. No answer.

SAMMY

You're being a big baby.

Read. No answer. He wasn't trying all that hard to sleep, but he was doing a Grade-A job of blowing us off.

SAMMY

Seriously. The biggest.

Read. Then—the typing dots! The only sign of life he'd shown this whole time, but it was followed by nothing. No response ever came.

Ugh! God, why is this boy so frustrating? He didn't know how lucky he was, and he was pissing it all away. So what if he was missing out on a little bit of football? He could play again; his mom told us the doctor said it might be possible. What was a little bit of downtime? At least he hadn't been killed...

I shut my eyes, jaw clenched, and a slow, deep breath escaped me. Dan was an idiot for driving drunk, and Jared was an idiot for letting him. And all the rest of us were idiots for not noticing he was headed in that direction before we left that night. Maybe there was something more we could've done, but we didn't.

The desperation Mrs. Tomlin felt for her eldest son was easily discernible on her face. She apologized again on his behalf. "At least you can say you tried."

I sat quietly, staring at my phone, waiting impatiently. I knew he knew we were there.

"We won't give up on him, Mrs. Tomlin," chimed Birdie.

Looking unsure—of us or of herself, I didn't know—she thanked us. With that, we understood it was time to go. Everyone piled up in Sarah's car, and one after the other, we were dropped off at home, defeated and frustrated.

That night did a number on all of us in some way. As annoyed as I was with Jenna today for backing out and not making an effort with Jared, I understood she was going through something. I myself still couldn't believe Dan had been carted off by police from the hospital. He hadn't been hurt, but the sight had been jarring.

Wasn't that always how it worked? The driver barely suffers, even when their passengers—or worse, others on the roads— suffer greatly. Dan walked away with nothing but a scratch and wouldn't go to jail.

Jenna had passionately told us all about it earlier that morning. Apparently, he was deemed an alcoholic, and the judge sent him to a special rehabilitation program called South Texas Life Restoration. People called it STLR, pronounced "stellar." According to the legal system, in Dan's case, rehab was a more suitable place for him than jail or prison.

Based in various major cities throughout Texas, the program just opened a new branch about an hour north in a not-so-major town called Beeville. With as many prisons, hospitals, and mental health facilities as that place apparently had, it was either the most dangerous place to live in the whole state or the safest.

But whatever. Dan was going to get past this. He was going to get the help he needed to get sober. As soon as his stint in the program was complete, he would be sitting pretty. Jenna would get her boyfriend back and all would be right in their world again. Yeah, that night had done a lot of damage to all of us, but some had suffered a lot more than just a summer setback.

And *some* of us weren't being huge babies about it. But Jenna and Jared definitely were.

Pulling me from my thoughts, Ronnie tapped on my open door. "Hey, Sis. You doing okay?"

"Yeah, just frustrated." *My new norm.*

"Wanna talk about it?"

"No, it's fine. I'll deal."

He cleared his throat. "You remember what's happening tomorrow?"

How could I forget? Even if Claudia was still only my aunt, we all knew what her visits meant. No peace at all for the duration of her stay.

Ronnie's question was two-fold, though. After our spat at the breakfast table, I gave my parents permission to tell Ronnie and Caleb the truth. They were surprised, but like the awesome brothers they are, they took turns hugging me and giving me their love. They vowed to never treat me differently, and I vowed to hold them to it.

"Unfortunately, I do," I said. "But just because she's coming doesn't mean you guys have to leave. It would be really great if you stayed, in fact. Super great."

"We would if we could, Sam, but that's not why we're leaving. We have to go back to work if we want to keep our apartment. And I need to pick up that summer course I was talking about."

"Did you know you can go to school online from anywhere you want?"

The corner of Ronnie's mouth—Dad's mouth—quirked under sad eyes. When he came to sit beside me, his tall, built frame pulled the edge of my bed down. I gave him my best puppy-dog impression. "Can't you guys stay?"

He shook his head. "Please don't ask me that again. I don't know how many times I can tell you no."

"But that's what I want." I gave him a sad, scheming smile.

"It's not what *I* want. It's not what I need. Caleb and I, the only plan we have is education. If we didn't have that we'd be—"

"You'd be no better off than me."

"I wasn't going to say anything like that." He swung into my shoulder with his. "You could still come with us. Audit the first semester and apply for spring. You know there's always room for you at our place. Even if you take a year off before enrolling like I did."

"I don't even know what I'd do at college, Ronnie. I'm not an academic like you guys."

"You've never really enjoyed school like we do, I know that."

He hadn't said anything we didn't already know. It was a simple truth—I did hate school. Being a professional student was not my thing like it was theirs, and that had never bothered me until now. Him pointing out that difference between us just served as another splash of vinegar in the wound.

I'm not like them. I'm a mess, like my "real" mom.

Claudia Ballard was no substitute for the woman who raised me, and I really had no desire to get to know her. She made her decision eighteen years ago and would never make up for the time she'd lost with me. I really didn't care if she wanted to. The last thing I wanted was for my brothers, my rocks, my only source of stability left on earth, to leave at a time like this, but I wasn't going to get my way. Not this time.

I'd gotten along my whole life just fine without her, with hardly ever a thought about whom she would turn out to be because I was satisfied with my life. I knew that, whatever the case, I was given up for a reason, and it was for the best. I could lodge no complaints there.

Then, to discover my birth mother was my deadbeat aunt, well, then I cared even less. Six days out of seven, I could even convince myself she was my aunt and nothing else for how different we were.

Only now, I'd never felt more like the wrong woman's daughter. I couldn't help feeling like my waywardness was letting my parents down, and Claudia's presence was not going to help that.

"Hey." Ronnie squeezed my shoulder. "You can be anything you want. You don't have to be anything like us for us to love you."

I pondered for a second, shaking my mind loose of the clouded emotions. "Can I be a unicorn?" He rolled his eyes, realizing his mistake. "No, wait, what about a penguin? Aren't they so cute with their flippers and all the waddling? I could totally pull that off."

"You win this round, Sammy. But I'm not giving up. I think you'd make a great student if you wanted to."

"My transcript would beg to differ."

"Like I said, if you wanted to." His knowing smile made me roll my eyes. I threw a decorative pillow at him, and he snatched it mid-air before tossing it back. I caught it with ease.

"I'll see you later."

"Later," I said, clutching the small pillow to my chest as he left. Soon, he wouldn't just be moseying down the hall to his room. He would be leaving town to return to school, taking Caleb with him.

It was just another punch to the gut that I didn't want to deal with yet. One would come in, and two would go out. I would give anything to have the reverse. Somehow, having them home for the summer, especially after my birthday news, made it all more tolerable. I needed my brothers.

Meanwhile, my subconscious kept trying to correct my words. Tabby and Ronald weren't my parents but my aunt and uncle. Ronnie and Caleb weren't my brothers but my cousins. That's how it was by blood, but how much did it matter? It wouldn't do me any good to disconnect myself from them right now, even if I was still mad. Which I was.

But family was family…

After Ronnie left, I only lasted about fifteen more minutes at home. Every second that ticked by brought Claudia closer to my house, into a life that actively rejected her. Nothing good was going to come out of it. She didn't want me then, and I was convinced she didn't want me now. And I, sure as the sun rose each morning, didn't want or need *her*.

For a while there, we all thought she might not even come this year because we usually heard from her long before now. It wasn't until last week that my dad finally got the phone call from somewhere in California where she'd been booted from the apartment she shared with her latest conquest. Thus, her bad circumstances were bringing her to my doorstep after all.

My irritation consumed me until it had grown into full-blown rage. I considered rearranging my bedroom with a sledge-hammer but decided on a different path of destruction and debated going back to Jared's house.

SAMMY

Last chance, Tomlin. Wise up now or pay the cost.

No response. He didn't even open the text this time, but I'd bet anything he wasn't asleep.

Alrighty then. My course was charted. Decision made, I drove back to Jared's house.

I parked down the street so I could sneak up to his window without being heard or seen. I couldn't stand it anymore. He could tell me to go away to my face. If it was up to me to demand sense return to that boy, then I was more than up for the task. Better to be with Jared's issues than at home with mine.

JARED

16

I HELD OFF AS LONG AS I COULD. STILL LYING IN BED, I POPPED MY next dose of painkillers. I remained laid back with my phone in my hand, staring at the text on the screen.

Annoyed, I tossed my phone aside, after merely previewing the new text. Sammy had been messaging all day long, even when I could hear them all down the hall. At my mother's request, my brother had come and told me I had visitors and should come out. I didn't, of course, holding fast to my refusal, breaking my TV remote in the process, until at last I heard the shuffling and murmuring of goodbyes.

Finally, I had thought to myself. *Now, maybe I can get some peace.* Only I knew I wouldn't. I hadn't had *any* peace since the accident.

I was so beyond tired. Every time I closed my eyes, the memories resurfaced. The sounds of the screeching tires on the pavement, the scraping of Dan's truck against the exit barrier. Shattered glass in my face and lap. Frenzied shouting as I teetered in and out of consciousness.

I closed my eyes and pressed my fists against my ears, beating them until I couldn't hear anything but a dull ringing. Once I cleared my head—though it would never be enough—I opened them again, only to see a shadowy figure behind the blinds of my window. Then, there came a light tap, and my heart raced. What the…?

"Open up," came a harsh, feminine whisper. "I know you're awake in there."

Sammy? Wow. She was nothing if not tenacious.

As for me, I felt defiant, petulant even, like a child. I folded my arms across my chest and stayed put and silent.

"I'm getting impatient. There's a lovely assortment of rocks out here, and I ain't afraid to use them." There was a momentary pause. "Awww, a gnome!"

My head fell back, plunking against my headboard, and I sighed in defeat. I believed her. Throwing back my comforter, I slid out of bed. Eyeing the crutches propped up on my nightstand disdainfully, I stood on one shaking leg. Using the support of my knee brace, I hobbled past the stupid crutches, steadying myself with my hands along the walls and furniture as I went.

Yanking my blinds up, I intended to peg Sammy with a rueful look, but my efforts were thwarted when I saw her face.

"Finally," she said. "Now, if you don't mind, could you open up and let me through? I'm getting weird looks from your neighbor's cat." She was irked, yet she exuded her usual confidence, which stripped me of all of mine. Instead of being cross with her, I found myself hyper-focusing on her strong, pursed lips, suddenly recalling the last time we saw each other.

The beach. The kiss.

I forced a scowl. "What are you doing here?"

"Making good on my threats."

Rolling my eyes, I counted to five in my head before unlatching and lifting the window. "You really can't take a hint, huh?"

"No, I can," she said, as if an elaboration was coming, something to explain why she was ignoring my requests to be alone, but all she did was climb through my window. "Phew. That was actually kinda fun. A little bit of a thrill. Now I know why authors are always writing that stuff into books. It's effective."

"Yeah, at irritating people." I turned, gritting my teeth, and broke out into a sweat as I walked back to my bed, avoiding looking as helpless and pathetic as I felt. "What is it you want?"

Collapsing as if I'd just completed a triathlon, I worked to steady my breathing. Unfettered, Sammy lithely walked around my room, inspecting with her eyes as much as her hands.

"You have a lot of stuff," she said casually, continuing her perusal.

Slow breath in... slow breath out...

"Oh, wow," she said, reaching out to grab something. She turned toward me with a football in hand. "Don't tell me this the ball from the last game?"

"The very one." I scored the final touchdown that night, ending my high school football career on the highest note possible. Of course I got to keep that ball. "How could you tell?"

She held it out more. "The signatures gave it away."

"Oh. Right."

"That was an epic catch," she continued. "How many yards was it again? Ten?"

"Twelve."

Sammy nodded, turning to glance at me. "Epic."

"Can you put it down?"

She looked suddenly startled. "Oh, it probably has good luck on it or something, right? Don't wanna be rubbing that off." She stuck the ball back in its cradle. "I'm just teasing. That was a really strong finish to a great year. Glad I got to see it. It was cool for all of us seniors, in a way."

"You were there? I don't remember seeing you."

"I wasn't with the girls."

"I know because they came down to the field afterward and congratulated me. Who were you with then?"

"Adam."

"Alvarado?" The surprise in my voice, coupled with the look on her face, explained why she hadn't said that from the beginning.

"The very one," she threw my earlier words back at me.

"Why in the world would you go out with that tool bag?"

"Aw come on. He's really not so bad."

I scoffed, nearing laughter. Why was I annoyed she was defending him? "The guy made it through one season of football freshman year, and pretended he was everybody's best friend until he wussed out after one concussion and bailed."

"You're mad because he figured out the hard way that he didn't want to play football?"

"Not at all; it's not that he quit the team. It was the little punk way he behaved afterward. You don't treat your brethren like that. Once a Titan, always a Titan."

"I guess he was never truly a Titan then. Not everyone has the same kind of school spirit."

"Pfft."

She continued her casual inspection of my room and everything in it, coming across a photo of my family—back when it included my dad. I was almost eleven in that picture. Unbeknownst to us, Dad would be gone just five years later.

"Aw. You look so cute. You were even more blond back then." She turned back to me, and though she was jovial, I could see a hardness in her eyes.

Let's just cut to the chase already. "Alright, for real. What do you want, Sammy?"

Shoulders sinking, Sammy came to stand at the edge of my bed. "You weren't returning my calls, texts, or voicemails. You wouldn't let us in to see you."

She was correct. "And?"

"And enough is enough! Quite frankly, your attitude sucks. You need us, Jared. Look at you. You're not okay, but you easily could be better."

"I'm sorry, what?"

"You have people here who are trying to care for you, Jared. From the sounds of it, you're not even cooperating for your mom. Do you even *want* to heal?"

"You have no idea what's going on with me or between me and my mom. And it's a little convenient for you guys to give a crap now, isn't it? Where were you guys when Dan and I were in the hospital?"

Her brow scrunched, and her eyes narrowed. "In the lobby. Like, the entire time. You didn't know we were there?"

"No."

"We asked to go in, but your mom told us no. She said you were struggling to stay conscious. Was that true?"

"Somewhat. But she never told me you guys were there for me. I thought..." I felt too stupid to finish that sentence.

"Spit it out. You thought what?"

"I thought it was just Jenna there waiting for Dan."

Sammy knocked her fist into my shoulder. "You thought we left you to rot?"

"Kinda, yeah."

She laughed. "Well, that explains a lot. No wonder you've been such a butthead." Sammy sat down next to me on the bed. The motion jostled my knee in an unfavorable way, and I hissed without realizing I'd reacted.

"Oh my gosh. I'm so sorry." She placed her hand onto my shoulder. "Are you okay? Can I do anything to help?"

"Sit still," I said through tight teeth.

"Right. Still. I can do that." She withdrew her hand and slowly placed it into her lap, forming a statuesque posture.

"Level with me. Why are you here?" I asked again, although less demanding this time. Apparently, bossing around the boss didn't work.

"Remember what I told you during spring break at the beach?"

Umm. Did I? "What was that?"

"That I'm your friend."

"So?"

"So, you can't be forgetting it. Being a friend means being there through thick and thin and making a total nuisance of yourself when they try fruitlessly to shut you out and all that good stuff."

"I'm starting to comprehend the nuisance part of it especially."

"Good. It's really a lot easier on everyone if you do."

Surprising myself, I laughed as I leaned back and adjusted. The hinges of the brace seemed to add fifty pounds to the heft of my leg, adding to my pain. We were shoulder to shoulder by the time I finished getting myself situated, and then my pain was replaced with something else entirely. I couldn't imagine if she was as aware of where our skin touched as I was. Was she also thinking about that silly—or not so silly—kiss?

"Does it hurt really bad?" came her gentle inquiry.

I shrugged. "I've endured worse." My mind's eye flicked to the family portrait on my bookcase. "But yes, actually, it hurts like crazy."

"I'll bet it does," she said, but her voice trailed off as she spoke. I suspected she wasn't referring to my pain anymore. "I tore a couple of things in my day on the court, but nothing this serious." The look on her face changed. "To answer your real question, I'm not entirely sure what I'm here for. I just acted on impulse."

"Why? What does that mean?"

"Let's just say you're not the only one with big, ongoing drama right now."

"Wow. Vague much?"

She exhaled hard and turned, staring into the room. "I just don't want to talk about it."

"I can tell. But maybe it would help."

"Doubt it."

She could dish it but not take it, was that right? "Well, too bad. I'm going to give that *you gotta be a nuisance to be a good friend* system a try. So, Samantha, tell me how you're feeling today. What's on your mind?"

Her eyes squeezed to slits. "I'm feeling something like steamrolled horse manure that got vacuumed up and poured into an ice cube tray and then busted up and ran over by an Army tank."

That was quite an emotion. One that I felt I actually understood. "And then collected and thrown into a volcano, right?"

"Exactly."

So, she really was going through something pretty big and

dramatic. I picked at a thread on my comforter. "You know that my dad died in the middle of junior year, right?" Unsure why I blurted that out, I avoided her stare.

"Oh, no, I didn't know that." Her hands flexed in her lap, captured by the corner of my eye. "Sorry, I didn't mean to bring all that up for you."

"No, it's okay. I'm telling you because I want to."

For some reason.

At my sides, my hands squeezed and released lumpy sections of my bedsheet. "My dad has been gone for going on two years now, and most of the time, I'm actually okay, but it's times like now, milestones like graduation or possibly losing my scholarship when my mom starts crying a lot again, and I realize how much I still miss him. Stuff like that, along with Christmas and birthdays. I've gotten used to not having him around. What is really hard for *me* are the firsts and lasts without him. He'll never see *this* for the first time, and he'll never see *that* ever again…"

Sammy remained watching me intently, silently.

"Death is kinda funny," I went on. "A year and a half easily passes into more, and you start to forget how bad it feels. But then it only takes a second to bring you back, and it feels like it's happening all over again. Like no time has passed at all." I could see silent tears falling from her cheeks, but I still didn't turn. Tears? For me? For my dad?

"How did he…?" Her voice was quiet and softer than I'd ever heard it.

"Car accident driving home from the valley. He worked there four days a week, then came home for the weekend."

"I'm really so sorry."

"We were told it was an instant thing, so at least he wasn't in pain."

"Thank God for that."

Ha. No, thanks. God could've spared my dad's life after the accident if He wanted to. At any point in time, He could have intervened, or sent His angels of protection, or *something* that resulted in my father being here today. I would've thanked God for *that.*

My mom and I thanked the medical team who provided us with the knowledge of his pain-free death. We thanked the funeral parlor that gave us his cremated remains, and we thanked all the friends and family who attended his funeral. But I'd never thought to thank God for taking my dad from us.

Maybe He was responsible for killing Dad swiftly, but He's also the one who killed him in the first place. He could've stopped the collision. He could've taken anyone else. Plenty of those oil field guys don't have anything in their lives except work and a large truck payment. Not all of them had families waiting at home who wouldn't see them again. "God and I, we actually aren't on the best of terms anymore." I knew my feelings were unreasonable, but so was losing my father.

"Oh. That seems... understandable." Her tone suggested she desired to say something else, but it didn't matter. Whether it was understandable or not, that's the way things were.

She released a hearty sigh and wiped her face. "Sorry," she said, sniffling.

Respectfully, I gave her privacy and didn't look. You knew after just ten minutes with someone like Sammy Ballard that she wasn't the type who cried in front of people.

"Don't be. Listen, Sammy. I'm sorry I've been a jerk. It's just after the hospital, and then the fear of losing football, and all the pain and crap... I shouldn't have assumed the worst about you guys. I'm glad I was wrong. And I know you didn't come here for all this right now, but I figured I'd let you know that you're not alone either. Since you made it your mission to be such a good friend to me, I want you to know that I'll do my best to be the same for you. If you ever need to talk to someone about whatever you're going through, you can call me anytime… or text, or leave a voicemail." I chuckled, knowing she knew how to reach me very well.

"Yeah, but can I sneak into your window?" Her stuffy-nosed voice was charmingly adorable. I wanted to hug her.

"Anytime."

"Then, in exchange, will you come to me if *you* need to talk to someone? Remember I'm here, too, okay?"

"Sure."

"Don't say sure. I hate that word; it's so noncommittal."

I laughed. The old Sammy was back. "Yes, I will remember."

SAMMY

17

I couldn't believe what Jared shared with me about his dad, nor could I believe I cried—like a baby! He completely ignored it, too. A side to Jared I hadn't noticed was beginning to take shape, and I found myself wanting to see more of it.

Early on, his demeanor had gone from broody and bitter to tender and sweet once he'd learned we'd waited at the hospital for him. It was a rude move on his mom's part to not tell him his friends were there after the accident. I'd gotten a vibe from her when the girls and I were at his house earlier, but she'd been so convincingly upset that it was easy to overlook. There was probably something to unpack there, but one thing at a time.

By the end of my impromptu visit (In all fairness, I *had* warned him), I was experiencing a strange variety of emotions, not limited to my irritation or sadness. I could admit to myself that Jared was attractive. Maybe even *very* attractive, despite wearing a T-shirt I suspected he hadn't changed in a while, complete with the brace which bound his knee.

And, if I was being *extra* honest with myself, I struggled at first not to think about what another kiss with him would be like, though there would be no time to find out. What happens during Truth or Dare stays in Truth or Dare. Jared probably thought about cheerleaders or Sarah still. He wouldn't be thinking about someone like me.

Luckily, things with Jared felt a whole lot better after our talk, but there was still the matter of my problems waiting for me at home. As a result, I was in no hurry to get back there. I took the long way, opting to hit every traffic light on South Padre Island Drive, avoiding any route that would get me home too promptly.

While idling behind a long row of cars at the Staples intersection, I looked casually to the right. By some miracle, I was able to read the folding chalk sign out in front of Half Price Books. Cafe Calypso, the adjoined coffee shop, was hiring.

Throughout senior year, I hadn't done a lot of thinking about my future. I figured I might take the summer off and figure something out at the last minute, but I knew I wasn't interested in going to college. My family was more than interested enough for me, but I knew in my gut it wouldn't happen that way. As I told Ronnie, I was not a good student. Now that school was over and volleyball was gone, I wasn't that great at anything.

Seeing that sign seemed like more than a call to action. Immediately, I felt my luck changing.

Making a spontaneous decision, I threw my right blinker on and found an opening in the turn lane. Instead of making my slow way home, I turned onto Staples, wound my way back into the shopping center, and parked Roxy right in front of that chalk sign that had me filled with new ideas.

Customers came and went from the cafe, the door swinging open time and time again, but my gaze remained an unbreakable focus on the hand-written advertisement. Would my parents get mad if I came home with a job? I was a legal adult, so I could get one if I wanted, but wouldn't they know *why* I wanted? Not sure if I cared though. Pros and cons…

With a brand new goal, I unbuckled and reached for my shoulder bag from the passenger seat. Suddenly, I needed a job at this cafe I'd never been to before more than I needed anything else.

God, please have mercy on me and let me get this job. Don't make me be stuck at home with her. *Just give me some time, at least.*

Please…

Opening the cafe door, I was greeted by the typical cafe atmosphere. People littered the tables, engrossed in their books and other items. Coffee cups and food plates abounded. There was a line to the counter and two employees hustling behind it with fast feet and reaching arms.

The blonde woman spoke first, tossing me an immediate "Welcome in!" without hesitating in her work.

She and the shaggy, curly-haired brunette guy thinned the line with impressive speed. By the time it was my turn at the counter, at least two more welcomes had sounded, and someone was standing way too close behind me.

Greeting me with large, sky-blue eyes, the barista smiled. "What can I get you?"

"One application, please," I responded boldly, mirroring her chipper enthusiasm. When she blinked at me, I faltered. "And a, uh, bottle of water?" Yes, water was safe. I knew nothing about coffee, and giving her something to do for me while I was standing here hoping for a job didn't seem like the best move.

"You're applying for the open position? Here?"

"Yes?"

"You're hired! When can you start?"

"Are you serious?" Granted, I'd never had a job outside of

babysitting with Sarah before, but I was starting to think I was doing this wrong. My high school civics teacher branched out and taught us all how to craft a resume and fill out job applications. I had my resume at home on a flash drive somewhere. A lot of good it was doing me now. I even had three contacts in my phone marked to use as references. And what about all those mock interviews we had to do? Mrs. Caldwell never prepared us for an on-the-spot offer like this.

"One hundred percent. When can you start?"

"Okay, wow! Anytime, I guess."

"Great! Do you want to hang around for some on-the-job training right now?"

It was my turn to blink and try to force my jaw from gaping. My mom's sad face flashed across my mind, but I couldn't think about that right now. Exactly as I had hoped, I now had a job to do. "I sure can."

"Wonderful! This one is on the house." She handed me a water bottle along with her hand. "I'm Cindie Mitchell."

Cindie Mitchell had an impressive cascade of shoulder-length blonde hair and pretty blue eyes—not as striking as Jared's, I noted, but still lovely. She looked around my age but was probably a bit older and seemingly had pep for days. She was direct and to the point, and I liked her already.

"Samantha Ballard," I returned. "But call me Sammy."

"Nice to meet you, Sammy. Why don't you come around from there." She nodded toward the opening that would lead me from being a customer to an employee. "Then I'll run you to the back and show you where you can set your stuff and get you an apron."

In the break room, after I had claimed an empty locker and deposited my bag, Cindie turned to look at me, apron in hand.

"Do you have any barista experience?"

I swallowed. "Not actually."

"That's okay. What other job experience do you have?"

I thought for a moment, hoping to make it count, but didn't have anything better to share. "I can change a diaper in under a minute. Does that count?"

She laughed. "It says a lot about you, I'm sure. I don't know how to change a diaper at all. Babies and children are not my thing. It takes a special sort of person to keep other peoples' kids alive."

"So, it's not bad that I've never worked anything more traditional before?"

"Not at all. We're so desperate. You couldn't have come at a better time. You'll learn everything you need to as you go. Trust me and I'll get you grinding beans and slinging macchiatos in no time."

It sounded too good to be true. What a day it had turned out to be. Besides making headway with Jared, I had a new friend—because I already knew Cindie and I would be—and a great new job all at once. I suppressed the reality that today was also about a new mom. That part could go away.

"Oh, can you teach me how to draw little cream pictures in the coffee?"

"You're darn right I can. And it's called latte art, by the way." Cindie leaned out the door, peeking at what was going on. "We'd better get to it. Take a minute if you need it, and meet me out there when you're ready. We'll wait until after the rush and start your paperwork. You can stay as late as 5:00 p.m. if you're up for it."

"That sounds awesome. I'll just let my parents know." I held my phone up.

"Great. See you on the other side." She smiled and disappeared, leaving me alone.

Typing a quick text into my phone, I let my mom know I had gotten a job and would be home later. Quick and easy. I hated to wonder what responses I might get.

And then to Sarah, with entirely too many exclamation points:

SAMMY

I got a job!!!!!!!! Details later. Wish me luck!

Silencing my phone and stuffing it away, along with any negative thoughts that were trying to come for me, I straightened out my apron. Then, I took a deep breath and followed my new boss into the fray.

THAT EVENING, after my first crash course in coffee-making and a small stack of paperwork that made me feel like a real adult, I sat alone in my car. I smiled, feeling proud of myself and just a little bit smug. I hadn't intended for my spur-of-the-moment effort to work out so well. In one fell swoop, I was able to obtain the perfect alternative to spending time at home, and it came with a paycheck.

The minute I was through explaining it to my parents, who were equal parts happy and upset, I ran to my room to call Sarah.

"Hello?" she answered on the last ring.

"Hey. What's goin' on? You didn't text me back."

"Oh, yeah, sorry. I saw your text earlier. Congratulations! Where are you working?" Her tone didn't match her effort. I wasn't fooled.

"Cafe Calypso."

"How fun. Kevin told me good things about that place. Apparently, Tyler likes a girl that works there."

"Really? Is her name Cindie?"

"Yes, I think that's it."

"How cool, what a small world."

"Yep. But hey, can I call you back later?"

"That's fine. Is everything okay?" I probed.

"My parents are dragging me out for dinner tonight."

"You didn't answer my question."

"I'm fine, Sammy. I'll talk to you later. Congratulations again on the new job. You're going to do great."

I wasn't convinced, but there was nothing I could do. "Thanks, girl. I'll hear from you later?"

"Sure thing. Bye."

"Bye," I reciprocated, and the line went dead.

The longer I sat after our phone call, the more I didn't understand the truth of what happened between Sarah and Kevin, but the more I realized the seriousness of it. How was she dealing with what was going on with him, really and truly? It was so unlike her not to talk to us girls about these kinds of things. How could anything be so bad that she wasn't talking about it to anyone? I had to find out. And if one source was avoiding the issue, I would just have to try the other.

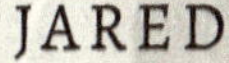

JARED

18

I KNEW WINCING AS I SAT DOWN TO DINNER WAS A MISTAKE WHEN I realized my mom saw it. Gracefully, she ignored it for the time being, and when I had propped my crutches up against the side of the table, she folded her hands, closed her eyes, and said the same blessing over our food that she's said ever since Dad died. The same one he used to say for us when he was alive. Across the table, Jeremy was a mirror image of my mom, even mouthing the prayer for himself from behind closed lids.

When finished, Mom spread her napkin on her lap and offered us both a roll. "How are you feeling?" she asked as though she didn't already know.

Why do parents always want you to be so vocal about everything? Let's not and say we did.

"Fine," I murmured, picking up my fork.

"I was surprised you turned your friends away earlier," she said, her tone indecipherable. "They all seemed very worried about you."

"Are you having a change of heart about them now? I know you don't like them, but apparently, you failed to tell me they were at the hospital after my accident. It would've been nice to know I wasn't there alone."

She whipped a fierce look at me. "You were by no means *alone*, Jared. Your brother and I were both there the entire time."

"Yeah, and I'm glad you guys were, but it would've been nice to know my friends hadn't ditched me in the first place. That's not something you should've kept from me."

"It was a very emotional time, Jared. I didn't want you to get worked up."

I didn't respond, so she added, "I did what I thought was best."

Give me a break. She could tell herself it was best all she wanted, but that would never make it true.

"But no, my opinion of your friends has not changed. I still think they're no good, but even I can admit it was nice of them to come and see you. You can't blame me for turning them away this time though. That was all you."

"I wouldn't have if I hadn't been mad at them, and I was only mad at them because you lied to me." It made me feel like junk for passing my bad mood onto them for no reason. I could absolutely blame that on my mom.

Even if I couldn't, I did anyway.

"I'm done arguing with you for today. I'm exhausted enough already." I didn't know how to take her tone. She was still mad, but it seemed her anger had shifted from them to me. I wasn't sure which was worse. She mercilessly jabbed a piece of broccoli on her plate. "Don't forget physical therapy starts tomorrow afternoon. I'll be taking an extended lunch to head out there with you, so be ready on time."

"I don't need a ride, Mom." I did, but I was too angry to let her take me. I'd hitch if I had to.

"Well, you know you can't drive yourself even if you were

pain-free, which I know you're not. You've been instructed to keep weight off of it unless you're at PT for a while longer. You're lucky you didn't need surgery. For crying out loud, Jared. Take this seriously."

I knew letting the pain slip when I sat down would come back to bite me in the butt.

"Fine, but I don't want you to worry about work. One of my friends will take me." Sammy specifically. She directly and without room for doubt insisted that I rely on her. So, I guess I would.

"Are you sure? Once I un-arrange these plans, I won't be able to drop everything and leave if they can't."

"I'm sure."

"Alright then."

Jeremy crossed his eyes at me obnoxiously and then stuck a large forkful of mashed potatoes in his mouth. "Hey, Mom?" he nearly spat, not bothering to swallow before he spoke.

"Yes, Jeremy?"

"Can I go to Xavier's house tomorrow when Jared leaves?"

"And how will you get there?"

"Jared's girlfriend can take me."

"Your brother doesn't have a girlfriend."

"Well, that's who was over here… just a bunch of girls."

Creating a fist, I sent my knuckles into Jeremy's shoulder. To his credit, he barely flinched. "Doesn't mean I'm dating any of them."

"Then who are all those girls? Is Dan the one taking you? He wouldn't mind driving me."

Dan wouldn't be driving anyone—least of all *me*—anywhere for a very long time.

At the question, my eyes darted to Mom. She avoided looking

at me, watching my brother instead. "Dan is out of town for a while. He's recovering from the accident, too," she said, her voice a callous frost.

Jeremy looked like he wanted to say something smart, so I rushed to his rescue. "If you don't want to be stuck here tomorrow, then just shut up now, and I'll see if you can get a ride with me."

We each turned back to our food, and the rest of the meal was uneventful. The strain wasn't gone, but at least nothing else came up. Mom excused herself first to start on the dishes, and after making Jeremy take mine to the kitchen with him, I hobbled my way down the hall to my room. I sat on my bed and reached for my phone, trying to come up with the best way to ask Sammy for a huge favor.

19

KEVIN SLOAN CAME OUT OF THE SECURITY DOORS IN HIS HIDEOUS orange tracksuit, and his face changed when he saw me. "Sammy? Wow, I didn't think I'd see you here… Wait, is something wrong with Sarah? Is she okay?"

We're jumping right in.

"Physically? She is just fine. Before either of us says anything else, I want your word on something." I sat down.

When I didn't continue, he joined me. "My word on what?"

"Sarah will never know about this visit. *No one* will ever know about this visit. Everything discussed during this conversation stays between us. The whole thing never happened."

Kevin's protest came rapidly. "I don't know if I feel right about that."

"Just do this for me because I'm asking you to. Please, one friend to another. What I came to say is important, but she doesn't need to know about it, at least for now. I'm sure someday I'll tell her, but I want to decide that. I don't know if she'd be angry with me or not, but I can't just sit around and do nothing anymore. Can you understand where I'm coming from?"

"Maybe I can."

"Then I accept that response as your agreement, and I'll cut right to the chase because they tell me we don't get a lot of time. I need to know what happened between you two."

He slumped back against his chair. "What do you mean?"

"What did you do to my best friend, dude? She's miserable, day in and day out. She fakes it so good that it almost looks like she's alright, but we know she's not. And it's got something to do with you, right? I just want to understand because I'm tired of seeing her this way. She won't talk, but something tells me you will if it's for her sake. Please, Kevin. What happened?"

Maybe it was something in my eyes that let him know how serious I was, or maybe my showing up was the opportunity to talk about Sarah he'd been craving all this time. I don't know, but he sang like a jaybird.

Heh. Jaybird. Like jailbird.

That's not funny, Samantha Olivia.

He reached into his shirt pocket. It had a flap but no button, and he slipped out a folded-up piece of paper. Dropping it on the table in front of me, he said, "Go ahead. Read it."

Curious, I didn't hesitate. Carefully but eagerly, I opened the folded edges. I recognized Sarah's handwriting:

Dear Kevin,

Where to start! I love you and miss you more than I thought was possible. I want you to know I'm not upset anymore. I understand why you did what you did. First, you saved me from Craig at the expense of yourself. Then, you saved me from yourself at the expense of us both.

You're so brave, Kevin. I see your sacrifices, and I accept them. More than that, I'm grateful. You have loved me so selflessly, it's the least I can do now to do the same for you.

But if I'm going to do this, you have to do one last thing for me. Focus on you. Take this time to find yourself, Kevin. Reconcile with who you truly are and learn to love him like I do. Like God does.

I'll think of you every day.
Love always + forever,
Sarah

"Wow." I folded the letter up and handed it back. "So, it looks like you broke up with her, and she sent you this?"

Silently, he nodded.

"And you keep this in your pocket just, like, all the time?" It wasn't entirely relevant, but inquiring minds wanted to know.

A quiet laugh slipped from the corner of his mouth. "Yeah, I do."

"Wow. I just… Jeez." I didn't know what I could say. They were both insanely in love. That much was obvious. It was disgusting and beautiful at the same time, although altogether useless since he was in here and she was out there. Of course, that's why he broke up with her, why she's behaving the way she is. Whatever they had was big.

"You really love her, don't you? Like, really, really?"

"Absolutely, I do." He didn't hesitate for a second.

"No wonder you told her what you did that prompted that letter."

"Yep."

"No wonder Sarah is so miserable."

Emotions were at war on his face. Poor guy. "So am I. But I'm doing my best not to be. It really sucks to hear she's not doing better."

"With feelings as big as hers, did you expect anything less than utterly crushed?"

"I prayed for it."

Hold up. "You prayed?"

"Yeah, I do that a lot now," he chuckled. "It's the only reason I've made it this far. I even graduated, you know. Not the same as you guys, but still. I'm taking college courses now, too."

"Wow." My vocabulary was stunted by constant surprise. "That's great, Kevin. Congratulations."

"Thank you. I can't tell you how badly I've wanted to share that with Sarah, with anyone who would listen, really, for so long."

"Do you have any, like, friends in here?" Boy, I felt weird asking that question. How do you even talk to somebody incarcerated? I really hadn't thought the visit through beyond knowing I needed to pay it.

"There are people I can tolerate more easily than others, but I don't know if I'd call them friends. It's not really like TV or movies around here. People leave each other alone for the most part because everyone wants to get out as soon as possible. Luckily, I do really like my cellmate. He's cool. I actually think Sarah would like him, too."

"Ha, that's a funny thought."

"You'd see it right away if you met him, I'm telling you."

"I don't know. It's crazy enough thinking of Sarah being in love with a felon, let alone becoming friends with more of them."

He shook his head with a sad smile.

"I'm sorry, Kevin. I didn't mean to call you that. I know why you're in here. You're not like these other guys here."

"Legally speaking, I am, and honestly, I don't feel too far off from it. On some level, I'm no different from anyone else here."

"*Ugh.* No, you don't deserve that. I'm really sorry."

"Don't worry about it." He waved it off, and then a look of something else crossed his features. Leaning forward, his voice took on an air of severity. "Hey, so, were you serious about keeping this visit from Sarah?"

"Oh, yes. A hundred percent." He nodded, gazing at nothing. "Are you cool with that?"

"Yeah, I think that would be best. She might get upset that I accepted a visit from you but told her to stay away."

"I didn't give you any choice," I pointed out. "But I was lucky you included me on your visitor's list. I don't know how I would've handled my mission if I wasn't. Maybe then I would've called to ask like a normal person."

"Pretty much every name I knew went onto that list. Doesn't mean I ever expected visits. I've gotten a lot more visitors than I thought I would. It's weird."

"Weird, why?"

"Having friends. People who care about me. It feels like some kind of strange extravagance I'm not worthy of."

"Do you have any plans for when you get out? Like, what happens with… Sorry, forget I asked. You don't have to answer that."

"It's okay. I would answer it if I could. I just don't know right now."

"Understandable." I didn't want to let the silence get awkward. "Well, anyway, I'm glad I came. You are absolutely worthy of *my* friendship."

"That's all that really matters then, I think."

I winked approvingly. "You think correctly, good sir."

The officer who let me into the room stood near the door with his legs spread and his hands clasped at his back. He announced that we only had ten minutes left. Kevin actually seemed saddened at the idea.

"And I'm appreciative that it can stay between us. It's not worth the risk of upsetting her over this. But you get that, or none of us would be in this situation."

"Yeah. For what it's worth, thanks for coming. It was nice to see you. And thanks for being so good to Sarah. I'm glad she has friends like you out there with her. To love and look out for her when I can't." His throat bobbed tightly.

"You're welcome, naturally," I teased again, tossing my hair behind my shoulder. Before I knew it, it was time to go. "Bye, Kevin. I'll be happy to see you in the real world again."

He laughed. "Same here." We both stood and exchanged good-byes, but before I reached the exit, he called out. "Hey, Sammy?"

I turned around just as the door buzzed open to let me escape. "Yeah?"

"Happy belated birthday."

A comforting warmth filled me. I could understand why Sarah had fallen so hard for Kevin Sloan. His heart was immense, but more importantly, it was genuine. He made accepting his birthday wishes easy, even though I had been more than ready for all thoughts of turning eighteen to disappear. "Thanks, Kevin."

All the way home, I prayed I would see the two of them happy together again. When it came to me and my auntie-mommy issues, I wasn't sure *what* to pray for.

20

"Don't embarrass me, or I'll have her drop you off at the fire station instead of Xavier's house. You got me?"

I pulled my shirt down over my head and then grabbed my crutches, which were leaning up against the edge of my bed beside me. My underarms would be thrilled when I didn't have to use the torturous things anymore.

Jeremy stood in my doorway, arms crossed over his tiny puffed-up chest. "I don't got nothing. You just try it. See what Mom says."

I snorted. "You'd tattle? Wow, how old are you again? Fourteen or four?"

I stood up and recoiled, but not from my busted knee. The evil crutches had caused so much bruising under my arms that I could barely stand to put weight on them.

"Does it really hurt that bad?"

"It's not my knee; it's the crutches." I leaned on my left side, put the crutches down on the edge of the bed, and lifted my shirt just enough for him to see. When I pulled it back down, I saw him grimacing.

"That looks hideous."

"It doesn't feel too great, either."

He nodded. "That sucks."

And that, ladies and gentlemen, was the closest to sincerity I'd gotten from Jeremy in a long, long time. I wasn't even tempted to squash it. "Thanks, bro. Let's go before Sammy beats us out there."

Jeremy was patient as I made my way out the door and helped me lock up and get down the steps. To my surprise, he even guided me down the drive. By the time we reached the curb, Sammy's little red-mobile came to a stop beside us.

"Hey, fellas. Need a ride?" she called through the passenger window.

Jeremy hastily claimed the front with an obnoxious, "Shotgun!"

"Seriously?" I groaned.

Sammy merely looked at me and lifted her shoulders. "He called shotgun. What are you gonna do about it, gimpy?"

Jeremy laughed, long and loud. "Yeah, gimpy. Better luck next time."

Sammy put the car in park and ran around the back. She met me at the door and opened it, though I was just fine on my own.

"I thought you might want to put your crutches in the back-back. I didn't know you'd be in the back seat though." She shifted her mouth to the side, trying to stave off a laugh. "It's up to you."

"They're fine here with me." I shot a glare at the back of my brother's head, wishing I had the laser eyes of Superman before ultimately deciding that would be too extreme. I'd damage Sammy's precious Roxy the Boxy.

"You got it," she said, closing the door behind me before going back around.

"Everybody buckled?" We echoed confirmations before she pulled away from the curb. "Let's roll then."

"Hey, thanks again for doing this. And I'm glad to see Roxy is back to proper working order."

Sammy affectionately petted the steering wheel. "Me too. And you're very welcome. I owed you, anyway."

She dropped off Jeremy first. Mom would pick him up after her shift, so I no longer had to worry about him.

I relocated to the front passenger seat when he got out, and now we were riding along on SPID, the busiest of all Corpus roadways, at what felt like warp speed. Besides my groggy ride home from the hospital last week, this was my first time in the car since the accident. My physical therapist was in the bluff, and even though that meant we were going in the opposite direction, I had to keep reminding myself we weren't going to crash. Sammy drove in the far right lane so she could go slower, but every time we passed a ramp, my chest felt funny.

I wouldn't have taken myself for someone with post-traumatic stress, but I kept looking over at her speedometer, thinking surely we were going at least forty over. My palms were sweaty, and when I went to wipe them on my shorts, my hands shook. The more I realized how fast my heart was beating, the harder it was to control my breathing.

I shoved my hands under my thighs and pressed back against the seat to brace myself. Closing my eyes, I tuned out the fact that we were in the car going eight hundred miles per hour. I kept my jaw shut, forcing myself to drag in heavy breaths through my nose and letting them out slowly. The last thing I wanted to do was draw Sammy's attention.

I'm fine. This is fine. We're almost there. Not much longer. It's fine. I'll be fine.

The whooshing in my ears drowned out everything else, and I was grateful. I couldn't hear the intense rushing of cars on all sides of us, speeding along as they decided their destination was more important than ours. Rationally, I knew that nobody on the road was out to get us, but internally, I had no rationality.

It took me a moment to realize we weren't moving anymore. I peeled my eyes open, and in front of me was the reflective glass of my physical therapist's office. My shoulders sagged as I released a pent-up breath.

Sammy's voice cut through me, and I jerked my face toward her. "You okay?"

I cleared my throat. "I'm okay."

I could see she wanted to say more, but I gave her a weak smile and stretched my still-jittery hand toward the door. If I got out, she couldn't ask me any more questions.

It wasn't all that long ago that my dad died. The idea that I might've recently followed him to the grave by similar means gave me a shiver that rocked my whole body. Picking my crutches out of the back seat, I had to shake it off. It was time to put in the work if I ever wanted to play football again.

I just couldn't think about the drive back home.

SAMMY GAVE me a measured smile as I climbed back into the car. "Welcome back."

I maneuvered my crutches into the back seat. "Thanks."

She put down her Nook and turned the keys, bringing the engine to life. "How did it go?"

"Fine. My leg hurts like crazy, but they tell me that's normal. Progress is pain or some junk."

"Yep, yep. They told me stuff like that when I broke my leg."

"I forgot you broke your leg. When was that again?"

"Junior high. I hadn't even been playing volleyball for very long at that point. In fact, I think it was only my second game ever. I ran into a teammate in a very bad effort to return the ball. Brilliant attempt. Terrible execution. Long night in the ER," she giggled. "My mom wasn't very happy."

"Yeah, mine isn't either, but she never is."

Oops. Did I say that out loud?

"I'm sorry to hear that. Is it because she misses your dad?"

"Maybe. She doesn't tell me anything. Just gets angry a lot."

"Have you ever asked her?"

I wracked my brain but couldn't come up with an instance where I had. In any event, I could only ponder for so long before I realized Sammy had driven us into a steady flow on the access road. We weren't going home on the freeway?

So, she had noticed everything.

"You know, you've already done me enough favors for one day. You don't have to take your time bringing me back like this." I gestured out the windshield toward the typical yet horrible traffic. A lot of time would be spent between traffic lights.

"Jared, don't."

"Don't what?"

"Don't get all pissy and self-deprecating. I'm just driving. You don't have to read into it."

"And it's just a freeway; you don't have to read into it."

I looked out my window, pouting like the toddler I knew I was being. I was acting more like Jeremy than myself, but I couldn't help it. Then, all of a sudden, Sammy put her hand over mine, lacing our fingers together. "Just shut up. You had a literal panic attack on the way over, and I'm not going to put you through that again. You've had enough physical exertion for one morning. You may not realize it, but that kinda stuff impacts your body. You need to focus on healing one thing at a time. There's no need to rush this part."

Once again, my tongue felt swollen, my face felt hot, and my hands were vibrating a mile a minute. The flutter in my chest felt heavy until there was nothing left in my head but dizziness. I tried to move my hands back under my legs, but Sammy just held on harder. I felt her will overpower mine, and I stopped. Everything. Even my breath paused.

"Breathe. It's okay."

Her voice was smooth and convincing. My lungs obeyed, springing back to life, and the more I focused on the soft touch of her hand on mine, the less I thought about where we were. The more I discerned her thumb rubbing against the back of my hand, the less I heard the sounds of the traffic.

Eventually, the ride got smoother. We weren't going as fast, and the panic had subsided enough for me to open my eyes. I peeked out the window and saw we were still on the regular roads. We stayed on them all the way from Flour Bluff to my house. I hoped she wouldn't be late to work, but I didn't trust my voice to speak. I didn't want to draw attention to my weakness. Nor did I want her to take her hand away, even after the panic had subsided. To my satisfaction—and astonishment—she didn't.

21

As soon as we reached a good spot on the lawn, Jenna plopped down. "When was the last time we hung out like this? No sand, no parties, no boys… just four friends sitting around, having a nice, simple time." She leaned back against her hands with her bare feet crossed out in front of her. Her painted toes wiggled happily in the evening breeze. The residual sunlight cast a warm glow across her smiling face. Someone was in a surprisingly happy mood tonight.

"A while," I said. And it would be an even longer while before we could all do it again.

"What movie is playing again?" None of us could remember. "It doesn't matter. I'm so glad to be out of the house."

"Same," Birdie agreed. "I know I'm only taking online classes, but I'm already not looking forward to starting them. I will miss having nothing but time on my hands."

Sarah looked at Birdie as they laid out another layer of blankets, creating a large pallet of comfort beside Jenna. "Don't say it that way, Birdie. It doesn't matter how you go to school."

"I know. I just mean I'm not moving away. It's going to be a bit easier for me, I think."

Sarah nodded in sad agreement. "It's going to be hard for me to leave. But I will be back often, don't forget."

I sure wouldn't forget. I'd have nothing but time to remind me, except for the couple of months I'd be in Mexico. I was sure at least that would keep me occupied enough to stop feeling sorry for myself.

It's not that I'm trying to be whiny, God. I don't enjoy feeling this way.

Maybe… Maybe if I told the girls about everything, I would feel better.

As the blankets and pillows were fluffed to perfection, the four of us piled together. Jenna was the first to dig into the food, unwrapping a giant dill pickle and pulling out a small bottle of Tajin. She dusted her sour snack with the zesty topping and then took a loud, juicy bite.

"Man, that sounds delicious," I commented.

"Have one. I brought tons," encouraged Jenna through her chewing.

"I most definitely will, eventually. I brought Hot Cheetos."

"Ooh, did you bring queso to go over them?"

"But of course."

Birdie Jo made a face. "You guys and your exotic foods. Doesn't anyone but me appreciate simple buttered popcorn anymore?"

I laughed, thinking about Hot Cheetos and pickles being exotic. "I do, but I'll eat anything. I'll actually take some now if you brought any."

Like Good Saint Nick in a Christmas movie, Birdie Jo procured a large container of popcorn from her bag, very pleased to have been asked. "I just made it fresh before leaving the house, and it's still warm."

"We've got The Pioneer Woman over here, guys. Bringing homemade popcorn to an outdoor movie night."

"I even made the most delicious seasoned butter to coat it. Mmmm."

"Give me some of that," Jenna demanded, reaching her hand into the container and cramming the buttery goodness into her mouth. After a moment, her eyes went wide. "Delicious indeed!"

We were still invested in snacks and idle chit-chat well before the movie started. As wonderful as the night had been, I hadn't the mind to ruin it with my home life drama. We were enjoying our last summer together. Sure, we would come together again here and there, but this, our last summer before starting our adult lives, inevitably marked the end of something great.

God blessed me with some truly amazing friends, each of whom I cherished deeply. There was Sarah, with her calm wisdom and gentle, loving heart. Then Birdie Jo, whose kind nature and old soul made her the sweetest person I had ever known. And Jenna, who embodied strength and resilience, paired with a fierce and unwavering loyalty. They all had incredible qualities I could only dream of possessing.

As we settled in to watch the movie, hunkering down and giggling, I decided we still had plenty of time before fall hit. There would be an opportunity to bring the party down later. Tonight, we enjoyed simply being together. On top of that, this was the perfect distraction from the chaos currently invading my home. If I wasn't there, I wouldn't be able to see her arrive. The time that distance from Claudia provided me would be well spent.

JARED

22

MOM MADE ME GO WITH HER TO HALF PRICE BOOKS TO PICK UP AN order and drop off a box load of old books she said she'd never read again. I argued, citing my strictest desire not to go, but she wouldn't have it.

She came into my room and opened the blinds, then tossed my comforter. "You're coming with me to run my Saturday errands. Let's go."

I let my arm fall heavily onto my face, blocking out the sun and her angry image. "I'm supposed to be resting." The excuse was weak, but so was I.

"You can't just lie around in bed all day and call it rest, Jared. You have to keep working your knee, too."

"It hurts. I don't wanna cause a need for surgery."

"You're not going to hurt it enough to need surgery by just getting out and about. Your doctor told you that himself."

That's not all he told me. As long as I kept up with my exercise and general restrictions—which included my stupid crutches—I would be able to start driving again by next week, earlier than he originally thought. Mom was excited for me and couldn't understand why I didn't have her same enthusiasm. I had no desire to get back behind the wheel, and I had no inclination to explain it to her, though part of me questioned why it wasn't obvious.

"I do get out. I go to physical therapy twice a week, remember?"

"You only just started, and you also have exercises to do at home. The work isn't only out there, Jared. It's here, too. It's every day. And I'm not going to let you avoid it like this, so get up. Up, up, up. Be ready in ten." She left my room, but not for long if I didn't listen.

On the way to the bookstore, I distracted myself with my phone, avoiding the unpleasant thoughts I was becoming accustomed to while in the car. Once we arrived, I saw that Sammy was there working. I smiled at her volleyball decal, which denoted the phrase, *If you want soft-serve, go get ice cream.* It was so her.

"I'm going to get a drink from the cafe," I said, breaking away from my mom the moment we were inside. She seemed satisfied with that or too focused on her task to question me.

I wasn't even through the doorway when Sammy looked up from behind the coffee machine, her rich brown eyes sparkling with activity. She smiled a welcome, and I moved behind the last in line to order, watching her in amazement. How anyone was expected to handle everything going on behind that counter was beyond me. It would seem that eight arms per employee would be necessary.

It was my turn next.

"Hello, hello," Sammy said cheerfully. "You come to say hi, or are you thirsty?"

"Both. What should I get?"

"Well, do you like coffee?"

"It's okay, but I'm not really supposed to have any stimulants while I'm on these pain meds."

"Oh, sure, that makes sense… That's okay, I can come up with something fun for you."

Putting my trust in her hands and my change in her jar, I let Sammy concoct something for me to drink. She pointed me to a table, saying she would bring it to me. A few minutes later, she emerged from behind the counter sans her apron.

"Your vanilla Italian soda, good sir." Sammy smartly presented the drink to me with a napkin and straw. Reaching slightly across me, her hair fell off her shoulders, nearly draping over me. The smell of her shampoo was startlingly pleasant, like a cooling summer wind. Her curve-hugging jeans and T-shirt outfit, which was outside the norm for Sammy "Sporty Spice" Ballard, was on full display without her apron.

"Thank you ever so much," I responded with a gentlemanly nod. "Are you off?"

"Just on break. Mind if I sit?"

"Not at all."

She sighed as she pulled out a chair and sank down into it. "Hey, Jared?"

"What's up?"

"Can I tell you a secret?"

I gave her a quizzical look. "Are you sure you want to do that?"

"Why? Can you not keep one?"

"Sure, I can. Fire away."

"You know I'm adopted, right?"

"I did not know that. But go on." The layers of this girl kept getting deeper and deeper.

"Well, my parents—my adoptive parents—had this deal with

me that once I turned eighteen, they would tell me about my biological parents."

"I gotcha. So, is it bad news?"

"Worse than you can imagine. They don't have a clue about my birth father, but my birth mom is none other than my awful aunt Claudia." Her face did a hundred expressions in that second. "Wow, I haven't said that to anyone yet. Wasn't sure I was going to."

"I thought you seemed a little funny when you showed up at my house the other day."

"What do you mean by that?"

"Nothing bad, just that you seemed off. Extra emotional, less like your regular grumpy self." I chuckled at my observation.

That one earned me a raised eyebrow. "You think I'm grumpy?"

"I know you are."

Her armor appeared ever so slightly chinked when she cracked a smile. "Whatever. Not the point."

"I bet it was a shock though. How are you feeling about it? If you want to share, that is."

"I got a job so I could be away from home as much as possible, and she happens to be visiting right now, so make of that what you will. She was only supposed to stay a weekend, but with her, plans don't mean much."

"I see."

"You see what?"

"What I make of it."

"Uh-huh. I'll bet." She fired me a fresh glare. "So, how is physical therapy going? You doing all your exercises?"

"More or less."

"Is it more, or is it less?"

Nervous, I fiddled with the straw in my cup, chasing around the ice cubes. That was twice in one day I'd been pestered about my PT stuff. Could the women around me not leave things alone?

I spent too long in my head, and she jumped on me.

"Jared, if you don't follow your recovery plan, you won't recover. Is that what you want?"

"No, *Mom*. It's not what I want."

She tapped her foot, her face showing her mind making a decision. "I get off work at two o'clock. I'll come over after that."

"What are you talking about?"

"I'm going to go over to your house after work, and we're going to do those exercises."

"No, you don't have to do that."

"It's okay, I don't mind."

She is relentless. "Okay, then. I don't *want* you to do that."

"I know, but it's a done deal. You need it." Sammy looked at her phone. "And as much as I'd love to stay and argue about it, my break is over." She stood up and pushed in her chair. "You gonna head out?"

"Yeah, I'd better. Apparently, I have things to prepare for." I left out the part about my mom being on the other side of the double doors, having dragged me out to shop with her. She would probably be done any minute, anyway.

She nodded, satisfied. "See you later, Jared."

I reciprocated her goodbye with a begrudging smile. "See you later, Sammy."

Interestingly enough, while her intruding on my life (again) should really annoy me, I realized if anyone was going to have the gall to do it, Sammy would. And I was okay with letting her.

JARED

23

"I… HATE… YOU…"

I ground my teeth. Sweat dripped from my forehead and into my eyes and mouth. My knee hurt, yes, but the pain was only part of it. Sammy's persistence, a thing I had thus far tolerated, had become the bane of my existence.

"Yes, yes. Get it all out, sweetheart." She sat beside me, each of us with a rolled towel under our legs. On her count, we did two sets of ten stretches. We were currently in our last rest period before the final set. Between Sammy's badgering and my general weakness, I was barely hanging on. There was no way I was this out of practice, so clearly, it had to be her.

"We're done after this, right?"

She reached over and came back with a stapled packet. Flipping through it, she hummed. "According to your write-up, there's still two more sets after this."

My brother's unceremonious appearance in the doorway interrupted my budding protest. "Hey, loser. Mom wants to know how it's going in here."

"Why did she send you?"

"She's fixing dinner. So, what do you want me to tell her?"

"You can tell her he's more than halfway done." Sammy patted me aggressively on the shoulder. "Until tomorrow, when he has to do it all again."

"Thanks a lot, drill sergeant, ma'am," came my unenthusiastic retort. Sammy only preened.

"Sounds boring. I'll just tell her you guys are making out."

"Jeremy, you little weasel!" I yelled out after him as he turned and fled. I hadn't the time to throw something at him. The twerp was getting faster. "Sorry," I muttered to Sammy.

"Won't she know it's not true?"

I shrugged. "Could go either way, but if she doesn't, we'll find out soon."

"Maybe he won't actually say that."

"Oh, he will." One could always count on Jeremy to be a turd.

"In that case, *I'm* sorry. If I weren't here, he wouldn't use me to cause you embarrassment."

"Trust me, it has nothing to do with you." I gripped the bands, anchoring them securely on the underside of my foot. "And I'm not embarrassed."

"Oh." From the corner of my eye, I endured her inspection. I would've killed to know what she was thinking.

Sammy fiddled with the timer on her phone, prepping it for its next count. "So, has Jeremy always been that way or only since your dad...?"

Nailed it. "No, he wasn't always that way. Not to the current degree, anyway."

She nodded in understanding, then rolled her shoulders back, ready for more. "Alright, maggot, look alive. Let's get through these last sets, and then I'll get out of your hair."

"Delightful. I can't wait for that."

She smirked. "Now—one… two… three…"

Pulling our bands taut, we flexed and released one number at a time, her reciting the timer out loud for my benefit.

Neither Mom nor Jeremy showed up at my door again, so I took that as a sign Sammy's honor remained intact, although I asked myself if being accused of kissing her would've been the worst thing ever.

24

THE NEXT MORNING, I WAS SORE. IT WASN'T MY KNEE THAT NEEDED work, but after doing those exercises with Jared, I felt like it was. Or maybe it was just spotting Jared the Grumpy Green Giant for the last hour and a half. The guy was huge and not easily supported; I felt sorry for his crutches. But he put in a good effort, and hopefully, with my lighting a fire under his rear, he would keep up the good work.

But if not, I'd stay ready with my matchbook and go back over there. I'd been sure to let him know as much.

I was just peeling myself up to go indulge in a hot bath and assuage my already sore muscles when my mom rapped her knuckles on my door.

"Hey, Sammy-Girl. You're home late."

Sitting up, I yawned. "I went to Jared's after work to help him with his PT. I'm so drained and ready for a nice long soak."

"That's kind of you. And how is he doing?"

"Fine, when he's not being a big baby."

She chuckled lightly. "Sammy, I wanted to talk to you about something for a minute."

Gee whiz. What ever could that something be?

"What is it?"

"Claudia is asking if you're going to be spending time with her while she's here."

"So?"

"So, we are out of things to tell her. Don't you think you could manage one dinner with her, say, tonight?"

Lord, help me.

"Mama, I don't want to. Why are you making me do this?"

"I'm not making you; I just asked if you would have dinner with her. Now that you know the truth, your father and I feel like it's worth getting to know her better, and you haven't exactly made an effort to do it on your own. But now it's not just us who's asking."

My mom didn't play fair. She knew if she came to me asking, with her pleading eyes and sensible request, I would most likely listen. But I didn't want to and had avoided it since she casually brought it up the first time. What did it matter how well I knew Claudia now that she was my *'mother?'* I didn't like her much before, and the news had made me like her even less. The idea that I came from a woman I'd known all my life as Hurricane Claudia did not thrill me at all.

"I'll think about it some more. That's the best I can do right now."

"And that's the most I can ask. Thank you, sweetie. If you decide to go, we already have a gift card for On The Border. You can use it anytime." She reached over and clasped my head, placing a kiss atop it before leaving.

After a muscle-soothing hot bath, I returned to my room still pondering dinner with Claudia. With latent frustration, I texted

Jared. Maybe if I had back-up, I could pretend a meal with her wouldn't suck.

SAMMY

Hey. What are you doing tonight?

JARED

Let me check my schedule…

Looks like a whole lot of nothing.

Why? What's up?

SAMMY

Want to do me a favor so huge I will owe you big time forever?

JARED

Wow. Those are exceptional terms. What's the favor?

SAMMY

My parents have asked me to have dinner with Claudia. I want you to go with me. (Their treat, don't worry.)

JARED

Oh, okay. As a date?

I balked at his question. A date? Jared and I? I laughed, but it came out pathetic. I cringed at myself.

SAMMY

As my adorable emotional support golden retriever, of course.

> Sorry, I'm not ACTUALLY calling you a dog, though Goldies have always been my favorite. I'm just in a weird headspace pretty much all the time lately. It's hard enough to deal with Claudia when she's only my crazy aunt.

> I just really can't imagine doing this alone...

I bounced my foot. Waiting for his response was taking it out of me. I felt so bad having asked him to be my emotional support *pet*. Ugh, what was I thinking? *Stupid! Stupid! Stupid!*

JARED

> Sorry, I was just putting my collar on. ;) What time should I expect you to pick me up?

Relief flooded my heart. Tears loomed, but I blinked them into oblivion.

SAMMY

> THANK YOU SO MUCH! I OWE YOU BIG TIME. AGAIN. I'M ON MY WAY RIGHT NOW. <3 <3 <3

WE PARKED in the back lot of the restaurant, away from the main road, and took a minute.

"Remind me why I agreed to do this," I pleaded with Jared, who had once again come to my rescue.

"Because you're Sammy The Bull Ballard, and there's nothing you can't handle. Because your mom asked you very nicely. Because you're already here, and I'm hungry. Is that enough, or should I keep going?"

"Nope. That's about good enough." But it didn't help my

nerves one bit. The only thing that did was knowing Jared would be with me.

"You ready to go in?" He checked the time on his phone. "We can get in there early if we go now."

"Okay. Let's do it."

"That's a good girl," he cooed, like I was a dog now, too. "You've got this."

"You butt."

He shrugged, looking smug. "You adore me."

"*Sure,* I do," I said, straightening out my clothes—I actually put a dress on for this—and taking deep cleansing breaths. One would think I hadn't seen this woman my entire life. Things really change when the truth comes out. *But if Jared said I've got this, then I've got this.*

"Oh, wait. Your crutches," I said, abruptly turning around.

"I'm not taking them inside."

"But won't you hurt?"

Jared caught me by the shoulders and spun me back the other way. "I'll be fine. I'll be sitting most of the time, anyway. Now, please, no more excuses."

Right. What he said. Onward, I walked. Time to face the music.

Inside On the Border, the hostess made direct eye contact and gave me a cheerful greeting. "Good evening! How many will be dining in tonight?"

Jared stepped beside me. "Three," he said, flashing the hostess a smile.

"Inside or out?" she asked.

"Outside, please." At least out there, we had the traffic in addition to the music and chatter to mask our conversation. The thought of being seated in a quiet spot where half the restaurant would be able to overhear us sent me into a panic.

"Sure thing. Right this way." The hostess peeled three menus from behind her desk and guided us toward the outdoor seating.

In true gentleman fashion, with barely a hitch in his step, Jared ushered me ahead of him with one hand placed tenderly at the small of my back. The intimate touch sent shivers up my spine, and when he strode in front of me to pull out my chair, something electric shot from my chest down to my toes.

If I didn't know any better, I would say this *was* a date, but I was soon reminded that it wasn't. I heard her before I saw her.

"Oh, thank you so much," her voice carried. "Even though I told you I knew where it was already." Claudia came barging through the door the hostess held open for her.

Closing my eyes, I breathed slowly, willing myself into a solid state of mind. *I can do this. Right, God?*

"See, right there," came her boisterous voice. "I'm with *her*."

"Very good, ma'am. Enjoy your meal."

"I'll enjoy my meal, but don't you be calling me ma'am. Thank you very much."

I flicked my glance up, catching a glimpse of the nice woman who just led Jared and me in. Her features were downcast as she retreated.

You're Sammy The Bull Ballard. You've got this.

Jared's pep talk came through as an encouraging whisper in my mind. He was right. I was. And I did. *God is with you, Sammy. So is Jared.*

When Claudia came loudly to the table and sat down with a crash of her large maroon purse, I met and held her gaze, if only by a thread.

"Hi," I said weakly. When I saw her eyes dart to Jared, my stomach dropped, but he stood right up and extended his hand.

"Hello, I'm Jared Tomlin. Friend of Sammy's."

"Right, a friend." Her eyebrows pinched together. "And why have you joined us?"

My mouth went dry.

"Well, to pay for dinner, of course." Jared smiled charmingly as he sat back down, handing her a menu.

"Well, in that case…" She accepted it, no doubt browsing for the most expensive meal possible. I'd have to pay Jared back as soon as I got my first check from the café if he didn't want my parents' gift card.

I didn't even know if he liked this restaurant.

She seemingly decided on something, put the menu down, then immediately turned her attention back to me. "So, Sammy… Long time no see."

Longer than I realized. I'd seen Claudia Ballard, sometimes on multiple occasions, for the last eighteen years, but never once had I seen *this* woman, the woman who birthed me.

25

I KNEW WHAT SHE MEANT WHEN SHE SAID IT. TO CLAUDIA, LONG time no see meant, "Hey, it's been a while since I broke up with my latest boyfriend and made my rounds crashing on your couch."

But of course, I didn't say that. "Yeah, what's it been this time?"

"Eh," she said, digging into her purse, then touching up her hair in a small mirror. "Maybe eight months."

"Wow."

Her compact slammed closed, and she stuffed it back into her purse. "Yep. Would've been longer if Jerry hadn't turned out to be such a slimeball. And I'd had such a good feeling about that one, too." She muttered it so loudly it bordered on yelling. I held back from looking around because I knew she'd recognize it as embarrassment and latch on. I could guarantee that after that, she would be twice as loud the next time she opened her mouth, just to spite me. Whenever anyone thought she was out of line, she did her best to prove them right.

Aunt Claudia was sort of the human equivalent of the expression, *"Hold my beer."*

Oh, jeez. I just had the most intrusive thought about Claudia partaking in a game of Truth or Dare with the others. *Shudder.* Nothing—and I mean *nothing*—good would come of that.

Claudia was talking a mile a minute, bouncing between laughing and berating the mere thought of her ex. From what I was able to listen to, she'd had "such a good feeling" about this Jerry fella before he'd taken her credit card and maxed it out by putting a down payment on a car he couldn't afford.

Then, plot twist: He had his *wife* co-sign the loan on it, so when he missed one too many payments, the wife was contacted, and she came hunting him down and found Claudia instead. Jerry had already taken off in his new Mercedes, and the last Claudia heard, he had avoided his warrant.

"Good riddance!" she spat. "I've never known a bigger deadbeat."

I was tempted to remind her about the deadbeat from last year and the one before that, but I just nodded to appear engaged. The second our server came by, I was elated.

Claudia stuck her face back in the menu. "You two go ahead. I'm still debating."

I made eye contact first. "Can I get the cheese enchilada plate with water and lemon, please?"

"Rice and beans okay?"

"Perfect. And can I add a side of guac?"

"You sure can." The server scribbled on her notepad. "How about you, sir?"

"I will take the steak burrito as it comes and a water."

The server's eyes came to rest on Claudia. "And for you,

ma'am?" she asked in such a sweet voice. I instantly felt bad for her.

Claudia was not happy. "Oh, no, y'all have got to quit calling me that. Do I look old enough to be a ma'am to you? Honestly."

"I meant no offense. It's just what I call everyone to be courteous." Another server with that horrified look on her face. I wanted to crumble into myself and disappear.

"You know what? Let me just get the fajita and shrimp platter, and don't be skimping on them shrimps, either. And a sweet tea."

"Certainly, m—" the server caught herself right in time. "No problem. I will just get those menus out of your way, and I'll be right back with your drinks." She managed a smile as she collected them, and she was on her way out quickly when Claudia turned and raised her hand.

"Oh, 'scuse me, *ma'am*," she bellowed. "Can you please add three spicy margaritas?"

My eyes went wide. "What? Jared and I can't drink!" I hissed in a loud whisper.

She turned to squint at me. "How old are you? Didn't you just have a birthday? I thought we could celebrate."

"Yes, I did... my eighteenth," I said dryly. Did she seriously need a reminder?

She shrugged and laughed. "More for me. I'll celebrate for all of us."

As she rotated back around to face us, I watched the server depart with envy. Jared had managed to scoot his chair close enough to where his knee was touching mine, and the simple contact kept me grounded. Boy, I wondered what was going through his mind. What did he think of my... Claudia?

Claudia sighed, high-pitched and drawn out. She leaned back

in her seat and slung one arm over the back. I took that moment to study her features, unsure if that was wise.

At first glance, Claudia Ballard was a beautiful woman. She had all the accouterments of beauty, such as carefully styled hair, well-selected clothing, and a loud assortment of jewelry. Her purse and all her clothes looked perfectly designer, but the thing about Claudia is that she didn't buy any of the things she owned. She had men do it for her.

Claudia was many things, and manipulative, persuasive, and cheap were some of them.

If I looked any harder at her, I might've started to see similarities in us, and I couldn't stomach it. What if I had her eyes? The shape of her ears? What if our eyes scrunched together in the same way when we smiled? If we shared things like that, what else did we share? I wanted nothing but a blood type in common with this woman.

"Girl, you are awful quiet over there." The way she stared me down, I felt sure she knew why. It was as if she could hear the direction of my thoughts.

"I'm pretty tired. Worked earlier today."

"Oh, you workin'? Where?"

"A cafe."

"Coffee, huh?" She clicked her tongue in distaste. "Not my thing."

And suddenly, I craved the stuff more than guacamole. Next shift, I resolved to start loving it.

"What about you, Jimmy?" she asked with a nod. "Are you making any money?"

"His name is Jared," I corrected. She rolled her eyes. "He's going to play football for Corpus Christi University in the fall."

Jared sat up straighter in his seat. "Hopefully," he corrected me this time. "I injured my MCL in a car accident recently, so I still have a ways to recover."

"Not so long," I countered. "A few months total if all goes well. He'll be throwing passes and making touchdowns in no time." We shared a quick smile.

Not quick enough. Claudia bounced unimpressed glances between us. She pointed as if she could be talking about anyone else. "Are y'all two hooking up?"

"Excuse me?" I responded, my voice raised. I was more than just a little shocked. From the corner of my indignant eye, I saw him prepare to speak. "Jared, no. Don't answer that."

"Oh, girl, you better be watching out for yourself. I am far too young to be a grandmother."

My. Heart. Died. For a second, all synapses failed to fire. I ceased to be. Jared, Claudia, and the entire restaurant around me fell away, and I floated in an abyss of distress. Because of being accused of doing something I most definitely wasn't doing, for sure, but mostly because she'd used the word "grandmother" to assert herself as my *mother*. Out loud. To my face.

Her laugh came out more like a resentful snort. "My brother told me they told you already. Pick your jaw up off the floor, child."

I did, my eyebrows knitting together in annoyance. Why was I listening to her?

"That's better. So, yeah, then it comes as no surprise, does it?"

Our food arrived at the same moment. I would've celebrated to see Mexican food put in front of me any other day, but I wanted nothing more than to turn tail and run. Anything but face the woman across the table who was both foreign and devastatingly familiar.

Jared was wrong about me. I am no bull, I'm a calf, and I don't got this at all.

JARED

26

I reached for Sammy's hand under the table, giving it a reassuring squeeze just like she did for me in the car. She didn't blink or turn toward me in the slightest. The only indication she gave that she even noticed was her fierce squeeze back. Above the surface, she gave nothing away.

Claudia was momentarily distracted by the influx of dinner. Two cooks brought out the meal as our server was nowhere in sight. *Smart woman.* I wondered if Claudia had the audacity to notice the young woman hadn't returned, but she didn't look up from her plate, let alone make eye contact with anyone handling the food.

I had a feeling she never truly *saw* anybody she came into contact with. No wonder Sammy had been so afraid to meet with her alone. The woman was a piece of work. I'd never seen anyone treat family and strangers the way I'd witnessed tonight.

Taking the opportunity to change the subject, Sammy gave quiet thanks for her food, then laid her napkin over her lap. When she looked up, Claudia was staring at her.

"They've really got you behaving just like them, huh? Mmm

mm mm," she muttered. "I thought that might've faded out by now. Are you sure there isn't a bit of me hiding somewhere in there?"

In all the time I'd known Sammy, I'd never seen her be this silent. She never held back, whether in word, tone, or facial expression. She didn't want me saying anything either, but how long could I hold out? Every time that woman opened her mouth, a new surge of lava threatened to break through the top of the volcano that was my patience. I could only imagine how Sammy felt.

"Boy, you sure are quiet for someone with no food in her mouth. What's the matter? Do I render you speechless?"

Sammy worked her jaw ever so slightly. "I'm just tired."

"You already used that one, honey. Try again." Claudia took hearty bites of her food, her fork scraping against the ceramic plate. "Don't you want to ask me anything?"

Why yes, thank you, I answered in my head, though she didn't mean me. *I'd love to ask why you suck so much.*

Sammy swiped a large forkful of enchilada through her rice and then shoved it in her mouth. "Not really."

"Mmhmm. I'll bet against that. Let me guess, you want to know who your dad is."

She rolled her shoulder, taking in another bite before she'd even finished chewing. "Not really," she said.

I had no appetite at all but suffered through the monotony of eating.

"Pfft. Yeah, right. You didn't want to come here tonight, did you?"

Sammy gave Claudia a look that clearly said 'winner-winner chicken dinner', but her tone came out placid. "I'm just overwhelmed."

"I had no idea when I gave you to them that they'd turn you into such a wimp."

Splotches of red flashed across my eyes, blocking out the parts of my brain that see reason. "Let me ask you something. Are you even aware of what comes out of your mouth when you open it, or is it anybody's guess?"

Turning her stare my way, Claudia raised her shoulders and looked down her nose at me. "Little boy, you don't want none of this."

"Trust me. Neither of us wants anything from you, including your company." Sammy let her fork fall against the plate, and she grabbed her purse. Without looking back, Sammy left.

"Oh…" Claudia's perfectly sculpted brows hiked up. "So, you *do* have some bite to you," she called to Sammy's retreating form. I could almost see the dust cloud kick up after her; she left in such a hurry. I didn't blame her one bit.

As I stood, I pulled out my wallet, true to my word, and left enough cash for the check and tip. "You've made a mistake here tonight," I told Claudia. "Enjoy your dinner, ma'am. Excuse us."

I hope that grates, I laughed to myself.

Kicking into a stiff jog, I caught up with Sammy around the corner of the building. "Hey, hold up." But she didn't. She was intent on departure.

"I'm sorry, Jared. I just up and left you behind like a sacrifice. I'm so sorry." She reached the car and paced back and forth in front of it. "We never should've come tonight."

"It's okay."

"No, I mean it. This was a huge mistake. I will *never* entertain the idea of providing her a relationship with me ever again."

"I don't think I could even argue with that. She's… something else. Can't tell you how many times I had to bite my tongue."

"Right? You can see how much of a problem she is after barely meeting her. I'm just gonna have to tell my mom I'm done with this. A girl only needs one mother and one father, anyway. Who cares about the biological set? I'm very blessed to have the parents who raised me. I know that. Don't you know I know that, Jared?"

I took her by the shoulders, bringing her ranting-pacing ordeal to a stop. "Sammy, enough. Listen to me. You don't owe anyone anything. Don't let guilt manipulate your love for your mom. You don't have to blindly do everything she asks just to make her happy, and it's not going to end your relationship with her if she's disappointed. If what she's asking you to do is hurting you, then be honest with her."

Her eyes closed, and beneath my grip, her shoulders rose and fell through a deep breath. Opening her eyes, she regarded me. "I know you're right. I can clearly see and understand that, but everything just feels so weird for me right now. I don't know who I am, and I feel like the more time I spend with Claudia, the more I'm going to hate myself. I don't want to be anything like her." She shook her head. "But what if I'm already just like her? What if the damage is already done, and all that's left is to see it? Jared, I don't want to see it."

Dropping my arms in exasperation, I couldn't suppress a laugh. "Sammy, are you kidding? I only had a partial evening with her, and it's so obvious to me. You are so far from being like her it's insane. She's abrasive, inconsiderate, selfish, and rude, just to put a few of her finer qualities into words."

"Which isn't so different from me. I'm bossy, blunt, loud—"

"You're sensitive, compassionate, funny, sweet, caring…" I ran the back of my thumb along her jawline, resting it briefly under her chin. "And smart, strong, beautiful."

Sammy's eyes nearly undid me. She looked as though she was hearing these things for the first time, but I knew that wasn't true. There's no way a woman this amazing didn't know all this about herself.

"Wow," she mused, searching my eyes. "I might almost believe you mean all that stuff."

Her doubt cut me to the quick. "I do mean them."

She fell back into her default setting, and a little smirk peeked out. "Better be careful, Tomlin. Someone walking by might think we're on a date because that sounds an awful lot like flirting with me."

That wouldn't be the worst thing, would it?

I shrugged. "Well, I did pay for dinner."

She laughed. "Oh my gosh, I'm so sorry," she started in again. "I forgot about the gift card! Do you want it? If not, I will pay you back."

"No, you won't. And before you try to argue, just save it. Get in the car. It's time to go home."

"Yes, sir," she mocked, going around to my door to gallantly offer me the passenger seat.

We took the long way home, laughing and talking about anything that wasn't the disastrous dinner. Pulling up to my house, I didn't feel ready for the night to end.

"Feels weird that you let me into the car earlier, and now you're the one walking me to my front door at the end of an evening together."

"What's weird about that?"

"Well, if this *was* a date, I would have done the door-opening and the driving and the walking."

"If you weren't a total gimp, you mean?"

"Right." I chuckled, reaching for my crutches. *I can't wait to burn these freaking things.* If only this dinner had happened a week or so later, when my brace came off, I wouldn't have needed them anymore.

When we reached my doorstep, I turned awkwardly to face her. "Something else crossed my mind." With one hand stuffed in the pocket of my jeans, I balanced on my good heel. "If this were a real date, I would kiss you goodnight right about now."

"Despite the intrusion of my severely unhinged, uh, family member, I can see how it was kinda like one." Sammy beheld me through dark lashes, and I didn't think anyone had ever looked at me quite like that before. "I can't thank you enough for enduring that when you definitely didn't have to, and for talking me off the crazy-ledge."

I leaned in. "I would do it all again."

She leaned closer. "Would you?"

And closer. "In a heartbeat."

"Hm. That does sound like a date to me then. What do you think?" Our eyes played chicken, neither of us looking away. I braced myself.

When I stepped forward, she didn't retreat. When my left hand reached out to cradle her neck, getting lost beneath her dark, loose tendrils, she didn't recoil. Instead, tilting slightly to the side, she welcomed my touch, and it was all the encouragement I needed. Leaning down, I—

Behind me, the front door opened so fast that the wind from the swinging door, combined with my surprise, nearly brought me crashing down. My idiotic, annoying brother stood in the doorway. "It's about time, gimpy. I thought you'd never get out of her car."

Sammy giggled. "Goodnight, Jared. Goodnight Jeremy. Good luck, kid."

"I won't need it," he boasted. What a dummy. He was *so* going to need it.

I watched her leave, and before I was ready, the night came to a crashing halt. Sammy left, and the answer to whether or not it was a date left with her.

SAMMY

27

Cindie and I were the only ones closing. The evening rush died out early, and we found ourselves shooting the breeze while the clock ran out.

"Hey, Sammy? Do you mind if I ask you about something personal?"

"Yeah?" I couldn't imagine what that was. We got along great and kept talking about wanting to get together outside of work, but so far, we hadn't made it happen. I wondered what kind of personal thing she could possibly want to talk about.

"I heard that you were, uh, well, adopted. Is that true?"

I ceased wiping down the counter and forgot all about my rag as I straightened and turned to face her. "Yes, it is. What makes you ask?"

She considered for a time and consulted the clock. "Let's sit down. I highly doubt anyone else is coming in at this point." She strode out from behind the counter and sat at one of the tables. She pushed the opposite chair out with her foot under the table.

Too curious of the sudden change in conversation, I was

powerless not to see it through. Taking up the seat, I watched her. "What is this about?"

She gave a small, warm smile. "I hope I'm not overstepping here. I know we are only new friends, but I wanted to share something about myself with you. In case it might help."

"Okay?"

"It's not a secret, but not exactly public knowledge, either, that I grew up in foster care."

"Oh, I had no idea." I was quickly itching to know more.

"It's a long, sorry story, but to sum it up, both my parents died when I was super young. I was raised by multiple foster families, some better than others, but I was never adopted. Had one close call when I was about ten, but in the end, they didn't bite the bullet. That's always kinda been how it is in my life. It looks like someone is starting to get close, to really decide to choose me, and then they just..."

"Swim away?"

She laughed. "Exactly. Just like the slippery fishes they are."

"I imagine that's why you took so long to accept Tyler's invitation for a date?" That patient man came into the café constantly just to order coffee from her and sit down to do his work. A girl got curious. I knew I was prying, but my instincts about the moment told me she wouldn't mind. It was the most personal I'd ever gotten with Cindie thus far, and I was enjoying her confidence. I liked to think that she was enjoying mine, too, or she wouldn't have approached me in the first place.

I already knew she didn't have a reason to worry with Tyler, that was for sure. The young youth pastor at Sarah's church was one of the most genuine human beings I'd ever known. If he said he was in it for the long haul, he meant the long haul.

She rolled one shoulder thoughtfully. I took her serene expression as a sign that I hadn't been wrong to ask.

"Part of it. Or rather, I guess all my reasons are bundled up into the same core thing. I've just grown up in a way that taught me to always get a good read on people before I trust them. I mean, I work at a coffee shop, you know? I see a lot of guys come and go, and do you know how many of them park it at my tables for days at a time, hoping to get my attention?" She shook her head, answering her own question. "I've lost count. I don't know why guys think it's fun to stake out for baristas, yet they do. But then there was Tyler…" Her eyes did that shimmering thing that Sarah's did whenever she talked about Kevin. I dared to hope whatever they both had was catching.

Could someone—Jared?—ever feel something strong like that for me?

"So, instead of days, he put in weeks, huh?" I giggled.

"Try months!" she corrected me, her grin spreading ear to ear. Actually, no, she wasn't correcting; she was bragging. It was kind of sweet. "He did nothing more than order and sit down for the longest time, and then he started dropping hints he was interested. And let me tell you, Tyler's hints aren't all that subtle."

I laughed. From all the times I tagged along to youth group with Sarah, I thought I knew just what Cindie meant by that. Tyler was many things, but subtle definitely wasn't one of them. He was unapologetically bold.

"What finally wore you down?"

"The fact that no amount of rejection had worn *him* down," she said with a calm finality.

"He chased you then."

Her mouth pinched as she pondered my statement. "I wouldn't say he chased. He *waited*. He proved a patient determination, and that turned out to be exactly what I needed."

"How did you figure that out?"

"I don't know," she confessed, her voice ticking up. "At one point, I just realized it was time to stop refusing because everything would be all right." I had to take a chance sooner or later.

"My mom would call that a move of the Holy Spirit."

She smiled thoughtfully. "I like that very much. I'd like to think so as well. Of course, Tyler says the very same thing."

Our attentions were drawn to the outside. A wayward patron of the bookstore walked by with his eye on the cafe door like he intended to come in, but he ended up merely slowing down and then moving on.

"Anyway," Cindie continued. "My point in telling you all this was just to say I'm sorry if you're struggling with your biological parents, and I hope that you know you're not alone in your affliction. In fact, there are support groups and all sorts of resources I can connect you with if that's something you'd ever want. At the very least, I'm always here, too."

"Thank you, Cindie." I wanted something more appreciative to say, but I could think of nothing good enough to express my feelings.

On one hand, I thought it was awesome we had similar circumstances in common. On the other, I was sad that anyone went through things like this. And, honestly, I felt the weight of my good luck. Cindie lost both of her parents. I still had mine, plus one, even if I didn't want her.

JARED

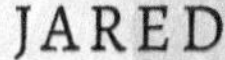

28

Man, I've really missed my independence. It feels so good to *drive.* At least, physically, it did. I could only wonder how long I would go without freaking out as the freeway stretched out ahead of us. As the lanes got smaller, the trucks got bigger, and things got louder. But I had Sammy with me, so admittedly, I worried less and less.

The first thing I did after getting out of my knee brace and off my crutches was call Sammy and tell her we were going on a road trip. She had spent the last few weeks carting me around, helping me out immensely. The least I could do was provide her with a fun day out to say thanks.

"Are you sure you're okay with driving?" Sammy asked, gentle measure coating her question.

"Yeah, I'll be okay. I need to get the hang of it again eventually."

"If at any point you want to swap, I will."

From the passenger seat, she glanced at the GPS, which told us to continue on our current route for fifty-three more miles.

We would be on I-37 North for most of the trip, and that's about all I had told her.

"So, where are we going?" she tried again, hoping to trick me into spilling with her pretty tone.

I wasn't falling for it. "It'll be much more fun if I don't tell you, won't it?"

"Yeah," she admitted with a sigh. It was endearingly comical how much she hated not having her way. It made the surprise all the more fun for me. "Unless you're taking me to a secret bunker where you'll bury me deep inside the walls and glaze over my remains with cement."

Eyes wide, I blinked at her. "You need to watch less true crime TV."

"Oh, I don't watch any. That's all me." She tapped the side of her skull.

"That's even more frightening. Now, I worry I'm the one being kidnapped, only to end up brutally murdered."

Glancing my way, she gave me a menacing smile. Then, she returned her attention to the road ahead. "Nah, you're safe. I could never harm that pretty face of yours."

"I knew my good looks would save my butt someday. They just had to."

We broke out into laughter. When it subsided, we were fifty-*one* miles from our destination, and my anticipation had not lessened; I found myself feeling anxious with excitement rather than fear of the road.

"You're really not going to tell me then?"

In response, I gave her a sympathetic look and reached over to pat her hand as it rested on her lap, causing me to once again ponder the tangible reality of her touch. "Just trust me." I intended to pull my hand away again, but it didn't happen. She nestled her fingers through mine instead, effectively anchoring me in place, providing a comforting relief we both knew I needed. "But if it will make you feel better, I'll give you one piece of information if you stop asking. Deal?"

"Fine. Deal." She smiled triumphantly.

I bit my tongue not to laugh. "It's somewhere not in Corpus Christi."

"You cheat!" She squeezed in disapproval, and I couldn't help laughing anymore. To assuage her, I brought her hand up and kissed the back of it. It was only a brief, innocent thing, but as I placed our hands back down, I could feel that it was a lot more.

"Only kidding! It's somewhere in San Antonio. And now that's the last I want to hear you asking about it."

"Whatever you say," she said with a dry smile.

MANY MILES ROLLED by in silence as I remained lost in my head, but Sammy's free hand reached for the radio dials, scanning for a station, jarring me back to the car. She caught something to her liking and left it, returning to her relaxed position against the seat. Her head bobbed, and her eyes closed as she danced along. I assumed drumming her thumb against mine was a subconscious reaction to the music, but I liked it. When she started singing, I found myself bewildered by her serenade, straining to hear it better.

Her voice was quiet but incredible. Every note emitted from her lips was on pitch and carried the loveliest of tones with a gentle, bowing vibrato.

"Get a load of that voice, Sammy. You can really sing."

Her mouth snapped shut, and she turned the volume dial until the song was merely a whisper. "How well could you hear me?" The horror in her voice was surprising.

"Pretty well. I'm on the other side of the car, not the other side of town," I ribbed her with a smile. "What? Is The Bull being shy? Are you finally showing your human side?"

She looked away from me. Her silence was confirmation enough. My initial instinct was to keep teasing her, but something else told me to leave her be.

Better yet…

Pressing on my steering wheel, I cranked the volume up. I didn't listen to a lot of music, but even I knew this one. Taking a hasty breath, I began to sing along. Sammy's jaw dropped as she watched me, listening and understanding what I was sharing with her. She didn't have to be embarrassed that someone heard her sing. Especially not when I showed zero concern for my underdeveloped throaty pitch. My voice wasn't *awful*, but hers was angelic.

When the chorus picked up, Sammy's voice joined in. I resisted the urge to cheer in victory, simply listening to her glorious sound. She harmonized above the band with expert tonality. The girl was a natural.

When the song ended, I remained awestruck. "Impressive. I can't believe you try to keep that talent locked away."

She rolled her shoulder, her cheeks taking on a barely distinguishable tint of pink. "It's nothing millions of other people can't do better."

"I find that hard to believe after what I just heard." She cracked a smile, and my heart swelled with pride.

My joy only intensified when I realized how long it'd been since I'd felt threatened by the highway. Somewhere along the lines of our friendship, Sammy had become a champion at chasing my fears away.

SAMMY

29

Finally exiting the freeway, Jared steered toward downtown San Antonio. "Have you been to the River Walk before?"

"Who hasn't?" I retorted.

"You never know."

"It has been a while though. Is that our final destination?"

"Nah, just a pitstop."

Frustrating, exciting male.

As Jared maneuvered carefully around the confined roads, he at last released my hand. I'd played it down, even in my head, but I had remained innately aware of the touch the entire drive up. His hands, bigger and stronger than mine, kept my heart warm like a blanket. And when he'd heard me sing and made the effort to soothe me, it felt so uncomplicated and normal. So very unlike *me*.

We found good parking with surprising ease. Then he rushed around the front of the car to my door, opening it. All I did was hop out and thank him, but the gesture had me feeling like mush

172

on the inside. If he kept doing and saying such gentlemanly things, I would…

I had no idea. Probably something stupid though.

When we reached the ramp to go down toward the river, Jared's arm found its way around my lower back. I looked at him, and he gave me a cheeky smile. "It's more for me than you," he tried to convince me.

For a moment, I was confused until it dawned on me that he didn't have his crutches. "How is your leg feeling?"

"Great so far, but I'm sure that could change real fast."

"Better safe than sorry then." I slipped my arm around him, too.

"Agreed," he said, his grip taking a firm, possessive hold on my side. To stop myself from smiling too hard, I bit the inside of my mouth.

"Since this isn't the main feature of our afternoon, we don't have to spend long here," he explained, and I was relieved for a topical distraction.

"The last time my family and I came, we saw someone fall in the river."

"No way!"

"Yes, way, and it was hilarious. There was a couple taking wedding photos over toward the mall. You know that theater area? Well, their photographer was across the water on the seating side shooting and took one step too many, and he plummeted right in, equipment and all. Even the photographer laughed."

"That sucks big time."

"I always wondered if the camera was okay and if they could salvage those photos."

"Hopefully. I'd hate to lose something that precious."

"You think wedding photos are precious?"

"Not everyone's memories last. They can come and go, but a photo will stay constant. Having photos is like having treasure only you and your loved ones care about, which makes it more special if you ask me."

"Hm." Thinking about it, his stance on the matter made sense. I recalled the photos in his room, most of which featured his dad.

"You don't think so?"

"Actually, I do. I just hadn't thought about it like that before. But you're totally right." *So sensitive. So sweet. I'm in so much trouble.*

A little while later, as we strolled along, deeply engrossed in conversation about the things we did and definitely did not miss from high school, we came across a large stone wall shaded by overhanging trees and lined with vendors. "Oh, look! They've got the artisan market set up."

"Do you want to stop by before we head back up?"

"Do I?" I yelped with excitement, skipping over to where the booths began. It was hard to take my time looking at everything since we still had somewhere else to go, but it was all so cool. There were wood carvers, leather workers, even iron workers, and jewelry makers, among many others. I was blown away by all of them.

"If only I could create stuff like this," I praised. "It looks so fun to do."

"You could learn."

"I don't think I have the patience for a new skill right now."

"Maybe in the future then," he offered.

"Maybe."

Enraptured, I bent over a tray of themed trinkets. There was a set of serving utensils with mother-of-pearl handles, a pair of decorative thimbles accented with the milky, misshapen orbs, and a gilded, pearl-encrusted baby booty. What really caught my eye was the random assortment of jewelry, also boasting my birthstone.

"Those are all handmade," advertised the woman on the other side of the booth. "All my jewelry is made with homegrown pearls from my family's oyster farm in Rockport, Texas, and all the metal is high-quality sterling silver. We never use nickel or other plated materials."

I smiled as I listened, running my fingers over an imperfectly round pearl strung through horizontally with a delicate chain. Simple, plain, yet so well put together, the pendant made the most beautiful necklace. "It's all gorgeous," I told the proprietor. "Pearls are my favorite."

"Did you recently celebrate a birthday by chance?"

"Yep."

Jared's smile contorted with curiosity. "How'd you know that?" he asked her.

"Pearl is the June birthstone," she explained to him.

"Ah. Right. Good to know."

"Thank you for letting us look. Take care," I politely told her before meandering to the next booth. There were a few left to look through before we took off for the rest of our plans. I didn't know what those were yet, but I caught myself excited over the suspense despite my typical opposition to surprises.

Shortly after, once I'd gotten my fill of gawking at the goodies for sale, Jared nodded toward the food trucks. "Are you hungry?"

I took a deep inhale of all the delicious smells. "I can always eat."

So we did, carrying our food in a paper bowl as we made our

way back up to the street. Spending time with Jared confused, bewildered, and befuddled me as well as tore down my carefully constructed walls, but so far, I wasn't going to complain.

JARED

30

"A BAKERY?" ASKED SAMMY, CURIOSITY SEEPING FROM HER.

I smiled. "Just wait," I encouraged. The grand finale of our road trip might not make much sense to Sammy, but when I'd decided to treat her to a day out, I knew I had to bring her here, to the bakery with a specialty cinnamon roll that had done so much for my family and me in the past.

We walked down the display cases stacked with sweet treats, and I noted when Sammy showed particular interest in something and added a couple of them to our order. Obviously, the cinnamon roll was for here, but the few little additions were to go.

So much had changed in my life since the last time I was here, but this place had stayed reassuringly the same. Either the owners appreciated being stagnant as much as I did, or a year and a half really wasn't that long. Either way, it made me grateful in a way I couldn't then explain to myself.

Seated at our table, Sammy was making noises of satisfaction, and it drew my delighted attention. She was heavily invested in procuring every bit of flavor off her fingers, wiggling in her seat like a toddler might if given delectable morsels of their own. It was freaking adorable.

"You like it, huh?" I asked, an unrelenting grin across my face.

"No, I love it!" she said assertively. "So delish. And what a cute place," she pointed out, looking around. "I will need to make a second round and bring home a few things for my parents, too. I thought about sharing these, but I'm definitely going to keep them for myself." Sammy patted our to-go box.

Shoving the very last bite of her half of our epic cinnamon roll into her mouth, she groaned. "It doesn't make sense why this thing is this good."

I totally understood. Mine was devoured in half the time. "It's the paragon of good baking and the crowning achievement of the whole place. At least it is to me."

"I might agree, though I haven't eaten any of the other stuff yet."

"My family and I would come up this way a lot for day trips, and we always stopped by here. It became a thing."

Sammy eased her napkin to the table. "Oh?"

"I'm not sure when it started, exactly. The cinnamon roll was our favorite. It kinda became its own member of the family." I laughed. "My parents would even sneak up here to buy one to celebrate special occasions."

"That sounds like a sweet way to celebrate. No pun intended."

"It was. If I got all As on my report card—cinnamon roll. If I won the spelling bee—cinnamon roll. Get a ribbon at the science fair? Cinnamon roll."

"I'd be so fat and happy if that were me. Maybe I'd be a better student, too." She giggled. "So, tell me, what is it we're celebrating today?"

This girl had no idea how much her laughter warmed me. "Just you."

Sammy's smile faded. "Why me?"

"Why not you? You're awesome. You've more than earned a cinnamon roll."

"I highly doubt that—these things are *really* good."

"So are you."

"If you say so." Her expression was indiscernible. She gave me a lighthearted glare before bundling up her trash.

I couldn't put my finger on it, but something seemed wrong. She seemed suddenly distant, guarded.

As if overcome by a new cheer, Sammy straightened in her seat and announced loudly, "I'm going to pick out a few things to take home and share. What else do you recommend?" She reached for her wallet.

I stayed her hand. "No. Let me."

"I can't keep letting you pay my way, Jared."

"Yes, you can. I took you out, so you can just put that thing away for the day."

"I'm more than capable—"

"I know you are. But today is my treat." My face softened, but it seemed like she still didn't know what to do with my hospitality, so I moved along before she could protest again.

Picking out the very best of my favorite treats for her family, plus a couple I snuck in there for her for later, I paid and made my way back to our table. She had her phone out but put it away upon my approach.

"Everything okay?" I nodded toward her phone.

"Oh, yeah, for sure. I was just checking in with the girls."

I had one to-go box under my arm, and I reached for the other. "You ready to get going?"

"Ready, Freddy." She nodded, smiling oddly. I held my free arm out for her to loop my elbow, but she either didn't notice or didn't want to. She walked right past me, on a mission to leave.

SAMMY

31

WE MADE JUST ONE MORE STOP ON THE WAY HOME, PULLING OVER at a rest area to stretch our legs. I took longer than I needed to return to the car because I was suddenly embarrassed to be around Jared. He kept catching me off guard by saying such wonderful things to and about me. How was I supposed to react to that?

At the bakery, I'd taken the opportunity to ask the girls about it during his brief absence.

SAMMY

Jared is being nice. Too nice.

JENNA

Define "too nice"??

SAMMY

He keeps paying for stuff and being cute and saying nice things.

BIRDIE JO

What a gentleman! Where's the problem?

JENNA

What the heck, Sammy, are you dating the guy now??

SAMMY

Not that I know of.

Though, this was not the first time we'd spent together that had felt awfully close to being a date. And, if I recalled correctly, that first time nearly ended in a kiss…

JENNA

Sounds like HE'S dating YOU.

After I'd read that last text, Jared returned, and I shoved my phone away. Even when we reached the rest area, I didn't dare take my phone back out for fear of what else they might've been saying. Jenna implied Jared was further into me than I would've guessed, but could she be right?

I couldn't help but notice Sarah was absent from the brief exchange. Was she busy, or had she held back her opinion for some other reason?

She couldn't possibly like Jared now, could she? If she did, if she'd given up on Kevin, then I was surely screwed. I'd never get the guy if someone like Sarah went up against me for him. She had so much more to offer him.

Did I *want* the guy?

Looking out over the vast nothingness of Southern Texas, I shook my thoughts loose and tossed a rock. It soared a modest distance before skidding along the nearly barren land. Resigned, I knew I had to return to the car sooner or later.

Jared was waiting in the car with the windows down when I

got back. "Hey," I said, sliding into the passenger seat. "Have you been waiting long?"

"Nah. I took a minute to do some stretches."

"Your knee hurting?"

"Surprisingly, no. I'm just hoping to make sure it doesn't start."

"Smart, smart… Hey, Jared?"

"Hey, Sammy?"

"Thank you for doing all this for me."

He shook his head. "There's nothing to thank me for."

"Seriously, there is. After the whole mother thing, I just wanted to run away. I tried to shift my focus so I didn't have to deal with what I'd learned. It didn't seem possible for me to deal with any of it until you began showing up for me. So, thank you for just being here—for being my friend. You know, I haven't even told Sarah and the others about all this yet. You're the only one I have to talk about it with."

"Sounds healthy," he teased, but I knew he understood. Something glimmered afresh in his eyes. "You're very welcome," he said, leaning his elbow against the center console.

I didn't know what sort of butterflies grew in an instant, but the sort Jared gave me certainly did. My gut was laden with their flap of anxious glee. Was I seriously considering kissing Jared Tomlin right now, at a middle-of-nowhere rest stop on the side of I-37?

Yes. Yes, I was.

Our eyes were locked as I leaned over, and before I could stop myself, my lips pressed against his. They were… *Hm…* They were certainly stiffer than I remembered.

Then came Jared's sudden laughter, vibrating against my

mouth and catching me completely off guard. My eyes popped open, and I pulled back like he was an electric fence.

Then I watched. The boy. Laugh.

"Wha..." I was breathless in my confusion, unable to form the words floating around my head like a buoy.

WHAT.

JUST.

HAPPENED?

I don't know how long I sat there before it became obvious to me that I should not have done that, and my shock turned into embarrassment before I, too, was laughing. *It's either I laugh or I cry.*

"I'm so sorry," I said, my hand on my mouth. "I don't know why I did that."

"It's okay," he said, his cheeks flushed. "I get it."

"What is there to get?"

"You're extremely vulnerable right now. We related to one another in a way you can't with your other friends. I'm devilishly handsome and charming... I get it."

I lightly punched his shoulder. "Your cool points are going down faster than they went up. Keep talking. I feel less like an idiot already."

"It's really okay, don't worry about it. We can forget it ever happened if that's what you want."

"Yes, please." *No...* "Let's do that."

"You got it." His supportive smile seemed tainted with disappointment. There's no way I was reading that expression correctly. Not after he just laughed in my face like that. I haven't had a lot of experience with guys lately, but I didn't think that was the reaction of a guy who *wanted* to be kissed by me. Seriously, who gets rejected mid-kiss?

What about our kiss at the beach though? Was that really only for the sake of the game? And what of our almost-kiss after dinner with Claudia? There's no way I mistook what was happening that night. Was I going crazy, or didn't we have chemistry?

Oh, well. We could forget about it. I was fine with that, or at least, I would tell myself I was until I believed it. Because if I ever questioned whether or not Jared and I would eventually be a thing, this confirmed we wouldn't.

I read you loud and clear, Jared. You're not interested.

He fired up the engine. "Ready to go home?"

Not really. Aside from going home with the shame of this mistake, I knew I wouldn't be able to avoid Claudia much longer. "Does it matter if I say no?"

"We could loiter around somewhere else a bit longer, but you gotta go home eventually."

And somehow, even after humiliating me a few seconds ago, he still understood me so well. "It doesn't even feel like home anymore," I said admittedly.

"I know." The expression on his face told me he really did. "But it will again soon enough."

The reminder made me think of his own situation with his dad, and all at once, I realized why I thought kissing him felt like a good idea. Maybe he was right that I was feeling vulnerable, but we really *were* on a whole different level, Jared and I. Our losses were not exact, but they were both a parent loss of sorts. As much as I loved Sarah and my other friends, they wouldn't understand what I was feeling like Jared did because he'd lost someone like none of them had. It was that simple. We were kindred spirits now, joined closer in friendship than I had ever expected we'd be.

But that's all we were. Got it. No kissing.

"Alright, then. Let's go home. I can do this."

"Yes, you can. And if you think you can't, text me. Okay?"

"Thanks, Jared."

"Anytime."

JARED

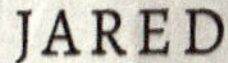

32

WHEN THE LAUGHTER I HADN'T KNOWN WOULD EXPLODE FROM ME finally subsided, and I'd finally gotten a look at Sammy, she'd looked less than happy—understandably so.

I'm such an indescribable idiot. Someone should give me an award for being the biggest one ever.

Sitting across from me with a meek helplessness on her face, I thought Sammy had never looked more vulnerable and hurt before, and it was my fault.

IDIOT.

"Hey, Sammy, all jokes aside, I'm sorry. You just caught me off guard."

"I thought we were going to pretend it didn't happen."

"I just… Where did that come from?"

"I'm not actually sure, and I really don't want to try and figure it out."

"Come on. We can at least talk about it. You're upset."

"Probably not as upset as you might think."

"Well, that's something," I encouraged, hoping to pull more out of her, but she remained silently obstinate.

As I'd suspected back at the bakery, some sort of switch had been flipped within Sammy. Based on how she'd been acting toward the end, it didn't make sense why she would just suddenly kiss me. My reaction was terrible, but it wasn't malicious. I would kill to have a do-over, but I didn't dare try anything. I'd screwed the day up pretty good.

Resuming the drive, I finally pulled out of the parking lot and curved my way around the lanes until we were once again on the freeway. At least my mind was preoccupied enough not to feel anxious.

My brain would not let it go. I got maybe twenty minutes into the drive when I felt brave (stupid) enough to broach the subject again. I had wits enough not to look her way, keeping my eyes glued to the endless ribbon of gray ahead. "Are you sure you don't want to talk about it?"

"Pretty sure."

I was taken aback by her tone and afforded a small sideways glance in her direction. She was focused on the traveling land out her window.

"Sammy. Seriously."

"Seriously, Jared. Drop it."

I considered her request; I really did. But nothing about it felt right. With a careful look at my blind spots, I flipped on my blinker and pulled over to the shoulder.

"What are you doing?"

When I stopped, I put the car in park and turned. "Talk to me, Sam. You don't have to hide whatever you're really feeling. It's just me and you here. What's up?"

The look she gave me was chilling. The air in the car churned. Her face was stone, jaw set tightly. Her dark eyes peered at me like I was public enemy number one. And under her scrutiny, I felt like it, too.

"I really don't want to talk about this because there's nothing to tell."

"But you kissed me."

"It was just something to do, I guess. No big deal."

"Then why are you so angry?"

"Because you won't let it go."

"Level with me, Ballard. Is it because I laughed or because you think kissing me was a mistake?"

She quirked her head. "Maybe a little of both."

"I'm really, deeply sorry I laughed. It truthfully is because you surprised me, that's it. Second, *why* did you kiss me? I think that's a fair question for me to ask."

She shrugged, providing an air of indifference. "Because I wanted to."

"And now you wish you hadn't?"

Her smile was mocking me. "And they say jocks are dumb."

"Jeez. That's real nice."

"So is laughing with someone else's face against your face!" she snapped, slapping one hand to another to emphasize her frustration, and it nearly made me laugh again. I felt terrible, but she was too cute, even angry.

"How many times do you need to hear I'm sorry?"

"I'm not asking to hear it at all. You can save it. All *I* want to know is why you laughed, and then I never want to talk about this again."

"I really was surprised. But, honestly?"

"If you would," she encouraged, annoyed.

"If you tried it again, I most definitely wouldn't laugh."

A strange mixture of anger, sadness, and disbelief washed over her features. "Whatever. You can say that all you want because you know I won't."

"But you could…"

"You know what else I want to know?"

"What?"

"Do you still like Sarah?"

I blinked. *Is that what this is about?* "Are you upset because you think I do? Did something I said or did today trigger that assumption?"

"Just answer the question."

"No, I do not like Sarah." Exasperation was catching up with me.

"It wouldn't make much sense if you did. You guys had a single date. The world's most terrible one, I might add."

"Yeah, I'm well aware. But thank you for the reminder."

"Sorry, but I don't get it. You act like Prince Charming all day long, and then when I finally… When I think you might be open to the idea… then bam, you show me just how wrong I was. And now, I really don't want to seem ungrateful, but I'd just like to go home."

"Fine. I can manage that." And little else, apparently.

Signaling back onto the highway, I gassed the car onward. After checking the clock, I was properly motivated to return. The sooner we got back, the sooner I could walk away from this uncomfortable situation. What would make her ask about Sarah out of the blue like that? Had she said something during their text exchange at the bakery, and that's why she seemed to change so quickly?

Somewhere between home and San Antonio, Sammy and I

had gone from the cusp of something amazing to two awkward people stuck in a two-hour car ride together. While I was grateful I was too preoccupied to be anxious about the drive, I mourned the absence of her comfort. I wouldn't get it, and I didn't deserve it, anyway.

33

On Sunday, I forced all the awkwardness between Jared and me to flee and brought him to church with me. He was being surly about it, but I'd gotten him there.

"I haven't been to church in a while."

By the way Jared's Adam's apple bobbed, I would guess that *'a while'* was an understatement.

"I don't always go, either, but my parents do. They're members somewhere else, but I liked going with Sarah to her church because the youth group was really fun, and now that I'm a legal adult, I get to help volunteer with the littles. Sarah already does it."

"And that's… fun?"

"It can be. Don't you like kids?"

His face contorted a dozen different ways before he settled on an answer. "Not really."

I chaffed. "Well, you'd better learn to love 'em because I bet you my next paycheck that they'll love you."

"Why would you say that?"

Giving him my smiling side-eye, I shrugged. "Just a hunch."

"Yeah, sure. But do we really have to attend service, too? This is going to take up half the day."

"Maybe a bit more. It'll be fine, I promise. Just because you're rusty doesn't mean you aren't welcome or that you won't enjoy it."

Jared turned toward the window and muttered something under his breath that sounded like he didn't care either way, but I chose to ignore it. I was committed to volunteering, and I was taking him with me. He couldn't just sit around and stew all day while I was at work.

Ever since San Antonio, his knee had been aching again. He might've tried doing a bit much too soon. Now, he needed something to occupy his time and get his mind off feeling sorry for himself and, in general, worrying about something other than that knee of his.

Besides, everyone needed some good old-fashioned church time. Myself included.

"I know you're not thrilled, and thank you for coming along despite that. But there's more to life than football, Jared. I'm glad you're going to live some with me."

"Well, when you put it that way, I guess I'll try to complain a little less."

Victory in hand, I reached over and patted his hair. "That's my boy."

"Hey! You can't mess with my hair if you expect me to get out of this car. At least play fair. I may lose my dignity being slave to a bunch of nose-drippers, but at least let me keep my style."

"Why do people always think children have a twenty-four-seven runny nose? It's like a universal thing."

"Because they do. They're dirty, snotty, and just plain gross.

That's kids. They're basically feral monkeys who might drip, spray, or throw something on you at any point in time."

Laughing at his endearing ridiculousness, I rolled Roxy into a parking spot. "Welcome to the jungle then, honey. You'll be fine."

"But what if I'm not? I have a preexisting condition."

"They're not checking you for life insurance, dude. Chill out. They're just kids, and they're gonna love you." I flipped the engine off, and just before I got out, I leaned over and whispered, "Just be sure to get yourself together first. They *can* smell fear."

Jared leaned back, glaring. "You're the worst."

It was hard to pretend the nearness didn't jar me. I warred with the memory of a similar motion that resulted in the most embarrassing moment of my life, but that isn't what I'd brought him to church for. I didn't want to recall that every time we were together. We'd agreed it didn't happen, so it didn't happen.

I had to go back to my old ways. Jokes were easier than honesty. Safer, too.

"Don't try to flatter me." I flipped my hair before turning and leaving the car.

Sarah graciously waited for us outside the entrance, and when I caught her eye, she was smiling. "Wow," she said, smirking as I stood off to the side with her, the two of us waiting for Jared to catch up. "You two look chummy."

"He's coming along nicely, isn't he?"

"Sure, but that's not what I meant."

"Oh?" I only asked because I knew she didn't have time to answer. Jared appeared beside us a second later.

"Hey, Sarah," he said, reaching out his right arm. She took him up on a friendly hug and greeted him.

"You seem great," she commented. "No more crutches?"

"Only if it's really hurting me, but I feel good today."

If his crankiness were any indication, I'd bet he was fibbing about that, at least a little bit.

Sarah clasped her hands together. "That's so good. Thank God. And you both are going to have a great time helping with the little ones today. I'm excited. I've been trying to get Sammy to come help me do this for ages."

He gave me a side glance. "Really?"

"Oh, yeah. It's been a long time coming."

Sarah beamed as we followed her in. I was so thrilled by her change of disposition that I completely ignored Jared's telling glare in my direction. So what if I had avoided Sarah's request to help out with children's church up to this point? And yeah, I might've let Jared's self-pity be the deciding factor when she asked me this time. He needed it more than I did. Either way, I figured we couldn't go wrong doing something for the church for a change.

SARAH'S CHURCH WAS DIFFERENT THAN OURS. OR, OUR OLD ONE, rather. Mom hadn't taken us since after Dad's funeral. It'd been over a year and a half since the last time I had to stand this much during a Sunday service, and my knee was already starting to let me know. I'd have to grab my crutches from Sammy's car before heading into the lion's den with the children for this after-church field day thing they were doing. I didn't want them, but better safe than sorry.

I'd done well keeping the physical stress down for the most part, but after I took Sammy up north, the knee began to lodge some complaints, so I put the brace back on to be extra careful.

I shifted again, trying to find more comfortable footing. Sitting down sounded like a good idea, but I didn't want to stand out and look weak. Even the elderly were up on their feet, some with walkers in hand. If they could do it, I could do it. The increasing discomfort on top of my anxiety started to make me feel hot. The more I fought with myself over the silly thought of whether or not God would forgive me for sitting down, the more anxious I felt.

Suddenly, an arm snaked around my back, and a shoulder positioned under mine. Her familiar warmth enveloped me and chased away my worry, replacing it with unexpected support. I adjusted, and Sammy stood firm, holding on to me and absorbing my every unsteadiness. I stood taller, confidence flooding through me with her help.

She leaned in and whispered, "I hope this is okay." Her wintery-fresh breath fanned my neck and cheek as the floral decadence of her perfume filled my lungs. It was more than okay. It was more than I deserved, considering my senseless behavior the other day.

"Thank you," I rasped, so close to losing myself and leaning toward her, her natural magnetism drawing me in. Luckily, the praise and worship came to vibrant life in my ears, and I was brought back. Sammy rocked naturally to the music, carrying me with her.

As the next song started, the hairs on my arms and neck stood at attention. I actually knew this one. It was one of my mom's favorites from when she still played music around the house—when Dad was still alive.

I found myself humming along while the screen at the front displayed the words that I'd heard plenty of times but never gotten to know. It was about the miraculous things God does, turning something bad into something good. The song was decent, and it had a catchy tune, but all I knew was if God really cared about making a garden out of *my* grave, my dad wouldn't be six feet under, rotting away inside one.

And with that realization, I mentally checked out for the rest of the service. I wanted to bypass the sermon altogether, even if that meant getting to the dreaded kids' event sooner. The girls ate it up, and Sarah's parents, too. How wonderful for them, and I meant that, but not everybody had a happy-go-lucky experience with the All Mighty. For my part, I wished only to serve my time in the seat beside my friends and get the rest of the afternoon over with, come snot or high-water.

SAMMY

35

By the end of service, I was in a growing state of turmoil. I think I'd just openly flirted with Jared in front of the entire congregation after I had sworn never to make a fool of myself for that boy again. Man, I was hopeless.

I'd put my arm around him because I'd seen him struggling and knew I could help, not to elicit any sort of reaction. But then he'd regarded me with the most intense expression, gratitude mixed with something I couldn't discern, and the very marrow of my bones had quaked as if I were the *Titanic* cowering before the iceberg. Jared and I were unexpectedly on a very certain trajectory, heading straight for something unavoidable that I hadn't seen clearly on the horizon.

But I'd been wrong before, as I'd come to realize.

What was I to do? Blow the whistle, ring the bell, and endeavor to turn the ship? Or stay the course and brave the obstacles ahead of us, of which there would be many? I had no idea how to be the captain of my own heart and mind.

"You guys ready?" Sarah's voice drew me out of my miry sea

of thoughts, and I blinked to attention. Her gaze was knowing, her smirk unmistakable. She'd grill me about this later.

"Yeah, totally." I reached to the floor and bagged up my Bible and the program with my notes on it. "Jared? How 'bout you? You ready to go join the circus?"

"Yep. Lead the way, boss." Jared rose to his feet, seeming less steady than before.

"You okay? Does your knee hurt?"

"I'm fine."

I flashed him a smile, and he faked one in return. It was pretty, as we both agreed he was, but it wasn't real. It made me falter, my heart doing a little flop. What changed between now and a half hour ago when he looked at me like I'd never been looked at before?

"Actually, I might swing by the car and grab a crutch. Just in case any of Sarah's monkeys get too rowdy."

"Are you sure you're up for staying? I know I've been giving you a hard time about it, but I don't want you to be in pain."

A sheet of affliction flashed across his face, right on queue. When he didn't immediately respond, I thought he would be calling for a ride home. "Can I just borrow your keys? I'll meet you guys back at the front doors in a minute."

I wanted to refuse and grab his crutch myself, but I knew I shouldn't. With each inquiry after his well-being, Jared seemed more and more unhappy. I didn't know the nature of his current state, but I understood its precariousness. His entire being screamed: *Handle with care.*

"Sure thing." I reached into my pocket and handed them over. "But don't meet us out front. Head down the hall to the kids' room instead." With a gentle parting smile, I left the row with Sarah.

When we were through the crowd and on our way to the kids' room, Sarah turned to me. "We're gonna talk about you and Jared later, but is Jared okay? He seems kind of… in a mood."

I knew it. Ugh. "I thought so, too, but I think he'll be alright. I can't imagine what goes on in the mind of a grumpy teenaged boy." I really couldn't. One minute, he was joking and playing around with me, looking at me in that way that gave me chills, and the next, he was, well, a grumpy teenaged boy.

Sarah glanced behind us, watching Jared make his slow exit. "I wonder if service had him thinking about his dad."

"You know about that?"

"I don't know details, but I remember when it happened. Jenna talked about it because Dan spent less time with her during that period. You don't remember?"

I shook my head. "He told me about it recently. I was completely surprised." Was I truly so unobservant or self-involved that one of our peers had brutally lost his father, and I hadn't noticed at all? How could I have been so blind to Jared's pain when he was right on the edge of my circle all this time?

"You two really are getting pretty close, aren't you?"

So much for talking about it later.

With a roll of my shoulder, I bit my tongue. I wasn't sure what I was comfortable sharing at that particular moment, but luckily, Tyler approached at just the right time.

"Hello, hello, ladies. How are you both doing?" Tyler Cortez, the youth pastor—the very same one Cindie was now dating—had a mesh net stuffed with various sports equipment slung over his shoulder. With the hefty cargo, he made the hallway look small.

"Great," Sarah answered for the both of us while I merely nodded in pleasant agreement. "We're very excited to do this."

"Ms. Diana has been getting the kids hyped for it all month. They're ready!" He looked around us. "Is Jared still staying for it?"

"Oh, yes. He just ran to the car real quick. He'll be back any second."

"*Bueno!* They are so excited to learn from a professional." He smiled. "Oh, and Sammy, don't let me forget before you go that I have your packet for the mission in my office."

"Oh, great. Thank you."

Jared came around the corner, and all eyes turned to him. "Ah, Jared!" Tyler adjusted the load on his back and put his hand out with friendly confidence. "Tyler Cortez, youth pastor here."

"Jared Tomlin, good to meet you."

"We are so thrilled to have you here with us today. Sarah and Sammy have talked so highly of you and your accomplishments."

"Really?" Jared's gaze bounced skeptically between us both.

"Yep. And the children can't wait to learn how to play football. It's so generous of you to volunteer your time and expertise like this. Thank you!"

Jared's jaw ticked, and his alabaster skin paled. "That's the plan for today? Football?"

"Yes, sir," Tyler said.

I bit my lip to keep from laughing, but I wasn't doing a good job. Did I feel bad that I'd sneakily conned Jared into doing something he wouldn't have wanted to do? No. But did I wish that I could have sat down and asked him in a mature way first? Also no.

Call me crazy, but I was enjoying this greatly. Not only would I feel a teensy bit vindicated for him laughing at my kiss attempt, but I knew deep down he would enjoy himself. He may not think he liked kids, but he loved football. If he really hated me after this, I would work on apologizing profusely later. For now, I stuck to my guns.

Here we come, circus!

36

Parents and pastors alike loitered at the edges of the makeshift field behind the church. If I had been a lesser man, unaccustomed to pressure, I might've had a serious problem with this situation. As it were, I stood up as straight as I could, leaning all my weight against the crutch and my good leg, and clapped, capturing the attention of my young pupils.

"Okay, everyone. Gather up around here, and I will start by teaching you a few choice terms. For starters, this tight-knit circle we've just formed, does anyone know what it's called?"

"Oh!" Sammy's hand shot into the air.

"Yes, Ms. Sammy?"

She widened her arms in a big circle. "A sphere of awesomeness!" All the kids erupted in laughter, and even the adults on the sidelines were chuckling.

"Good guess," I said loudly, trying to gain control of the crowd. "But no. It's called a huddle. The purpose of a huddle is to get real close together with your teammates and privately discuss what you will do next during an offensive play."

A little girl across from me in the circle raised her hand. She didn't wait long enough to be called on before asking, "What's an office play?"

"An *off-en-sive* play is when your team has control of the ball, and you're all trying to score." She nodded her understanding. "So, does anyone know what the opposite of offense is?"

"Me!" Sammy's hand shot up into the air again.

"Defense!" shouted one little boy, beating her to whatever punchline she had prepared. He couldn't have been more than ten or twelve, the oldest in the group.

"I was gonna say that," Sammy said, fake-scowling at him. He laughed.

"What's your name?" I asked him.

"Eli."

"You are correct, Eli. Good job. Defense is the opposite of offense. When you are playing defense, it means you're trying to stop the other team from scoring. You do things like block and tackle."

"Ooh, tackling? When do we get to do that?" Sammy rubbed her hands together like she couldn't wait to smoosh all the kids into the ground. They laughed and growled at her in return. I finally laughed.

"Well, we won't. We'll have these…" Reaching into the sack beside me on the ground, the one Tyler had placed there after introducing me, I retrieved a handful of flags. "Once we have split you all into two teams—offense and defense—we will Velcro these around your waists. If my assistant coaches could organize these into two piles, please?"

Sammy took them up readily and began sorting by handing all the red ties to Sarah and keeping the blue ones for herself.

"Ms. Sammy and Ms. Sarah here will be our captains."

"Aye-aye, sir!" Sammy saluted, wrapping one blue flag around her waist. Sarah did the same with a red one.

"Thank you," I said, shaking my head with a laugh. This girl was something else. "Now, have any of you ever played football before?" I directed toward the huddle. Two boys raised their hands. One of them was Eli, and the other was much smaller than him, maybe nine years old. His name was Orin. Very cool names. "Perfect, only two of you. That means you'll be our co-captains. Orin, you're with Ms. Sammy; Eli, you're with Ms. Sarah. The rest of you form a line, shoulder to shoulder, and we'll get the teams selected."

"I shall pick the teams," Sammy declared, approaching the lineup. She tapped the head of the first kid, skipped the one after, and then tapped the head of the third kid, continuing down the line to the end. When she had half of the kids, she handed them all blue flags.

"And the rest will come join me on the red team. Come get your flags, everyone," Sarah called, holding them up.

A short time later, we had everybody spread out on the field. Sarah dropped small plastic orange markers at everyone's feet where they should stand. I initially thought I would teach them all their positions, but that quickly became a mess. Keep it simple, I would.

I stood out of bounds right in the middle, where I could keep a close eye on the field. Tyler stood in the exact spot on the opposite side, acting as my co-referee, next to Ms. Diane. When I tried to explain what a referee does, Eli was quick to give us all an extensive rhetoric on how his dad explained it, which led me to the conclusion that his team always lost. Eli was a pretty funny kid.

The game forged on, and everyone gave their best, even Sammy and Sarah.

Sammy's team was ahead by two flags, and Sarah and Eli gave the last play their best effort, directing one of their red members to make a bid for Orin, who currently possessed the ball.

As a little girl pumped her arms with all her might, she reached Orin at the same time Sammy did. And when Orin tripped, dodging the little girl's reach, she and Sammy tumbled down with him.

I waved my arms like a flag and called for a time-out. Tyler, Ms. Diane and I hurried over to check on everyone. It wasn't the first fall of the day by any means, and the kids got up right away, dusting themselves off.

"Everyone okay?" Ms. Diane asked, looking carefully over her brood.

"We're fine," the kids chimed, nearly in unison.

Sammy sat up. "I'm good, too. I don't know what's harder, the ground or Orin's skull." She laughed, rubbing her head.

Tyler further asked after both of the kids, but not a minute later, Ms. Diane's timer rang out. "That's actually all we have time for today, but maybe we can convince Mr. Jared to come out and teach us some more another time. What do you guys think?"

All the kids jumped up and down, yelling, "Yeah!"

"Please, Mr. Jared?"

"I want to finish crushing these losers!"

I wonder who said that, I thought with a chuckle. "Just let me know when," I quickly conceded. There was no other choice. How could I disappoint a dozen small humans who had so graciously not gotten *any* snot on me? I still saw plenty. I was innately aware of its presence, but at least I wasn't wearing any.

Because of that afternoon, I could safely conclude that yes, children *are* snotty but also kind of cool. I wasn't sure if I would share that information with Sammy yet or not. I could already picture the gloating. Although, she *was* pretty cute when she gloated...

Decision made. I would tell her in the car on the way home and appreciate the way her eyes slit with impish appeal and the corners of her mouth upturned in satisfaction. And when she full-on smiled and said, "I told you so," I would be happily undone.

JARED

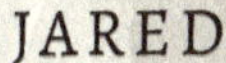

37

After Sammy brought me home from church, I came to another, more important decision: I wanted us to be together, and it was time I told her.

I was smiling like a cheesy mess at my phone when my mom walked into my doorway. "Hey."

"Hey," I said, putting down my phone and putting my hands behind my head.

"I hope you don't have plans this evening. I'm planning a nice dinner for us all."

"No plans. I'll be there."

"I was thinking I would make having a nice dinner together a regular thing, at least once a week. That way, if we're all getting busy, at least we have that to look forward to for reconnecting. You know?"

"That sounds good to me."

"Great. So, how was church?" She leaned her shoulder against the doorframe and crossed her legs.

"Not terrible."

"Well, that's good."

"Yeah. Sammy, Sarah, and I taught the kids to play football afterward."

"How very nice is that. Good for you. Is that what you were smiling at your phone about?"

"Ha, no." I swallowed. If I couldn't say it to my mom, I had no business saying it to Sammy. "I decided I'm going to ask Sammy out."

"You guys have been going out a lot already."

"Officially, I mean. I'm asking her to be my girlfriend."

"Oh," she said, coming to an understanding. "Sounds like a big deal. Are you sure about that?"

"Definitely." More than I'd ever been about anything else in my life.

"Okay then. I want to meet her."

"You kinda did. Remember the three girls in the living room? And she comes over to exercise with me sometimes."

"That doesn't count. I want you to introduce me to her properly."

"Yeah, yeah. I will."

"And, uh, make sure you're *careful*, you know."

"Mother, please. That's not an issue. I'm not even—just don't worry about it."

"Well, sorry. I know your dad would be better suited for this stuff, but I'm doing the best I can. Just be smart, that's all. And, of course, being smart means you know what lines you can't cross until marriage. Right?"

"Right." *Please just go away already.*

"Good. But regardless, remember, I'm always here, okay? You can talk to me about literally anything. Always. Anytime. Even if it's awkward."

I had to give her points for effort. "Thanks, Mom."

Satisfied, she made to leave before stopping herself. "Oh, and good luck with Sammy. I like how bright you've been lately."

"Me too."

"The girl gets my vote. Let me know how it goes."

"I sure will."

And with that, she actually left, leaving me stunned but impressed. The only thing that began to bring me down was not having Dan to tell my news to next.

It sucked not being able to tell him about any of this, and the longer that time went on, the more I felt guilty about it. He was the one who drove drunk and got arrested, not me. I had every right to be angry. Yet he was my best friend, and despite what he'd done to me, I'd abandoned him.

His parents had offered us his contact information at STLR. Maybe it was time I did something about it.

For now though, my focus was on Sammy. I may not have any news to tell him. As sure as I was about asking her to be mine, there was always a chance she would say no. Waiting until tomorrow evening to find out was going to kill me.

God, I hope she says yes.

38

THE STARS WERE OUT, SHIMMERING IN GLORIOUS SPLENDOR. JARED sat beside me, rocking the disjointed bridge of the big toy as I dangled my legs over the edge. He was acting weird.

I thought it strange enough that he wanted us to come to a park so late, but his behavior since picking me up at the end of my late shift was also questionable. He wasn't his usual confident self, and while he was normally a preppy dresser, tonight he looked especially snappy. His cologne had nearly choked me out of the car; I had to crack a window. Something was off.

I turned to him. "So, what made you wanna come to Cole Park?"

"I just like it here. The ocean winds and everything. Came a lot as a kid. Didn't you?"

"Not really. A couple times, but it was fun. I guess all parks are."

"Yeah. I just like it here."

I stifled a laugh. "You already said that."

"Oh, right. Sorry."

Eyeing him, I was increasingly suspicious. "Jared, is everything okay? And why did you take a bath in cologne?" He always wore some but applied it much less liberally. It usually aided his already impressive masculine allure. A scent that was all him, pleasing and musky, and not in the least bit offensive to the nose.

Suddenly, the bridge rocked under me as Jared turned. "Look at me."

"Huh?"

"Look at me—please?" he tried.

"Um, okay." Doing so, I brought my legs up and shifted, taking his offered hand. It was clammy and trembling.

Why'd I feel like he was about to break up with me, even though we weren't dating? He'd probably gotten so dressed up to soften the blow of bad news. What was it now? He was confessing his love for Sarah, after all? He was moving to another country? He'd found a new girl he was jazzed about and had to properly friend-zone me?

It would serve me right for getting my hopes up about a guy like Jared when I was who I was. I had too much drama going on to be deserving of another relationship I probably couldn't handle. And so what if—

"Sammy, I really like you."

Wait. "What?"

"A lot."

My head was spinning out of control. Of all the things my mind came up with to explain all this, his declaration was not among them.

"What do you think about that?" came his apprehensive question. "I've gone back and forth on what I think you'll say, but for me, I hope you feel the same."

My mouth went dry. "You... you've thought about what I'd

say?" I repeated dumbly as a sort of statement-question as shock consumed me.

"Of course I want to know how you feel. Do you really have to ask?"

"Don't you just know better by now?" Even his lack of awareness was shocking.

"Better about what?"

"About... how I feel."

"I don't, so just tell me."

I didn't. Instead, I scooted closer, the joints of the bridge squeaking under our shifting weight. Sitting up on my knees to be at eye level with him, I leaned in, but he leaned back, my heart quaking with sudden nervousness. Despite what happened before, his tentative expression did not deter me, and I pushed forward, making contact.

39

When her lips met mine, something incredible ignited, blowing away my hesitation, and I wound my arms tightly around her. Our lips melded together, sending a fire through me that singed every fiber of my being until it reached my soul in a way I could have only imagined. It wasn't our first kiss, wasn't even our second, but this third time was truly the charm.

Sammy's arms reached around my neck as she pressed herself in, and my hands slid down to grasp her waist. I was there for it; I was present. It was everything I had come to understand I wanted, and yet, a cold shard of doubt found its way into my mind.

Pulling back, I gently dislodged her arms. "Sammy, wait."

"What?" she asked, breathless and bewildered.

"As much as I've been wanting to do this, I have to know—do you know why *you're* doing it?" Before this went any further, I had to know what it meant to her. I couldn't stand to get excited about this if we didn't want the same thing.

"What?" she repeated, her tone taking on an edge.

"I've been trying to figure out my feelings for a while now, but once I finally did, everything made so much sense. I know what I want and that's why I'm here tonight going after it, but I want to be clear about what it all means to you."

She blinked as though different emotions were fighting for dominance within her. "Does it have to mean something?"

"Yes. It already does for me. I really care about you, Sammy. As a friend, a truly great one, but as way more than that, too."

"And you already know I care about you. It's pretty obvious, so why are you ruining this right now?"

"I'm sorry. I don't want to ruin anything, especially because I already botched one of our kisses, but how exactly do you feel about me? You said I should know, but I told you I don't. I can guess all day long, but I need you to just tell me."

"Oh my gosh, Jared. This isn't rocket science."

"And it's not that difficult to be honest. Do you care for me as more than a friend or not?"

"That's not—"

"Just tell me. Do you want me like I want you, or are you only kissing me as a distraction from everything going on in your life?"

She huffed, and I knew the frayed edges of our conversation were quickly unraveling. Shaking her head, she moved away and stood up. I wobbled back and forth when she stomped across the bridge. Calling after her, I followed suit. "Where are you going? Don't leave like this."

"Not everything is some big, cryptic thing, Jared. Sometimes people just kiss, and sometimes they just walk away," she said as if she were trying to prove me right.

"But *you* don't. You are the most emotionally calculated person I've ever met. I don't even understand how you function, but I recognize when you're doing it."

"Nice, good for you."

Ugh. Stubborn woman.

"Why are you mad?"

I was practically chasing after her at that point. Grounding to a halt, I refused to take another step her way. If she wanted to run off, I'd let her, and I guess that would be the answer to my question, but not before I said my piece. I had come here determined to be honest and upfront about my feelings tonight because Lord knew it was my turn to go out on a limb. But neither of us deserved to dangle alone.

"Samantha Ballard, you're being a major wuss. Grow up and come back here so we can settle this."

As anticipated, she froze in place, throwing me a menacing look over her shoulder. "Excuse me?" she demanded, just as I had hoped, and I had to battle the urge to smile. We would settle this. Tonight.

"Oh, you didn't hear me? Sorry, I'll say it louder so the stars can hear, too. SAMANTHA BALLARD IS BEING A WUSS," I shouted through my cupped hands.

She spun around and stomped toward me. "You have a lot of nerve!"

"I sure do. So much so that I'm not letting you out of this." Her slitted eyes followed me as I put myself toe-to-toe with her. "No more games, Sammy. No more hiding behind your brick wall. I see you, and I like you just how you are. I can see how the small pieces of your past could have grown into a hard exterior, and I can appreciate that because you've always thought you needed to be tough. Like you were always training for some kind of fight. But none of that is necessary with me."

Something twisted in her eyes—a nerve that I'd irreparably struck, I hoped. I smoothed one hand down her hair, leaving it to rest on her cheek. "I adore everything about you, Sammy, including all of that. But it's only fair I know how you feel about me in words. It's time you just admit your feelings, one way or the other."

Softening, her eyes closed and she leaned into my palm. "What if you don't like what I say?"

"Don't worry about that. I can take whatever it is, as long as it's the truth."

"I don't really know how to process these feelings, but yes, I admit, I have them. I'm not even sure when it happened, but when I look back on everything, I think it was starting even before school got out. Back when you were hoping to be with my best friend, and I knew I didn't stand a chance amid all that."

"I didn't know you felt that way. You gotta believe me, I haven't had any feelings for Sarah outside of friendship in a very long time."

"It's okay. I don't hold it against you that you once liked her; she's awesome! But I was always worried I would be a second choice."

"You're not."

"I think I know that. Now. It's just hard for me to let things go. And it isn't just the Sarah thing… It's me. I don't feel like I'm up to snuff. Not even my own birth mother put me first. Everyone, including you, is about to leave for college, and I'll just be here, besides Mexico, temporarily. I act like everything is okay, because I can't let people in and feel like they are only there for me out of pity. That would be even worse than having nobody at all."

"Yeah, but I see you trying. Just like I know, once you decide you're ready to tell your friends about your birth mom, you will have no trouble with it. As soon as your mind is set on something, nothing can stop The Bull." I tucked her fallen hair back behind her ear. "Maybe you don't see how brave you are, but I do."

"I feel like a big baby. Like a wuss, as some would say." She was getting her teasing voice back, and I was alight with hope.

"Two very different situations, but you've already proven you are neither. Now, about my question?"

"What was it you wanted to know again? My choice for president?"

My chest inflated with joy and victory. Our easy banter had told me I'd won, so I skipped the theatrics. "Be my girlfriend, Sammy."

Her eyes widened like she still couldn't believe me. "Your girlfriend…"

"Yes, girlfriend. You know, when a boy likes a girl, and he asks—"

"Would you just shut up so I can say yes?"

With a smile strong enough to break my face, I did just as she requested, and in return, she kissed me again. This time, there were no reservations. Since my accident, she'd been making me laugh, keeping my outlook from feeling as bleak as it could've. Now, she made my heart race. Samantha Ballard was mine, and I was hers. *This* kiss—our real first one, if you asked me—now sealed the deal. It was the truest answer to every question I wanted to know, and each one I hadn't thought to ask yet.

Slowly, I broke away, reaching into my pocket. "It's a good thing you said yes. I would've felt awkward giving you this if you'd said no," I said, presenting her with my closed hand.

With the most beautiful curiosity, Sammy held her hand out to receive it. Then, when the item revealed itself in her palm, she gasped. "The necklace from San Antonio?" With her other hand,

Sammy traced the silver chain all the way down to the crux of the necklace, the pearl. "How? When?"

"You were perfectly occupied looking at everything. I had plenty of time to hang back and buy it."

"You've had it all this time?"

"Yep. It clearly meant so much to you. I couldn't let you miss out on it."

"But all I did was look at it."

"And all I did was look at you. I could see it was supposed to be yours." I reached for it so that I could help her put it on. "May I?"

She nodded, letting me take it, and then turned. When she lifted her hair, I reached the chain around, clasped it, and traced the back of my index finger along her sensitive skin. Sighing with satisfaction, she tilted her head to the side, and I leaned down, placing two slow kisses on the base of her neck.

When she turned around, she touched the pearl with her finger. "How does it look?"

"Meant to be."

The way her eyes sparkled made my knees weak. Maybe she was right when she said there was more to life than football. If she stayed around to keep reminding me, I would be just fine if I never played again. I had something better now.

SAMMY

40

Jared had driven me home before, but not after a kiss like *that*. He'd walked me to the door before, but only as a friend. We had even had our hands linked plenty of times, but never as a couple.

What world am I living in? Jared Tomlin is my boyfriend! Mine to hold hands with and cuddle with and kiss whenever I wanted! I screamed internally, everything else in my life temporarily forgotten in light of my happiness. I could only pray it would last.

When I got settled in my room upstairs, I sent him a text.

SAMMY

Are we really doing this?

JARED

The Sammy I know doesn't ask stupid questions.

I'm just kidding! Yes, we are doing this. It is official. Mark your calendar. One month from today I'm going to bring you flowers. What kind is your favorite?

Never mind. I'll just pick, so it's a surprise.

My face hurt. I didn't think my smile would ever stop. I hoped it never would.

His good humor had me in stitches. *Dear Lord, I think I love this guy. That trouble I had feared has undeniably found me.*

I woke up the next day still feeling a million things at once, some of which were anxiety and insane happiness. More than anything, the intensity of the previous night and the accumulative craziness of my life lately reminded me how much I needed my friends, and an idea came to me. We hadn't had a sleepover in my treehouse since junior year. That used to be a once-a-month tradition to catch up on anything we might've overlooked during the day-to-day.

There were some things that a treehouse and your closest

friends just did best. It was amazing we got through our final year of high school without one.

I stirred up our group text with my decision.

SAMMY

Spur of the moment, I know, but I will be sleeping over in the treehouse tonight. I can't be the only one in desperate need of a tree-top confessional. Who will join me?

JENNA

Not me. Bizzy.

BIRDIE

I will. I need a good girls' night in.

SARAH

I'll be there, too! I was just thinking about the treehouse. We all need this...

Jenna...

JENNA

Fine. I'll come.

SAMMY

Awesome! See y'all tonight!

Nerves fired because there was no going back. I wondered what updates my friends would have about their lives and what they would think about all of mine. A lot could happen in a year that people might not want to share. Shoot, a lot could happen in a *week*...

What were they going to say about my relationship with Jared, I wondered the most. At that moment, it was nice not to fret about the rest.

WE WERE ALL PROPERLY squished in beside one another, our sleeping bags and backpacks taking up the entire floor of the 10X10-foot space. I nestled into my blankets, leaned up on one elbow as I reclined, and took comfort in the closeness of my friends. "I know we've all pretty much outgrown this kinda stuff. Thanks for coming."

"Um, I haven't. This is great!" cheered Birdie.

Sarah nodded her agreement as she finished chewing a handful of miniature pretzels. "I haven't, either. You can go ahead and mark me down for the next one right now."

I wasn't feeling brave, but I was plenty desperate. I wouldn't make it much longer before I spilled my secrets. Maybe Jared was right. Maybe they *could* help me if I let them.

Breathe in. Breathe out. "Well, I wasn't just feeling nostalgic, though that is a large part of why I wanted this."

"You have tea to spill."

I nodded at Birdie. "So. Much. Tea."

"Does this mean it's Confession Circle time?" Jenna read my mind from her side of the blanket and pillow heap, though she seemed less enthusiastic than the rest of us.

During past sleepovers, we gathered up in a cozy circle in the treehouse, away from everyone and everything, and shared something with each other. It could be a secret, a memory, or a funny story from class. If there was anything we'd been keeping from each other for any reason, however big or small, those things came out. It was our safe, pressure-free space.

"Maybe?" *Be brave now, Samantha. It's time to do this.* "Not maybe. Yes."

Birdie Jo raised her delicate hand. "If it's okay, I'll get us started because this has been killing me to keep it from y'all." She cleared her throat. "I finally got my license."

For a second, we all waited for the punchline until we realized she was serious.

"Birdie Jo MacLean, why is that a secret?" Sarah's face was marred with confusion as she called Birdie out.

Eyes averted, she twirled the sunshine-colored, curly tips of her hair between her fingers. "You guys know I hate to drive. I've been avoiding it as long as I can."

"So why now?" Jenna asked.

"After everything with Dan, I did a little research into STLR. It's a really admirable program, you guys..." We all flicked a not-so-covert glance at Jenna. "After reading up on it, I got a wild hair and applied to be a volunteer at the women and children's campus here in town. When I got the call that I'd been approved, my parents said I could only do it if I got myself there and back. My dad will loan me his car, but I have to drive it myself. So, I finally learned."

"Congratulations are in order then!" I said, throwing myself over the heap to pull her in for a hug. When I drew back, she was beaming. Sweet thing, she had been too nervous to be proud of herself. "We are so excited for you—for the license and for the volunteer work you'll be doing. It all sounds very rewarding."

The others took their turns congratulating her properly, and our darling Birdie Jo was nearly in tears. "Thank you, guys! I'm sorry I—Oops. Scratch that last part." Confessions made to the Circle were never judged, and no apologies were ever to be issued for secrets previously kept.

Jenna had her turn with Birdie last and looked to have some tears of her own, which were quickly wiped away and disregarded. "Good for you, Birdie. Also, we need to see that photo. Bring it out, girl."

"You don't have to ask me twice!" Hastily scooting over, Birdie dove into her backpack and fished out her wallet. When she had the object of her desire, she held it up for us to view, grinning from ear to ear. "I went to the salon and had my hair done that day and everything. I was determined to get me a good shot. What do y'all think?"

Looking at it, no one could deny it was perfection, just like Birdie was eight out of seven days. "Amazing," we all agreed.

"Thanks so much," she twanged gleefully, tucking the ID and wallet back into her backpack before shoving it away and returning to her spot. She sighed and crossed her arms, comfortably leaning against her pillows. "I'm so glad for a good chance to finally share that. Why did we ever stop doing this?"

"People gotta grow up sometime," Jenna said, her tone morose and dry. She was taking her separation from Dan worse than Sarah was taking hers from Kevin. Even she had begun to perk up recently. I wondered how long it would take Jenna to ease into her new norm without Dan. As far as we all knew, it was only temporary.

"Sure, but that doesn't mean we can't still do things like this." Birdie looked around. "Does it?"

"I don't see why not," I offered. "The treehouse is always open as far as I'm concerned."

"Good." Birdie was satisfied.

"Who's going next?" Jenna asked.

"I'll go." Sarah hoisted herself up so she was sitting and exhaled deeply. "Well, it's probably nothing you guys don't already know, but Kevin and I are no longer together."

I did know, but I wouldn't be confessing that today. Until it became important to share, that was just between me and Kevin.

Jenna nearly choked on a chug of water. Her hand beat against her chest. "You're kidding! Why? What happened?"

"When he called me after his arrest, he was very clear that he needed—"

"You mean *he* dumped *you*?"

"It wasn't quite a dumping, but he wanted me to take space from him while he's in there. It makes sense, and I think he was right, but I wasn't ready to hear that and fought him on it. He wanted me to focus on myself. I ended up sending him a letter saying I accepted his request, and I told him he better be doing the same."

"Wow... how long ago was that?"

"It was before graduation."

Pulling her by the shoulder and letting her head fall to mine, I gave her a squeeze. "I'm so sorry, Sarah."

"It's okay. I mean, it's not, it sucks how much I miss him, but I'm a lot better off than I was right after it all happened. I'm sure you've all noticed what a Debbie Downer I've been lately."

"What are you gonna do when he gets out?" Jenna asked. I would wager anything that she was thinking of Dan as she inquired about that.

"Slobber all over his beautiful face with kisses!" We all laughed. "Besides that though, I'm not sure yet. I'll be in school by then, but there's no way I'd miss his release. I might talk to his mom about working something out."

"Good. That's good. You have a plan. I'm glad." Jenna's voice was faded, a telltale sign of her downtrodden feelings. How fair was it for me to feel so happy with Jared behind their heartbroken backs? Jenna's boyfriend caused the accident that injured mine, and then he was sent away. Jenna must feel so alone. My heart ached for her.

I could feel she needed to get something off her chest. If ever there was a time, it was then. "Your turn, Jenna. How 'bout it?"

She looked sideways. "I don't have anything to share. But *you* said you did." She gestured at me.

So right she was. At the thought of saying those things out loud, my heart trembled a million beats per minute, banging around like it wanted to tip me over like an unbalanced load of laundry.

SAMMY

41

I STOOD UP STRAIGHTER, UNWILLING TO BACK DOWN. *I AM THE Bull. I've got this.* "Okay, well, get ready, y'all. There's a two-for-one confession from me tonight. Do you want the good news or the bad news first?"

"The bad," said Sarah. "So you can end on a positive note."

"Good idea. Okay then, I'm just going to spit it out. The night of my birthday, my parents told me who my birth mother is." Eyes wide, they all watched me with severe anticipation. "It's my aunt Claudia."

"Woah," impressed Jenna.

"You know, I always forget you're adopted. Did I ever tell you one of my cousins is, too? We love him to pieces. It never occurs to anyone that he isn't just one of us because he is. I'm sure it's that way for you and your family." Birdie's words were an unexpected comfort.

I turned. "I didn't know that. Which cousin?"

"Little Tay."

"Aw, Taylor? He's like, my favorite of your cousins."

She laughed. "He's everyone's favorite. So, what's that tell ya?

Family is family, girl. Ron and Tabby are always going to be your parents. You have no reason to doubt their love for you. If anything, their love for you is greater than our parents because they *chose* you."

"I agree that's the truth. You were their choice. That's so beautiful, Sammy," affirmed Sarah.

They chose me. That was a phrase I was particularly familiar with. I'd always considered it a stab at how my birth parents *didn't* choose me, but hearing my friends point it out with such reverence, I couldn't deny they were right. The upside to not being chosen by my birth parents was that I *was* chosen by the couple who raised me. That was something worth acknowledgement.

"I appreciate you guys saying that. They said something similar, too."

"I don't think my parents would've picked me if they'd known how expensive I would end up," Birdie giggled. Funny though she was, I could only imagine the price tag that came with keeping a proper beauty queen like Birdie put together.

"I just couldn't really take it in, I guess. Claudia isn't an easy pill to swallow."

Jenna nodded. "That does sound interesting. She's kinda like the OG party animal, isn't she?"

"Pretty much. I grew up not having any respect for her at all. I've never thought I was anything like her. I certainly don't want to be, but then I'm told I'm her daughter? I didn't deal well." I chuckled at my mild rendition of the truth.

Sarah used her careful voice. "That's understandable, but that kind of biology doesn't define you. You have brown hair and brown eyes, and those things could've come from her. You do share Claudia's DNA, sure, but you are not some carbon copy. You're still your own person. You don't inherit her behavior just because she gave birth to you. You know that, right?"

"I mean, I *do*, but it doesn't stop the intrusive thoughts."

"They'll stop on their own eventually. You have to adjust to life changes over time. You can't just wake up one day and accept them blindly. People don't work that way," Sarah said.

"Eventually," I echoed.

Silently, Jenna reached for my hand. She gave me a tender smile, her caring nature coming from beneath the surface. In some aspects, she had a tougher exterior than me. "Alright, so, if that's the bad news, let's hear the good news," she encouraged with a pat.

"Oh, right. There's good news." I laughed, rolled my shoulders, and cleared my throat. One Band-Aid off, one more to go. "Jared and I are dating."

Jenna's jaw dropped the furthest. "That's *good* news?"

"It's about time!" shrieked Birdie with a big smile on her face.

I hardly had the opportunity to enjoy Birdie's favorable response because I was fixated on Jenna's surly attitude, which felt disappointingly like judgment. So much for the safe zone of the treehouse. "What's that supposed to mean?"

"I knew it. I've been picking up on those vibes." Birdie was thrilled with herself for having seen it coming.

"Not you, Birdie," Sarah whispered, interceding on my behalf.

"What the heck, Jenna?" I couldn't let it rest. She wasn't getting away with a hit-and-run like that. She would explain herself.

"I don't know if y'all have noticed, but ever since Jared joined our group, there's been drama after drama. Everyone seems to have forgotten what he did to Sarah, but I haven't. And how can you not understand it's because of Jared that Daniel got sent away?"

Empathy was probably a better choice, but my anger wouldn't let me attempt it. "Jenna, are you kidding me? Do you even hear yourself when you speak?"

"It's *true*. The only reason Daniel got put in the program was because his passenger was injured. Had it only been himself in the car, the judge wouldn't have ordered it. He's a first-time offender. He should be home with me right now, not stuck in some rehab program he doesn't even need until next freaking year! He's going to miss everything!" She was borderline hysterical now.

My voice was on the rise, matching the boiling of my blood. "First-time offender? Jenna, your boyfriend has a real substance abuse problem. There's no way you don't know that. But you're right about one thing. The outcome would've been different if he'd gotten what he deserved, which was a DUI and suspended license. Tell me exactly how any of that is Jared's fault? You can't. Dan drove drunk and crashed his truck, and Jared was the passenger who got hurt. That's as black and white as it gets."

My tone was menacing, and I didn't care to try and help it. Jenna was delusional, wallowing in aggressive sorrow she had no right to feel. *She* wasn't physically hurt. *She* wasn't the one sent away for that entire year she complained about, away from her friends and family, to a facility to dry out because she had a serious problem. Those things happened to *them*, not to her.

Her eyes hardened into slits. "You're only being pissy because Jared is suddenly your boyfriend now, and you think you know something about loyalty. I've been with Dan for almost two years. We've been through a lot more than you and Jared probably ever will."

"You're being willfully ignorant, Jenna. We're not comparing anything here. I simply said crimes equal punishments, and that's what Dan got. There's no excuse for driving drunk. Zero. None. It wouldn't matter who was in the car with him, or even if nobody was. Do you not understand how easily he could have killed somebody? Would you still be up in arms on his behalf then?"

Her nostrils flared, eyes blazing with her fury. "Fine, *Miss-Know-It-All*. You accused me of having my own confession earlier. Are you happy to know you were right? Would you like to hear it?" Before anyone could begin to form a response, she blurted out, "*I'm* the one responsible for the accident in the first place."

Our shock was undermined by our silence. What the heck was she getting at now? Only Jenna Rodriguez could find a way to spin something into being all about her. "That's not even cute," I said, trying not to let the depth of my annoyance bring me down to her level. I was getting dangerously close.

"I'm not trying to be. It's the truth. Daniel was drinking heavier than ever that night because of me. We'd been fighting a lot lately, and on your birthday, he spent most of the time pestering me, asking what was wrong, and I didn't want to tell him. I *shouldn't* have told him." She sniffed.

I think we all realized she was crying at the same time. For as emotional as Jenna was, it wasn't often we saw her tears. We were all stunned.

Sarah's voice pierced the confused silence. "What are you saying?"

She sobbed, her words coming out in a broken frenzy. "I-I just... When I finally told him why, I guess he couldn't handle it. I just wish I could talk to him now. I miss him so much, and he probably hates me like everyone else should." Jenna put her face down and hugged her knees, her body wracked with emotion.

Birdie was the only one who knew what to do and extended a motherly hug to Jenna. When it surprised me, I questioned myself. Shouldn't that have been my first response, too?

God, am I a terrible person for not jumping to do the same?

Birdie cooed, rubbing Jenna's back. One deep breath turned into many, and eventually, her breathing returned to normal. "What's going on, Jenna?" Sarah ventured. "Why were you guys fighting?"

"Because I'm pregnant."

There it was. The reason behind the reason that put Jared's future in precarious balance. Jenna and her never-ending drama really did play a part in causing the accident. In one fell swoop, she helped change the lives of several people in one night.

And now, there was going to be a *baby?* I could scarcely wrap my brain around that one. The poor thing. Its home was broken right from conception. In a way, I could relate to that. Never in a million years would I have considered my home or family broken, but that's because I only knew the half of it.

The moment I realized I couldn't turn off my negative feelings, I wished I'd never had this stupid sleepover idea. All three of these girls were my best friends, but one of them had just broken my heart—for Jared, rather than myself, but forgiveness didn't come easy for me.

Confession Circle or not, safe zone or not, I was struggling. I closed my eyes to the scene unfolding in front of me and just took a moment.

God, please soften my heart toward my friend and let me forgive her for her mistakes. I know I'm judging harshly right now because of my feelings for Jared, and even though I know that's wrong, I can't make it stop. I'm so mad...

The night wound down quickly after that, and I, for one, was grateful for it. Based on the familiar sound of their sleep-breathing, Jenna and Birdie were out cold. Sarah was staring wide-eyed through the slats in the ceiling, the same as me.

I scooched closer slowly, careful not to wake the others, until my head rested on her welcoming shoulder.

Her soft whisper came next. "I didn't get the chance to say it earlier, but I'm really happy for you and Jared. I want you to know that."

"Really? I can't help but feel like maybe I should've talked to you about it first. I haven't been very upfront about Jared, mostly because, for a while, I didn't know how I felt about him. Or maybe I didn't *want* to know. That's entirely possible."

Her shoulder moved softly with her laugh. "Yes, it is. Now that I think back on it, it's obvious you've always had a soft spot for him. Which I think is fantastic. He's a great guy; you're a great girl. You both deserve so much happiness. *All* of the happiness."

"You and Kevin do, too."

"And I believe we'll get it. Even if it takes a while."

"I believe you're right. Still, I'm sorry. With the stuff that happened with you and Jared, I worried he might still be into you like I would never—"

"Please, don't. You owe me nothing like that, and neither does he. I'm so beyond happy for you both." Sarah slithered her arm around me with a squeeze. "Your happiness is my happiness."

"Wish I could say the same for Jenna."

"She's hurting really bad. And she's pregnant? I can't imagine. We're probably only seeing the surface of what all she's feeling.

We're all worried about our post-summer plans, but she has to worry about a whole lot more."

"I hate it when you're right."

"Oh, gosh. Then you must be eternally unhappy."

With one final muffled giggle, we said goodnight and adjusted back to our own spaces. But before I followed Sarah and the others to sleep, I grabbed my phone.

SAMMY

I told the girls about us.

I still couldn't believe there was an *'us.'* What a turn of events.

JARED

How did that go?

SAMMY

Mostly fine. Jenna actually got pretty upset, but she's not happy about much of anything lately. I thought *I* had problems... I wouldn't want to trade for hers.

JARED

I'm sorry to hear that. She's probably real torn up about Dan still.

SAMMY

Yeah... I doubt that'll ease up anytime soon.

JARED

Must be really hard.

SAMMY

You're very sympathetic toward her, considering... Does it not bother you that her boyfriend was the cause of it?

JARED

Dan isn't Jenna's boyfriend to me. He's my best friend. We've been best friends for years, longer than he's known her. But I mean… Yeah, I'm still upset with him. I'm upset about a lot of it.
Doesn't mean I don't realize she's hurting, too, in her own ways.

SAMMY

I'm so sorry about what happened to you, Jared. I really am.

JARED

I know. I'm learning to be okay with it. It helps to have you.

SAMMY

I can't imagine why I make up for any of it, but I'm glad.

JARED

Me too :)

SAMMY

Talk tomorrow?

JARED

You know it.

JARED

42

"So, how was your night in the treehouse with the girls?" I asked as we walked along the seawall. The tide was low, exposing much of the jutting walkway as white, foamy waves crashed against its base. Every once in a while, a wave would ricochet up high enough to spray us.

"Nothing like it used to be. Probably the most intense and confrontational we've ever gotten, but it was pretty great, too." Sammy sighed, pausing to look at the horizon. "Did Dan ever tell you why the two of them were fighting?"

A vision of headlights brought me back to Sammy's birthday. I reached for my knee without thinking. "He was in the process of telling me when he lost control." I swallowed the hard lump in my throat. "But he didn't get the chance to share."

"It's funny that the last one to join the group is the first to hear everyone's secrets. More or less," she added.

"It's my pretty face, isn't it?" I took the opportunity to forget the gloom and remind her of her compliment, palming my cheek. "It makes people want to trust me."

"It does." She laughed, giving me a shove, but her expression changed quickly. "Jared? I would like to share another secret with you if I could."

"Is it serious?"

"Very, but it's actually not my secret this time, which makes me feel guilty about sharing it. I just don't want to be responsible for this weight anymore, and I think you need to know."

"Whatever it is, I'm here." Sensing her distress, I dropped her hand in exchange for a tighter hold around her waist. It had become second nature to touch and comfort her any chance I could. "Are you okay?"

"Yes, I'm fine. It's not about me. It's not even about you, but it will have an impact. Maybe. I just…" She straightened her shoulders. "Jenna told us what happened the night of the accident. The thing they were fighting about that had Dan so upset."

I rubbed the back of my neck, telling myself no matter what she said, I could deal. "Yeah?"

Releasing a puff of air, Sammy blurted out, "As crazy as it sounds, Jenna is pregnant."

My jaw hung loose in shock. That explained so much. And yet, holy cow. "Wow," was the best I could manage.

She shook her head. "I still don't believe it. On one hand, I do because they were never modest about their relationship, but you never expect to see that happen."

"It's surprising. They're smart people, but seriously, how does that kind of thing happen on accident?"

"Right? Everyone knows where babies come from. Getting pregnant in high school just doesn't make sense. I keep having these conflicting thoughts about it. I'm mad at her for being stupid. She's not ready for this, and neither is he. But I'm also trying to be compassionate because I love her."

"I know what you mean. Dan messed up. I feel really let down by him, but I have no idea what he's feeling now. I keep telling myself I'll call him or write, but don't. I'm not sure what I'd say."

Now, I'm even less sure.

"I don't blame you."

"Did she say anything about how they felt about their, uh, situation? Or what their plan is?"

"Not really, but she was a serious mess."

"I had been watching their interactions that night, and it was obvious something was wrong. He really cares about her, and he's always putting up with a lot. I don't mean to say anything negative about her. I know she's one of your best friends, but she doesn't seem like the nicest girl he could've been with. Dan is a really awesome guy. Even if I'm mad at him now, I'm bound to forgive him eventually."

She wound her fingers through mine. "Jenna is an awesome girl, too. She's just incredibly emotional and not very good at dealing with it. And now, she's trying to deal with the absence of her boyfriend and their approaching child, all without him." She appeared thoughtful. "I wonder if her parents know or if she is getting any support at all."

I wondered, too. Sammy's apparent sympathy was a stark reminder of the negativity I was still clinging tightly to. Here, I had been feeling callous toward Dan, my *best* friend, and so consumed by feeling mad at him for what he did. I hadn't thought at all about what he intended to say before crashing. And Jenna… all those texts she sent me in the hospital made sense now. She had been in a delicately tough situation all along.

Sammy straightened with excitement. "We should do something for her. Yes! Like a baby shower! The girls and I can probably throw it at my house. It could be a surprise thing."

"That's a great idea."

"What do you think about having kids?" As quickly as she'd asked, she turned away.

We continued walking, and I placed my arm around her shoulder. Her cheek was warm with embarrassment when I kissed it. "I don't think about it at all right now, but as a thing in the future—way, way in the future—kids are a definite possibility."

She leaned her head against my shoulder. "Is it because I made you teach the peewees at church how to play football? Did that seal the deal for you?"

I laughed. "It might've helped. But I still don't want kids anytime soon."

"Me neither. But I do want a big family someday."

"You do?"

"Maybe not as big as Birdie, but I want at least three kids, like my parents."

"Three is a good number. So, as far as you and I go… You're happy how we are right?"

Sammy took her time responding. "If you're talking about what I think you're talking about, then yes, I'm very happy." She glanced briefly at me. "Are you?"

"Of course. I'd be happy with nothing but your hugs and kisses until the day I die."

43

Later in the week, I played a voicemail through the speaker: *"Good morning, Jared. This is Carly with Dr. Fitzgerald's office at Victoria Orthopedics. I was just calling to let you know we've had a cancellation, and the doctor would like to see you tomorrow afternoon if that works for you. Please give the office a call back before 3:00 p.m. this afternoon, and we'll get you scheduled. Thank you, and take care."*

The recording went dead, and I immediately called my mom at work.

"Hello, is everything okay?"

"Hey, Mom. Everything's fine. The ortho office just called and said they can move my appointment up to tomorrow. They want me to call them back right away with an answer."

"Oh, Jared, that really is some timing. I can't take off tomorrow, but I really don't want you going alone."

"It's fine. I'm sure Sammy will tag along with me."

She sighed heavily. "I really wanted to be there for this one." Her disappointed voice lanced my heart.

"I'm sorry, Mom. It's just that, if I can get cleared tomorrow,

I'll be able to start preseason with the rest of the team. I'm really hoping not to miss too much of this stuff." If I didn't reschedule and waited for my original appointment, I would just barely be getting in on time. I didn't like how it felt to be left up against such a make-or-break deadline.

Even if I went tomorrow, and even though my knee was feeling greater than ever, there was still a chance I wouldn't be cleared. Who knows what could happen? Something could be detected on a re-scan that we didn't anticipate. Maybe I hadn't done a good enough job with my PT or home exercises since I'd been so hard-headed about them at first.

Good thing Sammy was even more hard-headed than me, or I might not be as well off as I am.

"If they can see you sooner, I know that's what you'd rather. Go ahead."

"Thanks, Mom. It'll be all good."

"You'll call me as soon as you get out, won't you?"

"Sure thing, I will."

"Great then. Thank you." Pretty sure I heard her sniffle, but I chose to block that out. She'd softened up lately. What part of this made her so upset, exactly? The fact that she wouldn't be able to attend the appointment, or the fact that she assumed I'd be cleared to play and didn't want me to leave?

"No problem. I'll see you later."

"Love you."

"Bye, Mom."

Hanging up with her, I then dialed the doctor's office. When the appointment switch was confirmed, I then called Sammy.

"Why, hello," she answered with the silliest sultry voice I'd ever heard.

After a good laugh, I responded, "Hello, to you, too. What are you up to?"

"Just hanging out. You?"

"I just got some interesting news. Are you free tomorrow?"

"Tomorrow is my day off, so yes."

"Perfect. Are you up for taking another road trip with me?"

JARED

44

THANKS TO SAMMY'S PRESENCE MAKING THINGS BETTER, THE HOUR and a half drive to Victoria felt like ten minutes, and we arrived with a little bit of time to spare. After I checked in, a nurse came out to take me back for my follow-up MRI. Sammy had to wait behind.

When I returned, we were waiting maybe five minutes before a new nurse opened the door and called my name for the second time. Impulsively, Sammy stood with me. I could tell she was feeling my nerves, her anxiousness feeding off me, from my bouncing leg to my fidgeting hands.

The nurse looked between us. "She can come back with you if you want." Sammy smiled and followed.

The exam room was a fate worse than death. I'd much rather have waited out in the lobby instead of in that tiny room, forced to stare at diagrams of various bodily structures and listen to the ugly crinkle of the sanitary paper underneath me. Did everyone unlock unpleasant memories of that sound, or was it just me?

Insisting on a distraction, I turned to Sammy. "Ten bucks says I can chug a Slurpee faster than you."

"You're on, Tomlin. First gas station we see on the way out, let's get some and find out. Your treat."

"My treat? But you have a job. You're the one with the big wallet."

"Then you shouldn't be the one with the big mouth."

Teasing and laughing with Sammy was as natural as breathing. When the door opened, I realized I'd been successful in my quest to become blissfully ignorant of my surroundings.

"Hello, Jared. So sorry to interrupt."

My head whipped up to find a smiling Dr. Fitzgerald with a tablet and manilla folder in hand.

I straightened my back. "Hey, Doc. Nice to see you again."

"And you, Jared." He sat in a wheely chair across from me, placing down the contents from his arm in favor of typing on the computer. "I've reviewed all your records from the hospital, and gotten excellent reports from your physical therapist back in Corpus. I'm so glad to hear you've been following your treatment plan so diligently."

I glanced at Sammy, then gave a curt nod. "Thank you. It was rough to start, but we've gotten a good handle on it, and I'm feeling great. It's all for the game, sir."

With an understanding smile, Dr. Fitzgerald stood from his chair, and I watched it roll away rather than focus on him walking to the light box on the wall. Now it was obvious to me what was inside the envelope.

Sure enough, he withdrew a black and white translucent image from the folder and stuck it on, striking the light switch with ease. "Alright, Jared. Here again is your MRI from right after the injury." He paused, turning to be sure I was paying attention. When I nodded, he kept going, facing the film again. "As you know, your MCL was about a grade 2 tear but did not warrant surgery. Luckily, no surrounding ligaments were impacted. And you're very lucky that the blunt trauma of the accident didn't cause any fractures to the bones. Despite all that, your knee has gone through a whole heck of a lot."

I nodded, my tongue a knotted, useless thing in my mouth. Sammy silently reached for my hand.

"Now this," he said, retrieving and sticking up a second film, "is your knee today. You see the difference?" As he circled the offending zone, I thought I could.

It looked... better. Dare I hope this was truly the news I wanted? "Is it healed?"

"It not only healed, it healed beautifully. Besides a slight loss in mass on that side, there's virtually no trace left of the injury. There's barely any visible scar tissue."

My heart pounded. "So, can I still play football?"

He smiled with an accompanying nod. "I don't want you jumping right into it just yet, but yes, you certainly can."

Thank You, God!

I jumped to my feet, letting my excitement burst forth. "Yes! Thank you, thank you, thank you!" I shouted. Dr. Fitzgerald said you're welcome, but I wasn't talking to him.

"I'm happy to deliver good news," he added.

Turning to Sammy, I leaned down and scooped her up. Oh, it felt so good to hoist her high and hold her. I was so glad she was here with me, hearing this good news, and able to celebrate.

She giggled and kissed my cheek. "Congratulations, jock-head! Now put me down before you tear something new."

"I'm feeling invincible."

"But you're not. Let me make that clear," said the doctor. "You have to refrain from football or overly strenuous conditioning for another eight weeks."

"But the preseason stuff begins next week."

"You can attend and participate as you're able, but nothing too strenuous and no actual football for another eight weeks." His voice stressed the importance of his directions. "Don't let yourself go backward out of impatience."

"So, by Labor Day, I can play again as normal?"

Dr. Fitzgerald referred to the calendar on the computer. Considering it, he eventually agreed. "Make it 'til then without doing anything to re-injure the ligament, and I'll be happy with that."

"You were very lucky when all you sustained was a good amount of bruising and a partial tear. You've been able to recover completely, but that doesn't mean you're walking out of here without on-going risk. Even though your scar tissue is minimal, it will never be the same as the original ligament. If it is excessively hit again, you could end up with another tear or worse. You must realize you are in a dangerous contact sport, and this is going to continue to be a risk."

"Yes, sir, I understand. I've always known that."

"Good. Then this is where we part ways and hope to never see each other again." Dr. Fitzgerald shook my hand compassionately, answered all my final questions, and wished me well.

I called my mom once we stepped outside, and she was overjoyed. I was grateful for her enthusiasm. But Sammy was surprisingly quiet.

45

THE END OF MY SHIFT HAD AT LAST ROLLED AROUND. I GOT OFF A bit early so I could get ready for an evening Sunday service with Sarah. Pastor Brian and I needed to discuss more legalities for Mexico. I was swapping my apron for my purse when Cindie popped into the break room.

"Hey, glad I caught you. I keep forgetting to ask: Are you and Jared free sometime after the 4th?"

"Besides work, I know I am. I'd have to ask about his schedule though. He's starting up with team stuff around then."

"Okay, well, Tyler and I thought we might double date and spend an evening at the bowling alley."

Her sweet offer stopped me in my tracks. "Really?"

"Totally, doesn't it sound like fun? It'll be the first time I've gone bowling since reaching adulthood. Not that twenty-one is all that adult." She chuckled. "But anyhow, if y'all are up for it and available, we'd love to hang out."

"It sounds great to me, but I'll let you know when I confirm with him."

"Okay, just text me, and we'll figure it out." Out in the cafe, the door chimed. "I better get back out there. See ya later, Sammy!"

BACK AT HOME, I readied myself for service. When I was finished showering and getting dressed, I had ten-ish minutes left before Sarah arrived to take me, and I was already running behind.

In the end, we weren't late; that was the important thing. But it was already quiet, everyone standing for praise and worship by the time we got there. I quietly filed into the aisle beside Sarah and smiled a silent greeting to her parents, who'd arrived early, as always. More prepared than I, Sarah handed me an extra notebook and pen for taking notes.

And take notes I did.

By the time Pastor Brian had us stand for the closing prayer, I'd filled an entire page. It wasn't anything to rival Sarah's, but it didn't matter. It was more than I expected to get out of a random evening service, that's for sure.

"We come humbly before You, Lord, seeking Your forgiveness. There are some here today who haven't done that in a while, and I beseech You on their behalf for the expunging of their records right here and now. Let no one walk out of here today still stained, Lord. Let Your powerful mercies and grace wash over them until they know they're clean. Let them seek Your absolve, expect it, and rejoice in it. Provide for everyone here, as only You can. We ask all this in the precious name of Jesus, amen."

"Amen," I raised, not even recognizing my voice. I didn't know I was crying until I opened my eyes and felt warm tears roll down my cheeks. Sarah reached over and squeezed my hand, her eyes red with the sting of her own turmoil. The sniffing and sighing coming from all around me signified the same was true for many there that night.

"Don't worry about it. I cry after most sermons." Sarah smiled.

"I never worry," I joked, raising my chin in mock defiance.

"Oh, no. Me neither," she agreed good-humoredly. Then she turned to bid farewell to her parents before returning her attention to me. "Want to take the long way home and talk about it?"

"About what?"

"Whatever it is you're not worried about."

"Sure." I sighed. "Yeah, okay. Let's do it. I just have to go get those forms first."

"Right. I'll meet you in the car?"

"Okay." I glanced up toward the altar, where Pastor Brian was laying hands on someone. "Hopefully, it doesn't take long."

She followed the direction of my thoughts. "It's okay. I've got a book with me if it does."

Parting ways with Sarah, I walked up the aisle and stood off to the side, listening to the soft background music as I waited.

When Pastor Brian had gotten through the few who remained, he approached me, smile on his face, hand extended. "Ms. Ballard, it's always a joy to see you."

"Thanks, it's nice to see you, too. Great sermon tonight."

"Well, thank you. What can I help you pray for?"

My palms got sweaty. "No, no, I'm not here for prayer. Remember I spoke with you before about coming by for more Mexico paperwork?"

"Of course. I have those prepared for you. They're actually in a folder right there, ready to go." He pointed at a seat at the end of the front row. "If you have any questions as you fill them out, just let me or Tyler know."

"That sounds great, thank you." I remained there, my eyes on the folder, which contained documents that secured me at least one step forward. A step I had told everyone I was taking but couldn't pinpoint why I was taking it. The weight of those final papers made me understand it even less.

"Samantha?"

"Huh?" My head whipped to face Pastor Brian again, realizing I'd spaced out.

His face was soft and understanding. "Would you let me pray over you before you go?"

What kind of jerk would I be to say no?

What kind of *bigger* jerk would I be to say no when I knew I really wanted to say yes?

Distrusting my voice, I simply bowed my head and stepped forward in surrender. His warm hand pressed against the crown of my head, and the moment he opened his mouth in prayer, I broke.

RED-FACED AND FULL-HEARTED, I finally situated myself and my folder into Sarah's car. Everything was silent, save for the melodic hum of the radio. She must've gotten a good look at me then.

"That really did take a while. You okay?"

"Definitely better than I was. I'm sorry for making you wait."

"Don't be." When we were on the road, Sarah turned the music down to a trickle. "You have the floor, my dear."

"I went up for my papers, and Pastor Brian prayed for me. I wasn't expecting it."

"That happens sometimes," she laughed. "How was it?"

"It was… something else."

"Yeah?"

"I think it's made me understand something. I thought about going on the mission trip when we first heard about it because I wanted to have a plan for the future like the rest of you."

"I was surprised when you brought it up on the beach that day," Sarah admitted.

"Well, after that prayer, I realized that I really do have to go. I believe I was always meant to."

Sarah turned for the first time since we got in the car. For a moment, she looked between me and the road. "Keep going."

"I still need to talk to my parents about it, but yeah. I don't know how to explain it… it just makes sense. I'm *supposed* to go. It isn't just some random thing to do anymore."

Sarah cracked a smile in the darkness. The light emanating from the traffic stop flashed green on her face as we started to roll under it. "So, are you really sure about this? Is that what has you worked up?"

"I'm one hundred and thirty percent sure. I've never been more sure about anything. God wants me to go. I can feel that. But no, it's not what had me worked up."

"That's really awesome, Sammy. What is it then?"

"Two months isn't a long time to be gone, but for Jared and me, it sounds like forever. It sounds like the death of a relationship."

"Why do you feel that way?"

"He's not going to understand my decision. When I brought it up at the beach, he looked at me funny, or at least I thought he did. I know it sounds dumb, but I get the impression he won't be thrilled about it." And Jared said himself, his relationship with God hadn't been in a good place for years.

"If I'm being totally honest, part of me doesn't understand your decision, either. Not that you don't have a good heart, everyone knows you do, but I'm just surprised. I will be praying for you the whole time, and so will your family and the church. You have so much support, and I know you're going to be smart and careful while you're down there."

Sarah's unwavering support breathed life into me, and I sat in peace for two intersections before either of us spoke again.

"Do you love him?" came her next question.

My blood pumped in my ears. Deep breath in. Deep breath out. Keep it steady. "We haven't said that to each other."

"But do you?"

"Yes." There was no point in denying it. "Truly, madly, deeply!"

"I thought so." She squeezed my heart with her tender tone. "Does he love you?"

"I..." don't actually know. Did he? Or did I only hope so? But the things he'd done for me... The way he'd held my hand—literally and figuratively—through some of the hardest moments of my life. He'd provided support I hadn't realized I was lacking. Every time he kissed me, it was like he'd die without one more. When we were apart I felt like I'd never be whole again. Surely, there's no way I could feel all of that without it being mutual. "I think... I believe he does."

"Then believe it will work out. Like you said, it's only two months. Don't let the fear of time apart stop you from loving each other."

JARED

46

ON JULY 4ᵀᴴ, SAMMY AND I FOUND OURSELVES DOWNTOWN AT THE American Bank Center, this time waiting for our friends to meet us for the big fireworks show over the water. Sammy and I had left the parking lot and found a nice slice of grass along Shoreline Boulevard to hunker down on. After laying out a blanket, Sammy wiggled into my side until my arm wrapped around her.

"Do you have any free time in the next week or so?" she asked. "Cindie and Tyler invited us to go bowling."

"Heck yeah, that sounds like fun. I'm sure I will. There's only so many hours we're allowed to do anything this early in the summer, even if I didn't still have restrictions."

"Good, I was hoping you'd say yes. You know, I was actually thinking about asking Cindie if she minds if Birdie and Nick come, too."

"That would be neat. I really don't know much about Nick."

"He's cool, but I haven't had much time with him, either."

"Is he coming tonight?"

"Yeah, but I'm not sure when. He might not show up with much time to chat.

256

"Is Jenna coming tonight?"

She must've felt me tense because she put her arms around me, too, caging me in. "Yes, she is. But you're thinking about Dan, aren't you?"

"Him, and I'm curious about how Jenna is doing with everything."

"I doubt she'll be talking about it, but as far as Dan goes, have you thought about calling him or going to visit?"

"Is he even allowed to get visitors?" I still wasn't sure, because I never did anything with the information his parents gave.

"I'm pretty sure he can. Birdie volunteers at the women's campus here in town. She would know for sure. Why don't you ask her when they get here?"

"I might."

I could feel her eyes on me. "You're still mad, huh?"

"Sort of, but mostly, I'm just confused. What would I say? For all I know, he's mad at *me*, and our friendship will never be the same. I'd hate to walk into a situation like that on the phone, let alone in person."

She squeezed my torso and kissed my neck. "I'm sorry you're hurting over this. I don't know what I'd do without Sarah, Jenna, and Birdie."

"It's not your fault."

"It's not yours, either. And being without a best friend really stinks."

"At least I have you."

"Yes, you do."

Sammy nuzzled deeper into my neck, peppering me with soft kisses that made me shiver. I turned, eager to reciprocate, when the corner of my eye caught Birdie and Nick's approach.

"Incoming," I said, leaning away just enough to dissuade her from continuing.

"Don't you two look cozy," Birdie teased, sauntering over with Nick by her side. "Is it safe to sit down, or do you guys need to be alone?"

"Well, if you're offering," Sammy joked, pretending to engulf me with affection. "Just kidding. Sorry, Jare."

Jare? I almost wanted to slap myself for smiling at the silly little moniker.

Standing up, Sammy hugged both the newcomers. "You guys didn't carpool with Sarah and Jenna?"

"No, were we supposed to?" Birdie looked to Nick, who lifted his shoulders.

"I just assumed you would because the traffic getting out of here is not going to be pretty."

"That's okay. My man drove." Birdie beheld Nick with a saccharine smile.

"Good then. Let's do something while we wait for the others."

"How long is it until the fireworks start?"

I checked my watch. "Forty more minutes."

"Jeez, we should have come later," Birdie complained.

Sammy shook her head. "You won't even be able to drive in later. Trust me, it was best this way."

Taking an opening while the girls further situated our blankets, I made a play to get to know Nick. Dipping down into my backpack, I grabbed a football. "Hey, Nick. Do you want to toss it around some?"

"We can try, but I can't catch to save my life."

"I won't throw it too hard then." I chuckled. I liked Nick; he had a great attitude. But I had a hard time not comparing him to Dan.

Stepping back from the girls and other crowds, we made room for ourselves. After a few passes, I could confirm what Nick had already suspected of himself: he couldn't catch to save his life. He even fumbled my slow underhand tosses.

"In my defense, I'm *really* good at math and science."

"How did you decide on marine biology?"

He slid the ball around in his hands. "I've always liked the ocean. Swimming is my favorite sport, probably the only one I'm not bad at. Plus, sharks are cool." He threw it back.

"That they are. Do you want to get down there in those cages and study them?"

"Sure do. But someone else is gonna have to tell my mom." He almost caught the ball that time, but it fell from his grip and bounced into his shin.

I laughed, palming his pitch. "I'd rather hang with sharks than face my mom sometimes, too."

"For real, she's going to flip out." Surprising us both, Nick managed to nab my return throw. "Finally! Bro, I think that's it for me. I'd like to retire on a good note. Besides, it's insanely hot."

"Sure thing. Good game, man." We shook on it and returned to the girls.

I'd been trying to work up the nerve to seek out Birdie, anyway. Sammy was right. I ought to just ask her about how things worked at STLR. It wasn't like inquiring about the policies automatically committed me to anything. Having all the information would simply help me make my decision. One way or the other...

Sarah and Jenna arrived then, offering the perfect distraction. Seizing an opportunity, I leaned toward Birdie, voice low. "Hey, can I ask you a question?"

Turning to me, she appeared curious, but she understood my desire to stay quiet. "Sure. What's on your mind?"

"Do you ever run into Dan when you're at STLR?" I knew that, in fact, she did not, seeing as how she worked at the women's branch, and Dan was not there, but I didn't know how to ask my real question. I would try a bad segue instead.

"No, I don't," she frowned. "I wish, but I only work the location here in town. He's up in Beeville."

"Oh, okay. So, you don't know how he's doing?"

"I've actually called him once."

Which was more than I could say. "How was he?"

"He seemed okay, but he didn't say much. I'm sure I'm not the one he wanted to hear from."

Guilt rose in my throat. With some effort, I swallowed it down. "Oh?"

She leaned in a bit further, tone hushed. "Jenna hasn't called him at all. She won't write, either. She claims she would visit if his parents would let her, but I think she's just avoiding him. I'm told you know why."

The pregnancy. But why Jenna would avoid working that out with him was beyond me. He wouldn't be gone forever.

"Wow."

She nodded, her face empathetic. "I know. Poor Dan. I can get you his number if you want."

I cleared the frog from my throat, hoping to reveal nothing. "Sure, thanks," I said, pretending I didn't have it.

With perfect timing, Sammy came meandering back from her conversation with the others. "Hey, you," she said to me.

"Hey, yourself. Ready to watch the show? It's starting in just a few minutes."

"So ready," she declared, getting comfortable beside me.

"I asked Birdie," I said.

"I know. I could tell that's what you were talking about." She bumped against my shoulder. "I think that's good."

"Me too."

"And I texted Cindie, by the way, and she said Birdie and Nick can go bowling with us. They are excited to go, too."

"Awesome. We'll all have a great time."

"Yep." She leaned up and pecked my cheek. She went in a second time, and I quickly turned, catching her lips with mine. She giggled in response. "You cheated."

"You liked it."

She rolled her shoulders, nonchalant. "Whatever."

The fireworks started a moment later, the first burst of light sailing into the sky, leaving behind a trail of sparks. Everyone, including us, murmured our appreciation like we'd never seen fireworks before. With Sammy cuddled snugly into my side, I smiled as I watched the display overhead.

Then, her sweet voice tickled my ear. "It's like the whole country is celebrating your good news, Jared."

"What good news?"

"Reconciling with your best friend."

"I will try, anyway. There's no telling how it'll go."

She covered her hand with mine, a maneuver I had grown so deeply fond of. "It will go exactly as it should."

Another pop and whiz in the air, and a large multi-colored spectacle illuminated the whole waterfront. It was probably the biggest one in the set so far. The end of it cast a blue glow around Sammy, and my heart choked with nerves. Reaching out to Dan wasn't going to be easy, but I had finally decided to do it. I had everything I'd ever dreamed of, and he was alone in there. I owed it to him, as his best friend, to let him know he had my support.

And I owed it to myself to give him my forgiveness.

SAMMY

47

Wise words from a wise friend. Sarah's good point followed me around every day since then. It was on my mind, even now, as I sat arms-deep in paperwork for my upcoming trip. I was so engrossed, eager to get it all perfect, that I didn't even look up through the slotted blinds when I heard a rackety car pull into the driveway.

Ever since Pastor Brian prayed for me, I couldn't deny the overwhelming confirmation that my decision was the right one. No amount of opposition, least of all from myself, would change my mind. Not when God Himself had so clearly and graciously endorsed it for me.

Obviously, He knew I took on the endeavor to escape a future that was looking pretty bleak, but things had started to change. I wasn't sure yet how, but the feeling I had was undeniably present.

"Hey, baby," came my mom's voice.

Dropping my pen, I turned. "Hey, Mama. What's up?"

"Your dad is downstairs in the kitchen. With Claudia."

"Oh. What's she want?" I twisted back to the papers on my desk.

"She came to talk to you."

"What for?"

"No idea. Your dad's keeping her company while she waits for you. We told her you were busy, and she insisted on staying. If you aren't feeling up for a visit from her today, well…"

"It's whatever. I could take a break from all this."

"Do you want me to look it over in the meantime?"

"Yeah, actually." I shuffled everything together, returned it to the folder, and handed it to her. "There's a lot, so better safe than sorry."

She took it and tucked it under her arm. "Go ahead downstairs. Let your dad know he can meet me up here, and we will tend to this together."

In agreement, I stood up and strode by her, trying to let the peace I'd gotten from church keep me grounded. If I let it, my anxiety would crawl out of the pit in my stomach and consume me, but I was dead-set against it. Claudia didn't deserve more power in my life than God had.

I SAT down across from her at the breakfast table in the kitchen. "My mom said you wanted to see me." Had I imagined it, or had Claudia's face fallen at my using that title for her sister-in-law? A sign of emotion from Claudia-Fraudia? I wouldn't be fooled so easily.

"I bought a car."

I blinked. "You bought a car?" I recalled the noisy machine

that had pulled into the driveway earlier. "The thing out there is yours?"

"Yep. All mine. Even the insurance payment."

"Wow. Okay." *And? What's your point?*

She looked irritated that I wasn't giving her the reaction she wanted, but God only knew what that was. Unless she came to finally give me the information she'd previously teased me with, lording it over me spitefully, then I probably didn't care what she had to say.

Might as well beat her to the punch. If she didn't come to play fair, she may as well leave sooner. "I don't know what it is you had in mind for this conversation, but let me just start with one simple question of my own. Do you really not know who my father is, or have you been hoarding the information just to torture me?"

"That is what I wanted to talk to you about."

"Okay, so talk," I urged impatiently.

"I have not always made the best decisions, okay?" She moved her shoulders in an unrepentant shrug. If this was her idea of an apology, it needed some major work.

"I'm aware of that much." Did that dry sound of boredom come from me? Oops. "Do you know who he is or not?"

Begrudgingly crossing her arms, she leveled with me. "No, I don't. I know that's not what you wanted to hear."

"But... how many could it possibly be? I mean, don't you know who your boyfriend was around that time?"

She ran her tongue along her teeth with a look of annoyance, but when she opened her mouth, I could tell she'd held back. "I've had my suspicions because of the way you look. You've always seemed more fair than the rest of us, but even if I had one or two potentials in mind, there are others I'm sure I don't even remember."

Me? Fair? I mean, I guess I could be.

"Are you saying my father might be white?"

"Some of us chocolate girls like vanilla from time to time. I've noticed you're familiar with that concept." She snickered.

I rolled my eyes. "Hilarious."

"He might also be green, pink, or purple, for all I know." Claudia schooled her face with a deep inhale. "I've never been preferential, nor have I ever been the monogamous type." Her voice faltered then, but I wasn't particularly startled until tears formed in her eyes. "It's taken me a long time to realize that the bad choices I made had such a profound impact on you and others, and that I should have tried harder."

"You mean, if you had known you'd end up with a kid, you wouldn't have slept around?"

She stared at me with a cocked brow, but again, when she spoke, it was impressively and surprisingly controlled. "I should have taken better care to know who I was with. I should have been more responsible. I should have been more protective over my virtues from the jump. I should have been a hundred thousand things, but I wasn't. The bottom line is that I wish I knew who fathered my child. I truly do."

The way she said it all, she was so tortured. I couldn't stand it. "You don't have to beat yourself up. I don't care who he is, anyway. I have a beyond-perfect father upstairs." And One further up, I discerned. But something *was* nagging at me. Worry or concern, perhaps, but not for myself.

"Yes, you do," she agreed. "My brother is the best man around. He tried to keep me safe, to look out for me, but I made it hard for him—for our mom. I've never been… good."

With a stiffened chin, one that I recognized all too well, Claudia swiped her faux-nail-clad fingers under her eyes. Her excessive jewelry clanged together as she moved. It was a ridiculous picture yet oddly comforting. It was so Claudia. She was who she was, but it came as a welcomed surprise that even *she* had feelings.

Claudia Ballard, though far from perfect or even admirable, was the reason I was given to her brother eighteen years ago. That alone had begun to sway my opinion of her, at least on a deeper level. She *could* have tried the motherhood thing herself. Who knows where I'd be if that had been the case? She'd done the only thing she could, and it had taken me this long to grasp that.

So, maybe she personally couldn't have provided the life I deserved, and I would never know my birth father. Maybe she didn't know how to love me then or even now. But in reality, she loved me as much as she needed to for my own sake. Are any of us allowed to ask any more than that?

I wasn't the only adopted person in the world, but I felt like I might be more blessed than most. If I doubted that, I could recount my conversation with Cindie. She had it bad growing up, and she never got adopted after losing her parents. I had so much to be grateful for, and the more I comprehended that, the more I knew I had plenty of my heart to give.

More than ever before, I was reassured that my decision to go to Mexico in the fall was valid and all part of God's plan. All I had left to do was pack.

And find the right time to remind Jared about it.

SAMMY

48

On the night of our bowling date, Birdie was already at my house for a sleepover. After Jared picked us up, we swung around to get Nick, then headed to the bowling alley to meet Cindie and Tyler.

Walking into the alley always felt like a blast from the past, no matter how often or recently I'd been there. The smell, unique to bowling alleys across the country, was an instant trigger, joined by the sounds of bowling balls soaring down the lanes and smacking into the pins. Together, the whole experience of simply entering the establishment created a distinct portal of nostalgia.

As a kid, I'd loved bowling but been so bad at it that I'd eventually trade my turn for quarters to use on the candy and small toy machines. A worthy sacrifice, if you asked me. Getting tattoos and stickers and handfuls of miniature chalky fruit was a way better alternative to chucking gutter balls all night.

Sitting down at the table near our lanes, we swapped our shoes out for rentals, except for Tyler, who had his own.

"You have your own shoes, huh?" I asked. "Are we all about to get our butts kicked?"

He laughed. "I might not be too bad. I have my own ball, too." As he stood up and removed his jacket, we saw his name and a team logo embroidered on his colored polo.

"Yeah, we're going down," Birdie said.

Nick patted her hand. "I already knew I was, so it doesn't matter to me. I really only came for the food. Who wants to put an order in with me?"

"I will," said Jared, standing up. "What would you like?" he asked me.

"Anything. Surprise me."

He raised an eyebrow. "Okay, I will." Shuffling over to Tyler and Cindie, they also gave him their requests, and Tyler slipped Jared his credit card for their tab.

A few minutes later, Tyler had the monitors decked out with everyone's initials, and the lanes were ready to go. Girls would be on one with the guys on the other. My abilities were hit or miss, and Birdie wasn't the absolute worst at bowling, but I secretly hoped Cindie was also in a league, or we might have found something the boys could beat us at.

We weren't on the beach anymore, Toto.

Surprisingly, we didn't do too bad in the first half. Tyler was leading the boys to a probable victory, but we were still having fun. Cindie made two strikes, and I discovered I wasn't half bad at picking up spares. Jared, the powerhouse that he was, clocked in with the fastest throws with a half-decent aim. Nick, from what Jared had shared with me, was more than making up for his lack of catching skills. And Birdie, who would've guessed, was an amazing bowler.

Nick gave her a double high-five when she walked off the platform after scoring a turkey. "Dang, Birdie, three strikes in a row? Is it beginner's luck, or have you been sneaking off to the lanes for years without telling anyone?"

"I've always played okay but never this good. I guess it's just my night." Sitting at the bar seating behind the platform, Birdie dipped one of Nick's onion rings into ketchup. A well-earned treat, if you asked me.

"We may just catch up with you at the helm, Birdie," Cindie cheered. "I'd love to beat Tyler and rub it in his perfect-form, polo-wearing face."

Tyler looked up from the ball return. "Hey."

"What?" She batted her eyes at him with an angelic smile plastered on her face.

"Just for that, I'm not going easy on you ladies anymore."

Birdie almost choked on Nick's soda. He patted her on the back. "This is you going easy on us?

He smirked and rolled up imaginary sleeves as his ice blue ball with flecks of yellow rolled out. When he picked it up, he cast a backward glance at Cindie, who crossed her arms and legs in smug anticipation.

Tyler assumed his position at the edge of the platform, lining up his shot in his head. When he began walking and drew back, Cindie suddenly shouted, "DON'T MISS!" Tyler was so shaken by the disruption that he held on to the ball a moment too long and ended up throwing it into the air. Losing his balance, one foot fell from under him, and he slipped, catching himself on his hands. We watched as the ball came to an unceremonious crash land onto the lane and skittered into the gutter. At least it stayed in, but only barely. Needless to say, he scored a zero.

After our initial shock wore off, we were laughing hysterically. Poor Tyler was crouched with his hands over his head like he was about to be bull-rushed by the bowling police.

Cindie, still wheezing with laughter, ran over to comfort him. "I am so sorry, Tyler! I had no idea that would work out so well."

"Look at that, Tyler. Pride really does go before a fall." Jared teased a pastor with a Bible reference. Impressive.

"Ha, and so it does!"

Cindie and Tyler stood up, and he yanked her in for a hug. "Thanks for the unorthodox reminder to stay humble." Tyler shook his hands out as they walked back.

"Maybe you need Birdie to step in for your second turn, Tyler," Nick taunted.

Birdie looked up from her food. "I totally could."

"It's okay. I have to finish what I started. That might still include kicking your butts, but I will do it more quietly."

After my latest turn, during which I scored a four—a *four!*—I decided a weightier ball might be in order. At the very least, if I used a heavier one, it could help do part of the work for me. After rolling a few around, I picked a pink twelve-pounder.

A male voice cut in behind me. "Sammy?"

I turned to see who had said my name. "Hey, Adam. Long time no see."

Adam Alvarado and I dated briefly senior year, and I hadn't seen him since graduation. I'd liked him well enough, but when I looked at him now, all I could think about now was Jared's general disdain for Adam and his poor sportsmanship.

Jared. Oh, no. All at once, I could feel his eyes burning a hole in my back.

Adam stepped in for a hug, and hoisting my ball on my hip, I awkwardly put one hand around his shoulder.

"It feels like forever. Was graduation really only a little over a month ago? Time flies."

"It sure does."

"You look amazing." He smiled. "Remind me again why we didn't keep going out?"

Heat filled my face as determined footfalls came up quickly behind us.

49

REDUCED TO MY MOST BASIC INSTINCTS, I STOMPED TOWARD Sammy and Adam like a Neanderthal, eager to put distance between the puny creep and my girl. Sidling up beside her, I gently removed the bowling ball from her grasp, placing it on the nearby carousel, before standing to my full height and sliding my arm around Sammy's shoulders.

I looked down at Adam with a smile on my face. "Hey, Alvarado."

He took a step away—a smart move. "Oh, hey there, Jared. How's it been?"

"Good, good. Just enjoying a date with my girlfriend." Pause for effect. "What about you?"

"Did you say *your* girlfriend?"

"Yes. Samantha is *my* girlfriend." As if on queue, she dropped her right hip and leaned into me, letting me pull her closer.

"Ah, okay. Wow, I wouldn't have seen that coming." He made an attempt at laughing, but it died quickly.

"Uh-huh." I stared him down, daring him to make another ill-advised comment.

He cleared his throat, shifting back another half pace. "Anyway, I'm just spending time indulging in my last summer break while it lasts. I'm enlisting in the spring, you know."

Cool. Get yourself far, far away.

Adam stared at Sammy, possibly looking for some reaction of remorse at hearing of his leaving. There was none.

"Right on. Well, it was nice catching up, man. I hope you have a good night. I know we will," I said, bringing about the end of the encounter.

With a slow, annoyed nod, Adam submitted to his defeat. "See y'all later."

Gleefully, I watched him remove himself from our presence, and Sammy turned to me. A second passed before she said anything. "As an independent-ish woman, I'm probably not supposed to like that."

"Like what?"

"Your little possessive caveman display."

"You looked uncomfortable. He put his paws on you." I stood firm and unapologetic. "I told you Adam was a tool."

"I wouldn't have tolerated him much longer."

"Oh, I know. But you can't ask me to just sit back and watch when somebody is treading on my turf. It goes against everything I know as an athlete and a man."

She rolled her eyes. "Caveman." Then, giving me a playfully satisfied look, she put her arms around my neck. "But like I was saying, I didn't hate it."

In response, I slid my own paws, welcomed and ardent, around her waist, spreading my fingers wide for optimum coverage. I leaned down for the kiss we both wanted when a crumpled napkin hit the back of my head.

"Take a chill pill, you two," Birdie cried, crumpling up a

second ball of ammunition in case we didn't listen. "It's been your turn for like eight years now, Sammy."

"Alright, alright, she's coming." Taking hold of her ball, I offered Sammy my elbow.

"Wow. From caveman to gentleman. What a quick evolution. Who knew I'd get the best of both worlds."

Winking, I walked her along. How ever the bowling scores ended up, and no matter what she may have thought about my interaction with Adam, I knew I was the real winner.

JARED

50

Whatever I thought a rehab facility was like, STLR wasn't it. A dark-haired woman from the front desk introduced me to Mr. Hawkins, the director, who then took me into his office and had me fill out a visitor's form and fork over my ID. There was a lot of leg work just to pop in and say hi, but there was no getting around it. God willing, I would leave there having made the amends I had recently acknowledged I was desperate to make.

God willing, huh? You're starting to sound like Sammy and Sarah.

Thinking little else of it, I finished the forms, put my ID back in my wallet, and waited to be told I could see my best friend. If we were still best friends after I left was yet to be determined.

"Okay, Mr. Tomlin," said the director, collecting a sticky name tag from a small printer and handing it to me. "This temporary accessory is for you and needs to be worn on the breast at all times while you're in the facility. If you're ready, I'll escort you to the visitor's patio now."

I stood, nervously brushing nothing off my jeans. "I'm ready."

Stepping back out into the heat of summer, I took stock of this *'visitor's patio.'* It was basically a sizable, fully fenced-in back-

276

yard, decked out with picnic tables and benches and covered by an expansive awning for shade. A few people were out there already, engaged in their own affairs.

"Mr. Schellers will be sent out momentarily. Please, enjoy your visit. If you have any trouble or need anything at all, one of our security staff can assist you." He indicated toward the various burly gentlemen patrolling the grounds.

"Thank you," I said, and the director took his leave.

I picked a bench near a small pond. In the middle, the pond had a water fountain shaped like a dancing cherub, the stream flowing steadily from his flute. The sound of the water and the hum of the wind eased my nerves until I heard Dan's voice behind me.

"Jared?"

"Dan, hey." I shot up quick as a light, and my anxious hands took refuge in my pockets.

Dan sat down on the bench, not appearing half as nervous as me. He was either now master of hiding his emotions or he had none left to show me. I didn't expect either of those options would foster a renewed friendship for Dan and me.

I stood there in front of him for an untold amount of time before he finally broke the silence. "I wasn't sure you'd ever come."

Here goes nothing. There was nothing left to be but honest now. "Neither was I."

"I'm glad you did though."

"You are?"

He nodded, leaning his bent elbows on his thighs. His hands draped down casually. "And I'm so glad to see you've healed. Did you wait to come visit me until then on purpose?"

Thoughts swirling, I slowly took a seat beside him. "No. But maybe that was a subconscious thing."

"Either way, it's helping. I would've hated seeing you like that, as selfish as it sounds."

"It's okay. I think I get that." If I had rushed to come see him, still fresh with the physical pain as well as the emotional, things might not have gone this well.

If that was, in fact, how things were going.

"Part of my struggle in being here was leaving the hospital thinking I'd ruined you for life. You didn't—don't—owe me anything, but I wish I had known how you were doing sooner. I'm relieved, and I'm glad for you. You were always more the sportsman than me. You deserved to keep playing. You *are* still playing right?"

"Sure am."

"Good. I don't know what I would have done if I'd taken that from you."

I was relieved I got to play still, but I admitted to acting less than sportsmanlike lately. If only Dan knew how much my mentality had suffered all this time, how much I'd complained and feared and resisted, or how much Sammy had to do just to help pull me out of it.

At that moment, I thought of Adam and how he'd quit the team years ago, then turned his back on all of us. He had the delivery all wrong, but perhaps his injury was a valid reason for quitting in the first place. If I was honest, it was entirely possible my real beef with him was the fact that he got to quit when he got hurt. He got out before he could get in too deep. In my current state, having healed in some ways more than others, his abandonment of the game was something more easily forgiven.

I shook my thoughts away, focusing on the here and now. The

happy. "I'm glad to report I was recently cleared to return to playing. Preseason activities have already begun."

"That's awesome, congratulations. I just want you to know I accept this whole thing was my fault, and I'm sorry."

"That's all I could've wanted. Thanks, Dan."

Putting my arm over his shoulder, I drew him in for a hug. He didn't hesitate to return it. When we drew apart, his eyes were wet.

He chuckled softly, pinching his eyes. "Sorry, man. Not much else to do here besides get in touch with my feelings and all that junk."

"I'm not gonna hold it against you. Progress is progress. It's been a crazy ride for me out there, too."

Dan sat up, looking more chipper by the second. "Well, tell me what's been going on. I'm desperate for—what is it the girls say? Tea? Hey, I wonder if the masculine form of spilling tea might be pouring beer. In that case, pour the beer, my friend."

"How can you stand to even joke about beer? I never want to think about it again." It made me laugh, but still. *Cringe.* I'd had enough of the taste, smell, and thought of alcohol to last until infinity.

Sighing, he dropped against the back curve of the bench. "Because if I don't joke about stuff, I will go insane in here. My life is under so much restriction and stress, so all I've got left is my wit. If I let that die, I might as well die, too."

Woah... "You don't really mean that, do you?"

Lifting and dropping his shoulder, he maintained a placid expression. "Not literally, I guess. But I don't see how else to stay sane, cut off from the rest of the world. My parents won't let me make any decisions since this was a legal thing, so I haven't seen or spoken to Jenna since I was arrested. I have no idea what's going on with her or the baby—which I may have forgotten to tell you about."

"Sammy told me."

"Pretty crazy, huh? I still can't believe it. I also can't believe I'm stuck in here for another ten months, dude."

"They sent you here for a *year*?"

"Yep. Twelve months solid. And if I don't pass all my screenings and play my part to perfection, I won't graduate the program. They'll extend my stay."

My heart went out to him. I had to let him know. "Jenna's doing okay, I think."

"Yeah? Is she really?"

"I think," I repeated. "Understandably emotional, but okay. I could pass along a message to her if you want."

"Tell her I miss her."

"I will do that. Anything else?"

"And I love her."

"Certainly. Is that it?"

"And I hope… I hope that she waits for me."

"You got it. Now, do you really want to hear my, uh, beer?"

"I sure do. Let's hear it all."

Feeling light-hearted, I told him everything that had happened from the time I woke up in the hospital to today. It felt so nice to confide in Dan again. Old times weren't so far away after all.

"You and Sammy, huh?" He shook his head with mirth. "You dog."

"How am I a dog?"

"You got with your crush's best friend? Ballsy."

"*Former* crush, Dan, as in, no longer."

"Eh. Still ballsy."

"It's not anything. We weren't even looking to start something. We just kind of... collided. We fit together."

"Hopefully not as well as Jenna and I did because let me tell you—"

"You *would* take it that way, but that is *not* what I meant. I'm not a total moron, unlike some people I know."

The ease with which we laughed was a comfort. I might not have had all of my feelings figured out, and parts of me were still recovering, but at least I still had a best friend.

And a best girl to return home to tell it all to.

JARED

51

Coach blew the whistle that signaled the end of our scrimmage, and immediately, all twenty-two of us were on the same team again. It was our first time running through a play in gear, and it went smooth as butter. High-fives and goodwill abounded, and many of my teammates slapped me with an *'attaboy'* on the shoulder or helmet.

"Nice run, Tomlin," Mac admitted, winded. He tore his helmet from his sweat-soaked head, his beaded, cheekbone-length dreads spilling over his dark eyes. "I almost had you though."

"Almost isn't enough. Have you seen these legs?"

"Only all the time in the locker room." Mac held his hand up as though shielding his eyes. "You need to get some sun on those drumsticks of yours."

One by one, the guys and I trickled off the field, each of us tired, sweaty, and ready to call it a night, but that was a great practice. Preseason conditioning and team building could only do so much for someone with the game in their veins. Experiencing it all again after coming back from an injury made it a class above. The air smelled better out here—a mixture of turf, sweat, and hard work.

Or it was all in my head. Either way…

Feeling my oats, I jogged over to my bag, bouncing with an appreciation for my almost fully-restored knee.

Teeth engaged, I popped the top of my water bottle. As I took a swig of the quenching liquid, Mac rapped his knuckles on my helmet, then pointed into the stands. "Hey, man. Isn't that your girl?"

I followed his line of sight and waved when I saw her, my chest inflating instinctively. How long had she been there? My smile took over all on its own. "It sure is."

Mac's brows hiked as he gave me a look of warning. "Better go see what she wants before the guys do. She lookin' cute today." He drew out the last word, rubbing his chin like he was considering a new play, one that entailed gunning for Sammy.

"Hey, now. Eyes off. She's mine."

He laughed and swung his helmet at me. "Better hurry up then, lover boy. Can't make a woman like that wait for long. But might be best to shower first. You stink, my dude."

With an eye-rolling laugh, I took off, and a few of the other guys hooted and hollered, some making atrocious kissing noises. I ignored them and mouthed to Sammy, "Be right back." She nodded. Then, breaking from the pack, I ran ahead. In the span of about ten minutes, I was showered, dressed, and jogging back to meet her.

Sammy was standing at the foot of the stands by the time I caught up. In her presence, I felt like a million bucks. "Hey, lady. What're you doing here?"

"Just wanted to come by and watch all the hype. I hope that's okay."

"Heck yeah, it is." I threw my arms around her, lifting her toes from the ground only briefly, her warm giggle hitting my neck as I put her down. "You caused a stir over here earlier. Did you hear all that?"

"Yeah, I did. Doesn't that man-hazing stuff ever get old?"

"We pretend like it does, but secretly, we all love it." I looked around. "Don't tell anyone I told you that. Might be a breach of bro-code."

"Your secret is safe with me," she whispered back.

"So, what do you want to do now?"

She held out a rolled blanket and a Ziplock bag of food I hadn't noticed 'til then. "I have some news. I thought we could have a little snack and sit out somewhere to talk."

My stomach thought that sounded like a great idea. "That sounds good to me. Why don't we go sit under the goalpost?"

"Are we allowed to?"

"I don't know." I laughed.

"Let's do it!" Laughing with me, she clasped our hands together as we walked. "You were looking great out there."

"You think so? We've got a really good team. They're going to have a great year."

"They are?"

"Oh, oops. I guess I'm still used to the mindset that it's not happening for me." I looked ahead, ignoring the slip.

"The team is good, but I was only really looking at you. You're very much in your element when you're all suited up, playing the game, doing what you do best."

I took the blanket and laid it out for us, pulling out the corners. "Thank you. It does feel good to be back at it."

After my last high school game, Coach Haworth told me football wasn't all I am, but how far did that get me if I didn't believe it was true myself? I wouldn't be so good at something and enjoy it so much if it wasn't the right thing for me.

"I'll bet." Sammy sat, fiddling with the sole of her shoe.

"You seem distracted. Everything okay?"

"I'm totally fine," she said, not that I believed her. She reached up and tucked a few strands that had fallen loose from her ponytail. The wind picked up as the sun was going down. "I keep thinking about something. Could you ever imagine, after the year we've had, that you and I would end up together?"

"If I had been a smarter man, I might've."

To think that I'd started the year with somebody else in my mind was crazy. I didn't realize there was a difference between my simple crush on Sarah and the girl who would one day occupy, consume, and emblazon my heart. The mere idea that anyone besides Sammy could've held my attention seemed ridiculous. I leaned out so I could take her in. There was none more beautiful than her, and she'd wanted *me*.

Placing my hand on her cheek, I marveled at how her skin next to mine wasn't contrasting but complimentary. Together, we were just two people, nothing more, nothing less. With deliberate gentleness, I cradled the back of her neck and drew her in for a kiss.

At some point over the course of our relationship, I figured out I would gladly do anything for her for the rest of my life. I'd even go back to church every single Sunday or teach every crusty-nosed child in all of Corpus Christi how to play football if that's what she wanted. All for this girl. For my Sammy.

A sudden desperation clung to my heart. My feelings for her were building up to a point where I couldn't deny their intensity anymore. It was the truest thing I'd felt in a long, long time, and the words clamored to be set free.

The realization reminded me of how my mom had once described feeling for my dad. Somehow, both loves—the source of her unrelenting unhappiness and my unwavering joy—stemmed from the same vein. Hers was gone, but mine was still here, and I needed to tell Sammy how I felt.

SAMMY

52

ONE LANGUID KISS TURNED INTO TWO, WHICH HURRIEDLY TURNED into three. He kissed me often, and each time was more wonderful than the last, but *wow*. What came before was nothing like that, like the air in his lungs wasn't enough to sustain him. And when I had spared a second to consider his urgency, I became aware I shared it. He meant the same to me.

Pulling back, we held each others' gaze. Something deep-seated shook me from the inside out, banging to be released. Something that I refused to acknowledge for many reasons before this moment.

"Samantha..." he began, a quiver in his voice. Every time he said my full name, the *way* he said it, that thing that had rooted itself deeper inside me grew a little bigger.

I looked up from under dark lashes. I couldn't shake the feeling that the same waves were rocking him. The oceanic swirls in his eyes were signs of the same trepidation I felt in my own heart. That, and the uncertainty beside it.

So many questions took shape in my mind. I hadn't even gotten the chance to tell Jared my mission trip was official. I was leaving at the end of the summer and would be gone for two months. Even now, the odds of Jared and me making it as a couple despite our vastly different life choices was bleak since our futures looked to be heading in different directions. Even after I returned from Mexico, Jared would be in college meeting new people all the time, living a life with school and football that I couldn't relate to. And what would I be doing?

He inhaled, his back straightened, as though he were hoping to use his spine to garner strength from the earth itself. "I—"

With a shrill cry, his phone rang out, interrupting what I recognized as something important and already fleeting.

Jared fished the incessant device from his pocket. It was his mom. Hearing her impatient voice on the other line, I didn't have to wait to find out he had been due back at home forty-five minutes ago, right after practice.

When he hung up the phone, his face filled in the gaps. "I'm so sorry. I have to go," he said with a tone of utter dejection. "I forgot about our family dinner, and now my mom wants to make it a game night as well. It's stupid."

A lump formed in my throat. He would've been on time if I hadn't come.

"It's okay," I offered. "And that doesn't sound stupid. It sounds nice. She's trying."

"I guess so, but it seems a little too late now. I'm pretty much only home to sleep. Why couldn't she have *tried* when I was living more of my actual life there and feeling miserable about it?"

"Better late than never. Don't be so bull-headed."

He raised his eyebrow at me. "Oh, if it isn't the pot calling the kettle black. Or, the bull calling the cow—never mind, it doesn't work."

I laughed, but not because of his precious bad joke. He was touching on nerves better left alone. There really weren't any similarities between Claudia and Laura, yet my mind was trying to make them.

"Whatever, I'm going," he resolved. "But be warned, eventually, I'm going to insist you come with me and endure a dinner with *my* mother one of these nights."

"I'm not scared. I'd love to formally meet your mom." Laura may have her own issues, but she could not be half the nightmare Claudia was, no matter what they may or may not have in common.

No matter how hard they may be trying...

"Alright then. Let's go run your car home. You're coming to dinner with me tonight. I've decided." A tender brightness shone in his eyes. The corners of his mouth curled up. "I hope you're hungry. We're having Italian."

SAMMY

53

Being nervous was a normal reaction to meeting one's boyfriend's mother, but what if I had made her very casual acquaintance before? I wasn't dating her son then, and she and I had never directly spoken. But there I was, in Jared's passenger seat, on the way to his house for family dinner and game night, an intimate evening to which I was not invited by the host. Evidently, it hadn't occurred to me to refuse.

Across the center console, Jared squeezed my hand. "You nervous?" He took quick peeks at me, even though the world outside was nearly dark now.

"A little, but mostly excited. I just hope she's not upset I'm tagging along."

"Eh, don't worry about that. I'm sure she'll just be satisfied I showed up at all."

"Has she ever asked about meeting me?"

"She has… But you know how I've told you she gets real spacey sometimes. In her own world and all that. She doesn't really notice much."

My heart pinched at the lamentation in his voice. "I'm sure she notices a lot more than you realize."

With a quick glance, he gave me a smile. It wasn't his usual dimple-producing, ear-to-ear exhibition of joy. It was smaller and more reserved but real nonetheless.

Clutching my hand, he drew it up for a kiss. "Thank you for your positivity, Sammy."

"Wait a second, I'm being overtly positive?" My eyes widened, and I shook my head, all *what-have-I-done* like. "Don't tell Sarah I'm creeping in on her job."

"I wouldn't dream of it."

Jared's house loomed at the end of a cul-de-sac, illuminated from the back with the remaining ripples of sunset. The blinds were still askew, and I could see Jeremy sitting idly in his chair while their mother checked and re-covered the dishes of food on the table.

Jared opened my door, a customary gesture, and as I climbed out, I felt struck by the scene through the window. Empathy seized my heart as I observed Laura. To me, she looked worn out. Her hair was done up at the back of her head with a claw clip, and much of it hung loose. She kept tucking it behind her ears rather than fixing it at the source. Her movements never ceased, and her features remained a strange sort of taut, schooled just enough for her to function, but the mask wasn't very convincing.

All that from one glance through the dining room window. This was going to be quite an evening.

Jared led me with one hand on the small of my back. I stopped just short of the welcome mat. "I've been here a handful of times, but why does this one feel so different?"

"Maybe you'd prefer to use the window." He gestured in the direction of his room.

Chuckling, I elbowed him in the chest. "That's probably it."

He unlocked and opened the door, pushing it open wide as he indicated for me to go ahead. I stepped inside the foyer, and he closed the door behind us and called out to his mom. "Hey, Mom. We're here."

"We?" came her curious voice from the other room. When Jared's mom rounded the corner, she looked back and forth at us in surprise. "Oh." Laura straightened her shirt and then tucked those masses of loose strands. She offered me a smile. "The famous Samantha Ballard, do we meet at last?"

"Yes, hi," I said, stepping forward and reaching out. We shook hands. "I'm sorry we didn't have time to arrange my visit ahead of time. I hope it's okay that I'm here."

"It's fine. I managed to keep the food warm, but let's not press our luck." She turned and waved for us to follow her. I elbowed Jared in the side again.

"Thanks, Mom," he said when he figured it out.

The dining room invited us in. The food was spread out across the table, atop a fine draping linen, as though it were a special holiday rather than an arbitrary day of the week. Jeremy looked up from his handheld gaming console when we entered the room.

"Sam! What are you doing here?"

"She's joining us for dinner, obviously. Scoot over and make room for her."

"But this is my seat."

Laura gave her youngest son a look and then withdrew a chair beside her. "Jeremy, don't be a baby. Move over here and let your brother sit by his girlfriend."

"And she prefers to be called Sammy, just so everyone knows," Jared added. My face flushed with heat at his defensiveness. It was true, but I was willing to go by anything as long as it kept the peace. I noticed the fragility of the atmosphere in this house more and more every time Jared opened his mouth.

Laura said a blessing over the dinner and thanked the Lord for my company tonight. My heart warmed, and with my head bowed and my eyes closed, I smiled, following up her prayer with my own sincere "Amen."

After we had all passed around the food and plated to our belly's content, Mrs. Tomlin turned to me.

"So, Sammy," she said with deliberation. "Will you be attending college soon?"

"No, actually. I'm a pretty unenthusiastic student." I laughed nervously.

"I understand that completely. I recently decided to enroll in some online classes to finally finish my degree. I gave up on college not even halfway through."

"You're taking classes? You didn't tell me that," Jared said.

She looked at him pointedly and rolled her shoulder. "You weren't around at the time."

"She told *me*," Jeremy piped in, casting a smug glance at his older brother. I could easily imagine that they were constantly at each other's throats. I had to pull my mouth to the side to quell a laugh. Underneath Jeremy's comment was the tension between Jared and their mother.

"What's your area of study?" I asked for my benefit as well as Jared's.

She sighed as though she was already doubting her choice to return. "Nursing." Now I understood why. That was a lot of schooling.

"That's really impressive, Mrs. Tomlin. You seem dedicated enough to make it happen."

"Thank you, dear. That's nice of you to say."

Wow. I really was becoming more positive.

"Do you have any alternative plans for this fall?" she probed.

"Well…" I smiled, sitting up higher in my chair and folding my hands in front of me. I'd been waiting all day to share this news with Jared, and now I would get to share it with his mom and brother, too. The more, the merrier! "Earlier in the summer, I applied to go on a mission trip with the church, and I just found out I was accepted." I redirected my gaze to Jared, craving his reaction more than any other. "It's official! I'm going to Mexico!"

A dark confusion settled on and clouded Jared's features. It threw me, so when his mom kept asking me questions, I scarcely paid attention.

"Congratulations, Sammy. That sounds like a wonderful opportunity. Have you always wanted to travel?"

"Not really. I never thought I'd be a missionary, either, but…" I rubbed the spot above my heart. "I really feel called to do this." It was about more than just running away, that much I knew to be true, but when Jared recoiled, doubts about everything else began pooling up inside my gut.

Laura nodded. "That's very nice. Good for you."

I greedily received her praise since I hadn't gotten any from Jared. He looked on fire for the topic, but not in the same way I was.

Laura continued, completely unaware. "How long will you be there? What sort of things will you do?"

"The trip is two months minimum. And I'm not totally sure yet. I just know it'll be like volunteer work. Helping the locals, maybe teaching some English or building stuff. Probably talking a lot about Jesus, too, but honestly, I'm still uncertain about the details because this is all brand new to me."

"I see. Well, that sounds exciting. And when do you leave?" asked Laura.

The pit in the bottom of my stomach grew. Now that Jared had given away his discontent at my news, I was afraid to make eye contact. "September."

"Aw, Sam, you're leaving? Are you guys gonna break up?"

"Shut up and eat your food, Jeremy," growled Jared.

Startling though it was to hear, it was a valid question. One, I had to admit, I didn't have the answer for myself, and that only confused me more. But maybe the mere fact that I was unsure was answer enough. When I considered Jared's odd reaction, what was I supposed to think?

Utensils clinked against plates as the table fell into momentary silence, save for the digital sounds of Jeremy's game. When I couldn't hold out anymore, I chanced a peek at Jared. Sure enough, his gaze was steely and harsh, his meal all but forgotten. How was I supposed to get through the car ride home, let alone leave the country, with the discord I already detected brewing between us?

"Don't let the fear of time apart stop you from loving each other."

Sarah's voice sounded in my head, but my obstinance fought her words. My fear had little to do with things when his behavior said loud and clear that he wasn't happy. It wasn't my fault that I'd happened to see it coming.

SAMMY

54

DESPITE MY INITIAL PRECONCEPTIONS AND THE AWKWARDNESS OF the post-summer plan talk, the rest of the evening went real well. Dare I say I even felt at home with the lot of them. Thanks to the skills I'd honed over the years with Ronnie and Caleb, gaming with Jared and his family was fun. I knew I'd scored points with Jeremy at least—no pun intended.

The car ride home afterward, however, was miserable.

Jared, for all his efforts to appear normal, couldn't convince me things were okay. My stomach remained in knots the entire time, and now, I was on the brink of complete disintegration.

"So, dinner was pretty nice, huh?" I hedged.

He nodded, muttering an agreement as he kept his eyes forward on the road.

"Were you worried it wouldn't go well?"

"Nah."

I nodded slowly into the darkness, growing weary of his distance, but I still lacked the nerve to bring it up.

By the time we were parked in front of my house, the negative mood had not subsided. I turned to him in my seat. "Please just rip off the Band-Aid already. I can't take it anymore."

"What Band-Aid?"

"I know you've been upset ever since I mentioned Mexico and we have to talk about it. Are you mad I'm going?"

"No."

"Then what is it? You weren't acting funny until then."

"I'm not mad. I just don't understand why you're going or why you waited until we were in front of my mom and brother to tell me about it. Why weren't you telling me about the process as it was going on?" I watched his upheaval morph into desperation. "Did I do something? Is this because I don't have as much free time as I used to? Are *you* mad at *me*?"

"No, I'm not mad at all."

"But you're something, right?"

"Maybe."

"Well, what?"

"I don't really know… Confused? I'm just trying to do right by this trip."

"What's that even mean?"

Oh, jeez. Where to begin?

I took a deep breath. "When I first signed up for it, I just wanted to be able to say I had a plan, something to do after the summer when everybody else went off to be successful." I looked out the window. "I didn't get into any of the colleges I applied for."

"Aw, Sammy… That doesn't mean—"

"Don't. It's fine *now*," I said, turning back to him. "But at the end of the school year, I was heartbroken and lost. Then, the moment I heard about the mission trip, I decided to try for it because it would get me somewhere. I would be able to say I did this awesome thing, that I didn't just sit at home and feel sorry for myself, feeling left behind by everyone. It was the perfect idea. I could even fib and say I chose it over college on purpose. I could pretend I had an ounce of control over my own life," I shouted, wondering at what point my voice had raised.

"And now that I'm committed to going," I continued, "I can't help but think while the timing is super perfect for me, it might be super bad for us. When Jeremy asked that question earlier at dinner, it was the first time I let myself really consider the possibility that we might not last… That we might not be right for each other."

"Slow down, you're saying a whole lot here, and I'm getting lost. At least, I hope I am. What are you saying?" His voice was like a razor blade to the sensitive parts of my soul.

"With everything going on, it might just be best if we didn't see each other anymore."

"I don't agree with that at all."

"Well, something made you react the way you did tonight. I didn't just imagine it all. You were upset I'm leaving, admit it."

"Okay, I already did, but I told you it wasn't for a bad reason. I was just surprised, and yeah, I'll miss you like crazy. That doesn't mean I don't want you to go. And it definitely doesn't mean we have to break up!"

"I was hoping you'd be excited with me. I even thought maybe one day you might want to join me on one if I continue going. Maybe being a missionary is my purpose, and if it is, we'd be taken away from each other a lot, one way or another."

"Those are all temporary things, and we don't know what the future looks like for either of us."

"You do! You have a football career now, Jared. Your dream is in the palm of your hand, and you have earned it. I haven't earned anything for myself. I don't know who I am!" My throat constricted, and I had to shout to get the words out. I surprised myself with the declaration, but it made the more stressed parts of me relax.

"Why haven't you come to me about any of this before? Sammy, I've always been here for you. Since you and I started this friendship, I mean really started putting effort into each other, we've been honest with each other. Why weren't you telling me about this?"

Jared's question, another well-founded one I didn't have an answer for, sent me spiraling deeper into the black hole my heart was becoming.

"I… I don't know. But as far as this trip goes, I feel like it's the right thing for me to do, and I don't want to feel guilty about it."

His brows and hands raised in defense. "Who's making you feel guilty?"

"I don't mean to say that you are, but it's how I feel regardless. You are moving forward with your life, and that's what you've worked for. You deserve to enjoy it and be happy."

"*You* make me happy!"

"I'm not making you happy now! And if we keep down this path, I'll only get in your way or hold you back. If not now, then soon enough. You know it's true."

"That's a ridiculous assumption, and you can't speak for me. I have my own part in this relationship, do I not?"

"Sometimes." My heart pinched. I couldn't believe I'd gone there.

"What's *that* supposed to mean?"

"Jared, I really don't want to do this right now. It's been a long day. Let's just sleep on this. I bet things seem better in the morning." I sure *hoped* they did.

"We're way past the point of no return now. Explain to me what you mean by *sometimes.*"

I breathed, slowing down so I could keep my voice steady. If we had to do this now, we would do this now. "I know how much you love football, and I'm so happy for you and proud of you, but I'm also a little sad for me at the same time. You are so busy, I've hardly seen you since preseason started, and when the real deal starts, it'll be even worse. It feels like you're heading in one direction, and I'm not going anywhere, not ultimately."

"You're mad because of football?"

"No, not really. I know I'm being irrational, and I know you're not doing anything wrong. It's me—my problem. I don't like how being jealous of your dream makes me feel, but I can't help it. And the closer I look at everything, the more I think what a bad idea our relationship was in the first place since you don't need me anymore."

"That's not true! I need you more than you know."

"You may desire me, but that's not the same. You basically used me to get over losing football when you thought you'd never get it back, and I used you to get over the crappy truth of my birth mother. All of that effort you mentioned we put into our friendship wasn't for no reason. So, in reality, we used each other. I'm at fault, too."

Jared tore at his hair. "For crying out loud, Sammy, that's not using each other; that's called being in a relationship. That's taking the hurt and turning it into something else. That's dealing with life's problems together. Isn't that what couples in love are supposed to do?"

I balked, his words slamming into me like a brick wall. "I know you did not just say that."

His expression turned like I'd never seen him before. All hints of his boyish charms were gone, leaving only a dark something else in its place. He must've anticipated a completely different reaction because my shock instantly aged him, transforming his youthful positivity into something weathered and glum.

In the end, he held my gaze firm, not backing down an inch. "So what if I did?"

"So, I don't want to hear it." But I did. Oh, God knew how I did. But it was too late now. Emotions were running too high, and I couldn't take it now. We both needed to go our separate ways for the night, if not longer.

But he was relentless.

"Maybe that's too bad," he said. "Maybe you need to hear it."

Shaking my head, I let my will pull me away from the situation. He didn't try to stop me when I opened the door. "I can't do this right now. Goodnight, Jared."

"I love you, Samantha Olivia Ballard!" he shouted before it closed, and I could all but picture the way he hung his head when I ignored him. I felt terrible, but *I* had to keep moving forward, too.

JARED

55

Long after Mom and Jeremy fell asleep, I remained wide awake, staring at the ceiling with my hands behind my head, replaying the night on repeat until I thought I'd go mad. My sound, rational brain couldn't process Sammy's logic, and even now, I fought the temptation to continue the argument, hoping against hope she would change her mind about ending things.

And that was the kicker. I fully supported her doing her own thing, but I couldn't get behind the way she was doing it. Leaving me based on her own misconceptions of my reality was not fair, and I didn't know how to convince her of it. I said I loved her, and I meant it, but that didn't magically give me all the answers.

God, what am I missing? What is she thinking? How can I fix this?

The prayer slipped out from the deep recesses of my mind. I almost didn't think to question it, but I blinked in wonder at my ceiling when I understood what I'd just done. I couldn't remember the last time I'd prayed; I almost didn't recognize it. Not just repeated a rhyme at mealtimes, but an actual speaking-to-the-Heavens prayer.

There came a light rapping on my window, rustling me from

my thoughts. Creeping over, I knew there was only one person it could be, and my heart spun around as if strapped into a carnival ride. I was getting another chance at this, so I had to really think through what I would say. We hadn't spoken since she stormed off in the middle of my first *I love you*, earlier.

All I knew was that I couldn't let her give up on us.

As I slid up the window, I gauged the look on her face, wishing her feelings were more discernible.

"Hey," I said, not much else coming to the forefront. *So far, so good. Just keep it cool.*

"Hey," she replied, her hands twisting in a nervous bundle in front of her. "Can I come in?"

"Always," I said and stepped aside, keeping one hand hooked under the window. When I closed it up, I asked, "Do you want to sit?"

"Sure." She turned and went over, sitting down lightly on the edge of my bed.

I stood in front of the window, arms folded tightly across my chest—an attempt to restrain the beastly, rapidly beating thing inside it. "What made you come back?"

"I didn't like how we left things, and I wanted to see how you were," she said, looking up at me, her question at the ready. "So, how are you?"

"That depends. Are you still breaking up with me?"

Her arms slightly rose, then fell in a heap into her lap. "Jared, I don't know how to make it work."

"It's easy: By committing to me, which you've already done. And by staying faithful, which I know you'd do. You'd get the same from me. So, I'm failing to see the problem."

"You don't think two months is a long time to sustain a new relationship on the phone? You will have even less time to spare than you do now, remember. It'll basically be like I no longer exist, and I can't expect you to hold back for me."

And we were back to this. My tether snapped, and I felt emotions rushing to my tongue, ready to run wild. There would be no holding anything back now. "Do you really think so little of me, Sammy? I just told you I love you, or didn't you hear it? Would I have said that if I was going to drop you the second things got a little challenging? And seriously, it's two months, not two years."

"How do you not see the differences in us? You are the embodiment of drive and direction and purpose. I only have Mexico, and I'm praying to God it gives me half of the direction and purpose you have. I need to figure myself out, Jared. This trip is the first thing I've been confident about in a long time. It's like it wasn't even a decision I made. I've never experienced anything like it. It all fell into place when I made the first step, even if it was with the wrong intentions. And I'm just plain excited to go now. God really wanted this for me all along; I know it."

As she spoke, I prepared a good and confident response for each statement she made until one specific comment smacked me like a rock in the face. "You weren't confident in *us*?"

Sammy sighed, her shoulders collapsing inward. "That's not what I meant."

"But it's what you said. You didn't—you *don't*—believe in *us*."

"I never said that," she whispered.

While she'd been talking earlier, I could see the point she was originally hoping to make, but now she was refusing to see mine. I stood and steeled myself. "Nothing about this seems right to me. You said you cared for me. We were insanely happy, but I'm suddenly just gone from the equation. You've made this big decision without me, which I guess is your prerogative since it's not like we're married or anything, but since we *are* supposed to be in a serious relationship, why am I not part of the discussion at least? I am your confidant and sounding board, Sammy. That means before I was anything else, I was your friend."

"I know, you're right."

"Then, we're not breaking up?" She didn't answer me, but the tears in her eyes spilled over, and her chin puckered, wobbling. My instinct was to pull her close to me and comfort her, make all her bad feelings go away, but her crying meant something bad for me, too. "I thought that you being here right now would make things better, but I don't think it has. Why'd you come? We could've just had this terrible conversation over the phone."

She reached out for me, taking hold of my arm. Out of desperation, I didn't move. "I tend to walk away rather than face things, and I didn't want to do that again. I didn't want you to have to go to sleep angry."

Oh, she had no idea just how angry I was getting. "Then why is this happening right now? We can still hit reverse. It can all go away."

"It can't, not for me. I'm starting to realize I'm good enough for God, but I'm still having trouble with trying to be good enough for people. It's hard to get out of my perfectionist mindset. I don't want to sort through my crap while you're supposed to be having the time of your life. I'm only going to bring you down. You don't need that."

"Stop doing this." Her tears had dried, and she seemed steadier than ever, which only made the way my heart spun out of control worse.

"I wish I could explain myself better. I feel a strange peace in mission work, and that's my path. It feels good and light, unwavering. God is my only certainty, and I'm not blaming you for that. I know I can make Him happy by doing this work for Him, and that's all I have."

"That is not all you have; you have me! And I'm not asking you to give anything up, Sammy. I don't know why you're prepositioning this as it's either me or God."

I couldn't believe I'd reached a point where I thought God and I were finally starting to understand each other, and now this? What a fresh blow.

First, He killed my father and took away my mother by way of her own broken heart. He narrowly missed stripping me of football and took away my best friend. Then, He gave me Sammy, only to rip her away from me in the end, too. I couldn't stand for it. I didn't want to do anything for a God that only ever gave me a hard time. Football was the only thing I'd have once Sammy left, and leave she would.

"I'm sorry." Her breath hitched, but she stood a little taller, fighting the newly formed mist in her eyes.

"You're really leaving just like that? I really get no say?"

"We can talk again when I get back if you still want to."

"I meant what I said tonight, but I'm not going to accept this. I want all or nothing. Right here, right now. If you leave tonight and we're not together, that's it."

So hard. It was *so hard* to watch her fight against the sting in her eyes. "I'm sorry I wasted your time, Jared. I wish this had gone differently."

"That makes two of us." Regret laced every syllable I uttered, but at that point, she probably couldn't tell. I barely could. I played the role of villain so well that even I believed I was a total jerk. If there was ever a chance God and I could reconcile, it felt long gone now.

With a heavy sigh, Sammy rose and stepped forward. With

her hands on my shoulders, she leaned up and kissed me on the cheek. I could only brace myself against it. "Goodbye, Jared."

Sammy's hands fell away, leaving a cold memory of her warmth. She left, and I felt more alone, more broken than I'd felt in a long time.

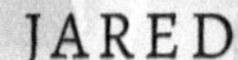

56

I MADE IT TO THE DINING ROOM AND SIGHED AS I PLOPPED INTO MY chair. Mom and Jeremy were still working on their breakfast, and a plate had been left out and covered for me. My fight with Sammy was still front and center in my brain, and I felt desperate to dislodge it. I had practice today, so I needed my head in the game and nowhere else. So, I attempted to shift my focus.

"Dinner last night was actually pretty good, Mom. Thanks for being cool about me bringing Sammy along. She really wanted to meet you." *Fail*. My focus would never be the same again.

"That's okay, it worked out. There was plenty of food and it was time I met her. She's very sweet and pretty. Seems good for you." Then, she looked up at me. "Wait, what do you mean by my food was *actually* pretty good? I've always been a good cook."

I suspected another fight was incoming, but I'd take that over thinking relentlessly of Sammy.

"Well, yeah, but it feels like it's been a while since we've really seen it, except for these fancy new dinners you make us do."

"That's part of why I decided to do the weekly dinners. At least we'll all be together once a week for a nice meal. But you know, you weren't even here on time, so I don't know where you get off being snarky with me. I got off work early so I could be home to make a nice dinner for us. I'm really trying here, Jared. Can't you cut me a little slack?"

"That's all I've been doing for going on two years now."

"You call what you've done cutting me slack? Do you expect perfection? Because that's never going to exist. It didn't even when your father was alive. Only then, it didn't feel like you hated me so much for it."

"I don't hate you."

She snorted, rolling her eyes, and the ends of her light brown hair dusted her shoulder. "Fooled me."

"I do hate how you act though."

"Oh yeah? And how do I act?"

"Like Dad was the only person who ever mattered to you. Like you can't enjoy your life just because he's gone."

Her throat quaked with a heavy swallow as her eyes pooled with tears. I didn't think I could take it once they started to fall, so I had to hurry, or I'd never get this out. Riding the waves of my break-up with Sammy was the worst time to be having a prickly heart-to-heart with my mom, but the floodgates couldn't be closed now. At least there was little chance it would go worse than last night. My mom couldn't dump me.

"You mope around the house, barely doing anything but cleaning and going to work, to the point that it seems like we don't even exist most of the time. There are entire days you don't look either of us in the eye." With a quick glance at Jeremy, I saw him shoot me a glare for bringing him into it, but he never refuted anything. "It's like you only love us enough to get mad, and that's the only thing you ever let yourself feel. Everything else is just gone. You don't smile or laugh. You don't spend any real time with us."

"That's crap. I care about you both as best I can."

"No, you don't, because I remember what it was like before. I've seen your best, and this isn't anything close to it. The way you've treated us since Dad died…" My hands fisted. "It's like we lost *both* parents. You've orphaned us with your lack of emotional stability. Frankly, the biggest reason I throw myself into football is to get away from here so I don't have to feel like such a burdensome afterthought to you. I realized when I injured my knee that I wasn't upset because I might not return to football again. I was upset because I might be stuck here at home."

One second bled into the next as she stared me down.

"Are you finished berating me? Is it my turn yet? Alright then, listen up. You may have a point, okay? I may have a heart so broken even my sons can't fix it, but that's not your fault and it isn't mine either. I lost my *husband*. Do you understand that? My true love, the man I pledged my life to, is dead and gone, and now one of the only people I have left is sitting here telling me what a horrible mother I am for still being hurt. I can't control this. I can't change how quickly I heal, but I can tell you I'm healing. It's slow and hard to see except in hindsight, but it's impossible to explain how big my love is for him or how daunting the hole in my heart still is now that he's not here to fill it.

"I know that I haven't been quite as Mary Sunshine as any of us would hope for, but does grief really make me such a terrible person? Do you really not know that I love you despite my shortcomings? Have I not shed endless tears for you and your brother? Do I not hope with every fiber of my being that there's a God up there so my prayers for your guys' futures are answered one day? Do I not work my butt off to keep your home paid for, taken care of? Do you and Jeremy ever go without any of your needs met, despite my *'lack of emotional stability?'* I love you both more than you could ever know, but you're going to have to stay patient with me. Someday, I will not be in so much pain. Someday, I will be better equipped to help with yours, but right now, you get me as I am. If it's not enough, then I'm sorry. Just know I'm working on it."

I. Am. Such. A. Jerk.

"Mom, I'm—"

"It's fine, Jared. You're allowed to be upset. But just remember, I am, too. And I don't think we need to talk about this anymore." She stood up from the table, scooting her chair back. She reached for the plates, mine having never been touched. Jeremy wasn't done with his and looked as though he might protest, but he remained still and silent. When she disappeared into the kitchen, he looked at me.

"Wow," he said.

I was at the same loss. "Yeah."

With a heavy sigh, I rose from the table and followed Mom into the kitchen, leaving Jeremy behind. This next part wasn't about him.

She didn't even turn when I entered. "I said I don't want to talk about it," she snapped, her arms already busy with the sink of dishes.

"I don't care!" I shouted. With an angered surprise, she turned and faced me. I hurried to continue. "You got everything you wanted to say out, but I'm not done. I didn't know how things were for you. I didn't want to make you feel bad. I'm *sorry*, okay?"

She crossed her arms.

"Say something."

"Your dad used to call me out like that." Her voice wasn't mad anymore, not even quite sad. "You got your bossy, dominant behavior from him." She laughed, almost like I wasn't even there anymore. "I hated it. He never let me just walk away. He always cornered me until things were resolved."

Just like I'd done with Sammy. "I guess I forgot that's something Dad used to do. He always made Jeremy and me work stuff out right away, too."

"As you always should." She sighed, the corners of her mouth soft and upturned. "He was a good man, Jared. And you're so much like him, more than you understand. He'd be proud you came after me."

"He wouldn't be proud I made you cry."

She chuckled. "He did it a time or two himself. Nobody is perfect. He would forgive you, and so do I. But one thing does bother me. Jared, I never cared whether or not you played football. I only wanted you to be happy. After your accident, all I wanted was for you to be safe and whole. Just don't convince yourself you're doing it for me. If you're not happy, then quit. Easy as that. If you're happy playing, then play. Doesn't matter what I like or don't like. Family is love, and that's all there is to it."

"So, you really don't care what I do? What if I decide robbing banks is the only thing that will ever make me happy from now on?"

"Don't overreact; that's not what I mean. I'm saying that you're my son, and my love for you will never change, regardless of your career choices. That's just the way it is. Now, I genuinely hope and pray for your success and happiness in life. I've always done so and always will."

"Thanks, Mom. I'll try to do the same for you."

She smiled. "Your dad would approve."

SAMMY

57

TWO SETS of eyes had been glued to me the entire morning, tracking my every move. Fed up with it, I pegged each one of my friends with an icy glare. "If you guys don't stop staring at me, I'm going to lose it."

On the outside, I was trying to be tranquil, joyous, and determined to have a nice time with my friends. On the inside, I was still thinking about the words Jared and I exchanged. My boyfriend and I had recently broken up. Did I really have the audacity to be this okay? My heart hurt, but I didn't feel like the world was ending around me. Did that mean I didn't ever love him? No, that wouldn't make sense. But maybe I had finally started to love *myself* somewhere in the midst of everything.

Yes, I believe I did. And I would enjoy my life to the fullest because what was the alternative? Utter misery? Unacceptable. Unthinkable. And out of my control. No amount of brooding was going to make things right between Jared and me, so why bother? Let go and let God, right?

"We're sorry, girl, really, but we can't just magically stop worrying about you. It wouldn't be natural. We love you." Birdie Jo averted her eyes long enough to tear a piece of tape off the dispenser and press it onto the end of a twisted streamer. Sarah did the same to the other side, across the room.

"Being loved is great, and I love all of you, too, but seriously. Enough. I'm not going to just spontaneously fall apart. You can all afford to worry a little bit less. Please, for my sanity." I needed it more than they knew—more than I wanted them to. The break-up was bad enough without my sweet but annoying friends constantly drawing attention to it. I would be okay, but they had to let me.

Birdie gave me a sympathetic look. "We're still adjusting to the news."

"I get that. Me too. Part of that adjustment is why we're throwing Jenna a surprise baby shower instead of throwing me a going-away party. Let's not forget why we're here." The only thing I wanted out of the day was normalcy, and apparently, that included throwing our barely eighteen-year-old best friend a baby shower months before necessary in peace. "Today is about Jenna and only Jenna. I need that. She needs it, too. Can we all agree?"

They exchanged glances as if conferring with one another if they'd allow it. In the end, I got a resounding, "Sure, of course." The decorating commenced without any more stares. *Thank You, God, for small favors.*

"Hey, how did you get your parents to let us borrow the living room for this, anyway?" Birdie Jo asked me. "My mom would never. Do they really know it's for a..." Birdie looked around as though the FBI might be listening. She lowered her voice. "...*baby shower?*"

"Yes, they know."

"Oh, wow. Are they cool with keeping it a secret?"

"They don't condone what happened or anything, but they're not here to judge or go spreading her business. They're not like that. And when I asked if we could turn my big going away party into a small baby shower for Jenna instead, even though I know it's traditionally too early to do this, they were willing to let me."

And thank God because we could all use a big dose of happy right now.

"That's really nice of them, Sammy. You're so lucky." Birdie Jo smiled, and I had to agree she was right. It was really big of them to be so accepting. They were even giving us the luxury of privacy. While the party was going on, they'd be hanging out upstairs and letting us be.

The three of us continued in quiet ease, letting the radio provide a soundtrack for our decorating. Sarah came up beside me and spoke softly, "I'll only bring it up this once because I know you don't want to talk about it anymore, but just try not to forget that you're not going through this alone, okay? It's normal if the people who love you, who *you* love, want to be there for you. Trust me. I'm speaking from experience." She supplemented this statement with a sweet, knowing smile.

"I'm trying, Sarah." *I'm really trying.*

Mom called out a minute later when Jenna arrived, and we all rushed out to meet her, swinging the doors closed behind us. She was entangled in one of Mom's hugs when we reached the entryway. Jenna was smiling but widened her eyes when she saw me.

"Mom, Jenna can't breathe."

Upon release, Jenna gave a nervous laugh, and Mom patted her cheek. "It's good to see you."

"Thanks, Mrs. B. You, too."

Turning to face the rest of us, Mom smiled. "I'll leave y'all to your fun. We'll be right upstairs if you guys need anything."

"Thanks, Mama," I said as she turned to leave. She disappeared up to their room, where Dad was watching the Cards win their latest game, hollering like the unapologetic St. Louis fan that he was. "So, Jenna. You hungry?"

She snickered. "Starved. Almost like there's a tiny, rapidly growing alien inside my body, stealing everything I eat before I get the chance to absorb it."

We all laughed.

Birdie sidled up beside her. "Ooh, I'm so excited for a baby!"

"You would be," Jenna countered. "I actually can't believe it wasn't you to go first."

"I'm going to be *married* first. You all know that."

"You say that now."

"And I'll say it later, too. I'm sorry, Jenna, I love you, but not everyone is a slave to their hormones," Birdie ribbed her. My eyes went wide with surprise, anticipating the backlash of the century.

So, imagine my shock when Jenna only laughed.

"I know, I know. You've got me there, Birdie. But unless somebody invents a time machine in the next five months, there's nothing I can do about it now."

"You never considered, ya know, an alternative?" I inquired, unable to avoid asking any longer.

"I may be stupid enough to get pregnant as a teenager, but I'd never get an abortion. Jeez, Sammy."

"Maybe she meant adoption," Sarah tried. "It is a topic close to her heart, after all."

"I meant both, actually." *Both* were a topic close to my heart. I just happened to be the best-case scenario between the two.

With a rugged exhale, Jenna shook her head. "I couldn't do that, either. I would always wonder where my child was. I would want her back. I know it would be a huge problem. It's just best if I get my life together before she's born."

"She?" I asked.

Jenna smiled, nodding. "I think so. I had a dream the baby was a girl. My mom told me a long time ago she always had dreams about the genders of her babies, and they were always right."

"Speaking of, does your family know yet? Or anyone else?" asked Birdie.

"Nope."

"You gotta have that conversation soon. You need pre-natal care."

"I'm taking vitamins and eating really good. I'll get the rest figured out eventually. I just need to take my time and do this right. When I think about rushing, I get scared. I don't want to tell my parents until I can prove to them I can do this."

Because she'll probably have to do it on her own, I thought. So sad.

"Jenna, can I feel?" Birdie was basically frothing at the mouth.

"There's nothing there to feel yet, but trust me, when there is, I'll give you first dibs."

Smiling, Birdie slung her arm through Jenna's, linking them together. "I can't wait."

"I heard that feeling the baby move is like gas bubbles," I offered. Everyone turned to look at me before laughter broke out.

"Thanks for that," Jenna said after catching her breath.

"You're so welcome."

"Didn't you say something about food earlier? So, like… Is there any?"

"Oh, yes! Right this way." We moved toward the family room, and I went ahead to stand in front of the French doors. It was as dark as we could make it inside, behind the frosted windows. "I just have one question for you first… are you ready to party?"

"Huh?"

As I flung the doors open, Sarah hung back and flicked on the lights. "Surprise!" we all shouted as decorations, food, and gifts came into view.

Immediately, Jenna was in tears. First laughter when surely there would've been blood, and now tears from our resident unfeeling ice-princess? Those pregnancy hormones were no joke. "You guys did all this for me?"

I pulled Jenna over to a spot on the couch. "We know. We're awesome, fantastic, and amazing. And you love us to pieces."

She laughed, throwing her arms around me. "Yes, exactly. I don't deserve friends like you. I know I've been awful. For a lot longer than this." She rubbed her belly. It wasn't even budding yet.

Sarah and Birdie flanked her other side. "Don't be silly. And even if you do get awful, which we're not saying you do, you're always deserving of us. We love *you* to pieces."

"I agree with Birdie," Sarah added.

"Agreed," I pitched in.

Jenna wiped her face and nodded toward the coffee table. There was a small collection of gift-wrapped goodies. "Are those for me?" She blinked her tear-coated lashes.

"They sure are!" I reached for one and let her dig in.

After Jenna finished opening her gifts, she sat back into the cushions and sighed. "I miss Daniel. And I hate him so much."

"That sounds not confusing at all," Sarah tittered.

"I know," Jenna wailed, throwing herself back. "Jared texted me the other day and told me about his conversation with Daniel when he went to visit. It made me feel better *and* worse."

Just hearing her mention Jared, reminding me that he was living his life, talking to my friend but not to me, threatened to undo all the joy I'd gained tonight. I couldn't let it.

"I wonder if his parents will let you visit when they find out about the baby."

"I love your optimism, Birdie, but that is *not* how that is gonna go. They already hate me, and with good reason. This will be the cherry on top of the cake."

"His parents do not *hate* you. You're a child; they have no right." Sarah tried and failed to convince her.

"But they really do, and it is what it is. For now, I'm just trying to keep things cool. If they want me to stay away while he's there, I'll stay away, but they can't say anything once he's released. I just have to try to get my life sorted as much as possible until then. Or who knows, maybe I'll move on without him, and Baby and I will be better off."

"You have time to figure it out," Sarah said, leaning her head against Jenna's.

"That I do."

SARAH WAS the last to leave that evening. Her hug lingered when we said goodbye. "You know, I've been praying for you. I think God is going to show up in your life in a big way soon."

"If you're talking about Jared, don't get your hopes up. He's so mad at God, I don't think he'd go for any miracles."

"You never know. You have to keep praying, too," she reminded me.

"I will. And I'm going to miss you all a ridiculous lot." This was our last hurrah before the end of summer split us up, even if it was only for a few months at a time.

"I'm going to miss you, too."

58

MEMORIES BREACHED THE SURFACE AS I RETURNED TO THE LOCKER room, and the hype from the field quickly vanished. I could barely pay attention to Coach's post-scrimmage pep talk, and nobody noticed. Good, I wouldn't want them to. How would I go about explaining things to them, anyway? They wouldn't understand how everything reminded me of Sammy, from looking out into the stands where she surprised me with a visit to the wind outside that used to whip her fallen hairs around, tickling my cheeks. I sounded pathetic, like I was living in some terrible 90s sitcom, but dang, if I wasn't telling the truth. I loved her, and I was miserable without her.

Looking at the small photo of her I hadn't removed from my locker flooded my mind with the memory of the first time I kissed her at the beach, the kiss that led to many others over the course of the summer. All over again, I was sent back to the beginning and forced to relive it all.

Maybe it was time to throw her photo away. Taped beside my favorite picture of my dad and me after my first win, it started to feel dark to have her up there still, like my locker had become a shrine to what was gone.

Tearing the picture down, I crumpled it up and shoved it in my bag. Then I stuffed my helmet and shoulder pads in my locker and peeled out of my practice jersey. When I reached for my phone, a text message from Sarah took me by surprise.

SARAH

You dummy.

That wasn't the kind of thing I would've expected to get from her.

JARED

What did I do now?

SARAH

You're really letting Sammy go?

Irritated, I ground my teeth. What choice had Sammy given me, exactly?

JARED

SHE dumped ME. And she's leaving the country.

SARAH

For two measly months, and the way she explained it, she didn't intend to break up with you. You forced yourself to break up with her.

JARED

That's BS.

SARAH

Is it?

Whatever the case, who says you can't still fix it? You want her back don't you?

More than anything.

I dropped my head hard against the lockers. The cold metal was a comfort to my heated flesh.

JARED

I don't know how to do that.

SARAH

Oh, Jared. Just have a little faith, will ya?

JARED

Trust me, if I have any left at all, it is, in fact, very little.

SARAH

Well, that's literally all you need. Remember the mustard seed?

Matthew 17:20. He said to them, "Because of your little faith. For truly, I say to you, if you have faith like a grain of mustard seed, you will say to this mountain, 'Move from here to there,' and it will move, and nothing will be impossible for you."

That even works for the mountains we place in front of ourselves when we think we know better.

Rising to the surface like a rogue wave rolling out from the depths during the perfect storm came the distinct timbre of my dad's voice...

"Don't worry about finding your own way, Jared. God already has the path marked for you."

But what the heck was I supposed to do with that?

JARED

59

September—First football game of freshman year.

In the locker room before our season-opening game, I should have been sharing in the excitement of my team. Rather than jitters, I had a pit of despair in my stomach.

Time to shake it off, Jared. You have a game to play. You have people counting on you. What are you if you're not a football player?

Getting my head in the game proved difficult. How did you throw your heart and soul into something when your heart belonged to someone else, and your soul was mere fragments of its former glory? The last month without her was terrible. I wanted to take back our stupid fight. I wanted Sammy to be there. I wanted her front and center in my life. I prevented myself from scanning the crowd because I knew she wouldn't be there, and not seeing her would feel like twisting a knife in my chest.

"Gather up, gentleman," Coach Evans shouted. "Go time in five minutes."

Some of us were seated on the benches, some were standing,

but all of us were gearing up and paying attention to our coach, who stood in the middle of the group. We'd spent the summer practicing, sweating, laughing, and working harder than ever, and this was the night it all came together. All our frustrations, on and off the field, would be present in tonight's game. Especially mine.

Colin took a seat to my right. Mac stood to my left with his arms folded, swaying back and forth on his anxious feet.

Coach smiled with a look of pointed determination. "Alright, men. You know why we're here. Winning isn't just what we do—it's who we are. It's what got you here, and it's what's gonna keep you here.

"Every name on that jersey means something. To your family. To this team. To every fan in those stands. And when that final whistle blows, people are gonna remember how you played today. They'll remember if you fought for every yard, every tackle, every single second on that clock.

"So, ask yourself—do you want to be remembered as a player who showed up or a player who took over? Because we don't just play this game. We own it. Now, get out there and prove it! LET'S GO!"

"Yeah!" shouted Colin, hands coming together in commendation.

Mac punched the air with his fist. A few others whistled or shouted their added approval. Coach Evans' words were met with unanimous applause and yelling, my own blending in with the rest. Finally, I was ready. This is what I needed. We were all feeling the coach's zeal at this point, chomping at the bit to be released onto the field to do what we did best.

I blocked out all thoughts of my mom's declaration that she didn't care if I played. Who cared if my girlfriend—correction, ex-girlfriend—was not there for me tonight? And what did it matter if Coach Evans' speech was the complete opposite of Coach Haworth's after my last game? That was high school. This was college. If we were lucky, this was the next step before the NFL for some of us. The only thing I couldn't figure out, and the thing I let the hype distract me from most, was whether or not I wanted to be one of those lucky ones.

WE WON. My first game of college ball in the books was a win. Not by a landslide, rather by the skin of our teeth, but we were victorious. The celebration in the stands followed us into the locker room, where the guys were downright chaotic with joy. I was happy to have played my part skillfully, knowing that my dad would have been proud. However, this time, I couldn't deny that my excitement was lacking compared to theirs.

The first thing on my mind when Trent made that final crossing into the end zone was Sammy's beautiful face and what her reaction would've been had she seen it. I imagined her pulling off my helmet to kiss me and the feeling of her arms squeezing around my neck as I spun her around. She would have joy to match my teammates. As I should.

Mac dropped himself onto the bench beside me. "Tomlin, man. You're aware we just won our opening game, right? You look like somebody just died."

Maybe it was me. Maybe that's why I felt the hollow void in my chest growing bigger by the second. If winning my first college game couldn't fill it, I didn't know what could. That had been my dream, my identity, for so long, and here it was in full.

And yet, all I could think about was the absence of the two people I wanted there most tonight.

The thing that really got me was that one of them could've been, were it not for me. On one account, at least, I did this to myself. Sarah had been right to call me out. I did want her back, even now, though I hadn't done anything to make it happen. I hadn't even prayed about it like she told me to.

I faked my way out from under Mac's scrutiny and casually excused myself from the post-game activities. I didn't bother showering, either; I just changed and took off, and before I could talk myself out of it, I drove to the cemetery. Desperate though I was to say hello to my dad just one more time, something weighing on my heart told me my only choice was to finally say goodbye.

60

I'd only visited Dad's grave a couple of times, and always with Mom. She'd brought flowers on his birthday but not on the anniversary of his death. She only wanted to celebrate his life, she'd said. The date of his death brought enough sorrow; she didn't want to emphasize it with floral embellishments.

It was a long walk from the road to his grave. The closer I got, the more I felt at ease, though I had no idea what I was going to do or say.

"Hey, Dad." I dropped to my knees, pressing them into the manicured earth blanket which covered him. "Played my first college game tonight. We won." Sniffing, I rubbed my nose. "I wish you could've seen it."

I sat back on my haunches, looking upward. Suddenly, the truth fell into my lap like a meteor from the Heavens. My nerves fired from every ending as it finally manifested in words. "For some reason..." I choked out the words through tears, now fallen. "It took this win for me to admit I don't want to play anymore. I don't want to be in the NFL. I don't want to be only football."

I can't believe I actually said that.

His headstone remained silent in front of me. Silent but comforting. "I hope that you're not turning over down there... Bad joke, but you probably would've laughed. I'd give anything for your advice right now," I added on a deep sigh.

Grinning at the new direction of my thoughts, I figured it was time I opened up about everything else. "I met a girl." I told him all about her, everything from her sweet and spicy personality to her unique adoption, down to the way she filled me to the brim with happiness like helium in a birthday balloon.

I even confessed how crazy stupid I was to have let Sammy go, just like Sarah said. "What would you tell me to do if you were here?" I beseeched the stone. "What should I do to get her back?"

Of course, Dad's grave couldn't talk back, and I was utterly alone in this cemetery. Still, something became abundantly clear to me just the same: If I let Sammy go for good, I would never forgive myself. I had to believe it wasn't too late.

She was still going to Mexico, and soon, so I needed to suck it up and work on my patience—something my mom pointed out I was sorely lacking. I could even try praying for her. All I knew was it couldn't end like this. I needed her back in my life. I wanted to forge whatever my new future was with her by my side.

Before going home, I rested my head against the steering wheel a moment, utterly exhausted mentally and physically. Then, I nearly blacked out when I saw my text messages.

SAMMY

Congratulations on your win. I'm so proud of you.

Oh, the things my heart was doing. I already had hope we

could make things right for us. It must be why this was the first I'd heard from her in weeks. *It's a sign.*

JARED

Thank you.

Be honest, Jared. Be bold.

JARED

I wished you were there the whole time.

SAMMY

I wish I had been, too. Would've blown that last game senior year out of the water, I'm sure.

JARED

As long as you didn't show up with Adam Alvarado…

SAMMY

Who knows? I hear he hasn't shipped out yet…

JARED

You wouldn't dare.

SAMMY

You're probably right.

She wouldn't usually back down from a challenge like that. Maybe this really was an opportunity for reconciliation. I had to jump on it.

JARED

I really miss you.

It took her a while to respond. The phone repeatedly told me she was typing and then not typing, and I thought I'd go mad watching it happen.

SAMMY

I miss you, too.

It was what I was hoping to hear, and yet it wasn't as reassuring as I'd wanted.

JARED

Then why are we doing this to ourselves? Why aren't we together?

If the will-she-won't-she of her typing was bad before, it was downright torturous now. So many minutes passed that I had turned my car on and prepared to leave the cemetery when my phone finally dinged again.

SAMMY

I'm still leaving in a few days. Nothing has changed.

JARED

I have. And I want you back. Please, I'll do anything to show it to you.

SAMMY

I want to believe you, but maybe it's just best this way for now. You should enjoy your season and we'll talk again when I get home, like I offered before.

JARED

That's not what I want.

She didn't respond again, and I had no choice but to head

home. However, her silence didn't register as rejection, and I remained undeterred in my determination to get her back.

Mom opened the front door and came outside as I was parking in the driveway. I met her under the alcove and sat beside her on the curve. "What happened to you after the game? We waited for you until I saw your car had left the parking lot."

"Sorry. I went to see Dad." I looked her square in the eyes. "Mom... I decided I don't want to play football anymore."

With a look of empathy on her face, she nodded. "I didn't think so."

"Are you really not upset?"

"Absolutely not. I told you I only want you to play football if it's what you love. You've worked very hard, so just be sure you know what you're doing before you make any official decisions. And in the name of parenting, I need to remind you that you're a scholarship kid. If you quit now, we can't afford for you to stay enrolled there, but I don't believe that's any reason to keep doing something so demanding if it's not making you happy. You just need to be sure about it, either way."

"I don't even know if college is what I want."

"Quitting football will be a huge change in other ways, too. You've been a serious athlete for so long. Are you ready to not be one anymore?"

"Yes." Without a doubt.

"So, what do you want to do?"

"I don't know. But I want to be with Sammy."

"Jared... Please tell me you're not throwing away your scholarship over a girl. Even one as sweet as her. You guys are so young."

"I'm not. I'm just talking. She's the only thing I'm sure of at the moment."

Mom watched me, looking unsure of what to say. Eventually, she patted my knee. "You're a sweet kid. And I think you are smart enough to make a decision I don't have to be afraid of, but you have to be smart about this. You need a direction with an attainable goal. If you wander aimlessly at this stage of life, you run the risk of never coming out of it."

I thought of Claudia Ballard. She had been an extreme sort of aimless at our age. Sammy had shared as much. Next, I thought of Dan and Jenna. Their aimless behavior had gotten them into some serious, lasting trouble, too. The sort that had spilled over and almost claimed the football career I now wanted to give up.

"I don't want to make any decisions for anyone else anymore, and that's kind of the point. She's not the cause of my change of heart. I just don't actually love it like I thought I did. I thought I had to love it to stay close to Dad and to make you happy."

Reaching her arm around my shoulder, she yanked me in. I felt her sigh against my chest. "I'm so sorry you ever thought that, Jared. And I'm so sorry you thought that about your dad. He's so close to us still every day, and he'll never go anywhere."

"I get that now."

"So then, what are we going to do next? What do you need from me?"

Taking myself by surprise, I said the only thing I could think of. "Prayers."

SAMMY

61

My heart was still hurting. I reached up and touched my necklace, which I refused to take off. I missed Jared so much, and knowing he missed me tore me up inside. He'd asked me a valid question the other night: Why aren't we together? I'd pondered it while we texted, and I still pondered it now.

When he said he wanted me back and would do anything, I desperately wanted to take him up on his offer. But my circumstances hadn't changed, and I didn't want to make decisions out of desperation. I didn't want to let the old me return when I was doing a decent job of accepting the new—*real*—me.

I'd made a commitment to myself, to God, to follow His will. And I felt like sometimes that meant taking no action at all. Before, I would've stomped headlong toward something *I* wanted for my own reasons. They didn't call me The Bull for nothing. So, why wouldn't I charge ahead with that same determination when it was His desires?

Because of my strengthened faith, the old adage rang more true than ever: You don't always get what you want, but you'll always have what you need. Jared still had a lot to work out regarding his own faith. I could never get in the way of that.

And *this* time, I said that out of love, not out of fear.

To help lure me out of my sadness or maybe to share a bit of it with me, Sarah video-called me while I packed. I intended to tell her all about my conversation with Jared, but I held it back. I knew talking it out with her wouldn't change a thing, and the further down my heart was on my sleeve, the more it hurt. I wanted to look forward, not keep glancing behind.

Sifting through my closet, I picked a handful of T-shirts and laid them across my bed. One by one, I rolled them up and stuffed them into my suitcase. Something other than Jared had recently returned to the forefront of my mind.

With a sigh, I plopped onto the bed, adjusting my phone on my nightstand. "Sarah, I have to tell you something."

She looked expectantly, endearingly. "What is it?"

"I went to visit Kevin in jail earlier this summer."

A glimmer of shock registered over her features. "You did?" She didn't appear *mad*, so that was encouraging.

"Yes, I did, and originally, I didn't want you to know about it because of how hard the whole situation was for you, but you've practically been your old self lately, and I didn't want any unfinished business clouding my mind while in Mexico. I want to feel free of all my burdens, big and small. Know what I mean? And I think you deserve to know now that it looks like you can handle hearing it. I just didn't want to cause you any additional hurt. I really hope you're not mad."

"I don't think I'm mad. I think I'm just surprised. Why did you go exactly? How was he?"

"Are you sure you want to know?"

"Definitely."

Inspired, I told her everything, how he showed me the letter and keeps it with him at all times. How he's reading the Bible and talking about God with his peers. How well he'd done graduating. Even how he wished me a happy birthday. The best part was telling her how obviously, deeply, and unapologetically in love with her he was. My divulging ended in mutual happy tears. It was unfortunate she wasn't around for a hug.

"You were so right to hold on to this until now. I couldn't imagine having waited all this time with it in my heart. Kevin asked me not to contact him, and that was the worst part of getting over him, but only to the point where I could function happily again without him. I could never truly move on from him. I can't forget him. He's my forever, I know it. If he had only let me stay in contact..." She waved her hands. "Whatever, I know he had his reasons, and I did my all to respect them. But, Sammy, I have a secret to confess, too."

"What is it?" I asked, just as curious and eager as she had earlier.

"Kevin gets out in October. Between making plans for school and my move, I've been making plans with help from his mom to surprise him when he gets home."

"So, *you're* coming home next month?"

"Yep! Just for a day or two. Long enough to spend some time with him, do my laundry, and go back."

"That's so exciting, but I'm sad I'll be missing it. I can't believe I'm about to go months without my best friends. I'm going to Mexico, and you're at college—*four hours away*, I might add. Jenna is becoming a mother; Birdie is invested in Nick and her volunteering... Growing up is hard on friendships."

"It won't be that hard on ours. I have confidence in the four of us. I will always need you guys, no matter what my life looks like."

"Ditto, girl. Love you."

"I love you, too. Oh, what about your job at the cafe?"

"Cindie says I can go back when I'm ready. It's all good there."

"That's awesome. I'm glad to hear it. But are you sure you're okay in general? I mean, this was kind of an eventful summer."

I chuckled. "It sure was."

"So, are you?"

I considered a moment. "Well, I don't hold anything against Claudia anymore because I see that, in her own way, she cared for me as best she could. I have no right to judge her for what could've been or should've been. She *could've* done a whole lot worse. At least I was born. At least I grew up knowing unconditional love."

And that was it. The difference.

Claudia loved me unconditionally because she made the hard decision to give me up for my benefit. My parents loved me unconditionally because they made the selfless choice to love me when they didn't have to. And Jared loved me unconditionally by showing up for me when no one else did, for having so much faith in our relationship he'd fight with me to try and save it, and for saying he loved me, sharing his truest feelings even in the middle of an argument when he could've easily kept silent to protect himself. All because he felt I deserved to know.

And *I* loved Claudia unconditionally by appreciating her sacrifice. It didn't matter if she was turning a new leaf now or if she went back to her old ways in a week. I knew where I stood and why, and I forgave her. I loved my parents unconditionally because I'd be nowhere, probably dead, without them. I could never, even during an internal identity crisis, denounce them as my parents. And I loved Jared, my sweet, silly boy, unconditionally because I had loved him enough to let him go. Like Claudia, I would give him up so he could live the life he had been working for.

My voice faltered slightly, but I managed to respond. "Yeah. Yes," I said more firmly. "I'm okay." Because that was the choice I'd made.

62

PASTOR BRIAN MADE HIS ANNOUNCEMENT, LED US IN PRAYER, AND everyone commenced loading their gear into the mid-sized bus that would take us four and a half hours to our destination. My heart was full of the luxury of solace. I knew I was doing the right thing, but I couldn't stop myself from missing Jared. In spite of myself, I wondered what it would've been like had he joined me on this trip. I imagined he would be here right now, his hand in mine, as we set off on a new adventure.

If only.

Getting into the line to load, I took one last peek at my notifications. I saw a few texts in the girls' group chat and another from my mom. But nothing else. With resignation, I pocketed my phone and took a deep breath, shuffling toward the bus door.

"Thank God I'm not too late," came a deep, familiar rasp from behind me.

When I registered the speaker, I was startled in the most comforting way. Turning around and beholding Jared, my heart almost burst. He wore an old Corpus Christi Titans baseball cap, a training tee, and simple jeans. But on his face, he wore the most beautiful, most perfect image of repentance.

I didn't protest at all when he tugged me by the elbow out of the line. "What are you doing here?" I rushed out in my surprise.

Standing in front of me, my back pressed against a towering live oak, Jared smiled. "I have so much to say to you before you go."

"I don't have a lot of time."

"I know, so first things first. I am so, so sorry for the way I behaved. I somehow managed to take my love for you and let fear twist it up into something ugly. I never should have pushed you away. I should have drawn you closer." At this, he stepped forward, twisting his cap around so the bill was pointing backward, then he let his hands resume their natural position on my hips. "I was hurting, not that that makes any of it okay. I shouldn't have made you leave me, Sammy. I should've fought harder for us."

I felt like I would float away if he weren't holding me down. I was inexorably caught in his gaze, held captive by his tender hands. When I managed to creak open my mouth, I hardly recognized my whisp of a voice. "You said if I left, we were over."

"But I didn't want that. I hoped by refusing to be reasonable, you'd decide to stay, and we'd make everything all better. I know it was stupid."

"Then what did you come here to say?"

"What I've already told everyone else: I'm quitting football and leaving the university."

"What?" I cried. "Why would you do something like that?"

"Because I don't want to play." He laughed. He *laughed?*

"I don't understand. Football has always been your dream."

"School isn't going anywhere. I can always attend later, and

I'm footballed out. It was my dream for a while, but dreams change. It just stinks it took me so long to learn that."

"You're serious about giving it up? Your scholarship and everything…"

"I don't feel like I'm giving up anything." I was made aware once again of his hands on my hips as his fingers tightened their grip. "I understand what you mean now. That strange peace you said you had about your decision, I have it, too. It's real."

"So real," I agreed, elated by his revelation.

"When my mom explained she didn't care if I played football again, I realized I was never playing for her like I thought I was. That was just a convenient excuse I'd made up for myself when I decided I couldn't deal with my dad's death. But my mom and I, well, we talk a lot more now. It's really helped.

"Once I realized what I really wanted, it was so easy to quit and say goodbye to the rest. Zero hesitation. Zero regrets."

Yes! My mind shouted, cheering for Jared. We all needed that sort of supernatural assurance, and now he had it. "So, what is it you want to do for *you?*"

"For me, since talking about things is so helpful, I want to start going to church again. Actually, my mom, my brother, and I will all start going again. But I have a lot to re-learn about God. Figuring out what I've spent so much time rejecting and why, then overcoming it is going to take a lot of work. I thought maybe Tyler could help me."

"Jared, that's so amazing. He's done so much work in your life in so short a time."

"Yours, too," he pointed out.

"Absolutely."

"And something else I want is to be with you. Forever. Or for as long as you will tolerate me. No, I take that back. Let's just leave it at forever. Final answer. And I want to go on a mission with you someday. For God, and for me."

As I listened, I bit my bottom lip in an attempt to school my features. "What if I say I don't want to be together anymore?"

"That will suck for my ego, but my heart can take it. And I'll consider it a temporary, minor setback because I have no plans to let you get away long-term. I love you, Samantha. That has not and never will change. But if you need to take your time in Mexico and think things over, I'll give it to you gladly. But just know, when you return, I'm going to be right here to pick up where we left off."

"Maybe we can let God lead us both."

"That's exactly why I'm here."

It was everything I wanted to hear and more. My eyes stung, but I was too joyous for tears, even happy ones. "I love you, too, by the way." It felt *so* good to finally say those words back to him. "And *I'm* sorry. I wanted to say I loved you the second you said it to me, but I was so eaten up by insecurity then. I never really wanted to break up."

"It feels so good to hear you say that."

Unable to resist any longer, I threw my arms around his neck, leaping up with so much force he had to grab hold of me to steady himself. I peppered his pretty face with kisses, making him laugh.

"Does this mean you *do* want to be together?"

"You bet your butt it does!"

EPILOGUE

SAMMY

WE MADE it to the mission compound right before sunset. Stepping out into the clear March evening, I beamed, taking in the surrounding vibrant culture. "I can't believe I'm in Mexico again or that I'm here with you this time."

"*I* can't believe I sat in that bus for so long." Jared stretched his back out, moaning and groaning like an old man. "I'm so out of shape."

"That's the kinda thing that happens when you're no longer a star athlete."

"Are you saying that from experience?"

"Does it look like I'm out of shape?" I eyed him questioningly, though his answer was irrelevant. I knew what I had.

Jokes. I had jokes. Mostly.

Jared smirked, and his Southern charm activated. "No, ma'am, it does not." Reaching for me, I gladly stepped into his embrace.

"I'm glad I'm here with you, too. This is going to be an interesting experience."

The stunning beam of deep pink that highlighted the upper trim of the compound seemed to agree with him.

"It would've been cool if you'd been here the first time. Your height and muscle would've come in handy while building this place."

The compound was a fair mix of necessity and comfort. There were dormitories, separated by gender, with bunks and a bathroom each. There was indoor plumbing for the toilets—thank you, Jesus—but the showers were cold. After a day of working in the sun though, I couldn't imagine showering in anything but ice water. And then, of course, there was a kitchen and a common room for prayer, worship, and team-building activities. Oh, and storage areas. Not all of that was finished by the time my trip ended last year, so I was excited to see how it all came together.

Too bad we were only serving two weeks this go-around, though it seemed like a decent length to introduce Jared to the lifestyle. It was spring break, and the community wanted us to put on a vacation Bible school for the local children. We had one week to set up, explore, and get to know the community, four days for the program, and the rest for outreach through our sister church.

Jared was worried he wouldn't do a good job, bless his heart. When Pastor Brian told me about this trip, talking about how much it would focus on the children this time, I knew it was something he would rock at. Whether or not he enjoyed sweating all day and cold showers every night remained to be seen, but I had confidence in him. He'd come a long way and was ready to serve God's people.

So far, VBS was a hit! Jared rocked at it, just as suspected, and now we were on day four, the outdoor finale. We had an inflatable water slide, water balloons, a sprinkler obstacle course, and my personal favorite, beach volleyball!

And by beach volleyball, I meant two kiddy pools filled with play sand on either side of a makeshift net. It was my awesome idea, thank you very much, and the kids were loving it. Anytime one team scored, their opponent would get sprayed with water guns. What's not to love?

This round, Jared and I faced off with a kid under our wing. It was me and Valentina versus him and little Rolando Jr. Two of our fellow missionaries stood watch at either end of the net, loaded arms at the ready. The score was tied in the third set, with only two points left to win. I would have to hand it to Jared; he had improved since our first days playing back home, and his young buddy did much to help out. But my girl Valentina and I would *not* be going down today!

Time to bring out The Bull.

"Why do you always force me to make you look bad in front of the children, Jared, honey?"

He sneered. "I know your tactics, Sammy, dear. Your remarks have no power over me."

I shrugged. "So says the loser."

"Think again. Today is the day I hobble The Bull, mark my words."

Making *'blah blah blah'* movements with my hands, I ended my jeering by blowing him a kiss. Then, to Valentina, I said, "Do you hear this guy? *Él está muy loco, no?*" She giggled, nodding in agreement.

As I was fixing to make my serve, Jared busted out with this: "Hurry up and pitch the ball, Ballard!"

I broke into laughter and faltered my movements, just barely getting the ball past the net. With the slowness of my serve on his side, Rolando lurched forward and spiked it right back over. Startled, Valentina and I sprang for the return but did not succeed.

"Ha! He made a basket!" Jared yelled with his arms up in the air in celebration. Rolando jumped up and down until he met Jared for a high-five.

"Not a basket! A spike!" Valentina shouted as though she couldn't believe her ears.

"And a match point, at that," I grumbled, still laughing. "But the game ain't over yet. How about we make this game a little more interesting?"

"What did you have in mind?"

"In addition to getting completely soaked by our lovely referees here," the kids both tittered with excitement, "how about we throw in a dare, too?"

"A dare? You can't be serious."

"Oh, but I am."

"Okay then. I guess The Bull has spoken."

"Time to serve up, Jare. Let's see how badly you want to be a winner."

LATER, as Jared sat drip-drying on the front porch steps of the compound, I stood up and faced him. "Okay, Soggy McGee. It's time for me to cash in on my additional winnings."

"Uh oh." He leered, looking suspiciously at me.

"I dare you to kiss me," I said, my hands folded sweetly behind my back. "And remember, you have to do it. Them's the rules."

Contemplation scurried across Jared's features until, at last, he rose, stepping toward me. "Well, no, I don't," he said, coming closer, taking my hand in his. "But I will, as long as you're willing."

Squeezing his hand once more, I nodded. "I'll always be willing."

"Good. But before this goes any further, I just need you to know something."

"What?"

He leaned down and whispered against my ear, "I lost on purpose."

"Yeah right!" I snapped up, accessing his features. "And why would you do that?"

"To find out what you'd dare me to do," he said with a snide grin, then ran his hands through his hair wildly, shaking drops on me. "Totally worth it," he said before leaning in for the kiss.

God had led us down wildly different paths than either of us expected. Having come through some of those changes already, we were so happy with the love we shared and so grateful to the Father who brought us together. He had His hand in our relationship from the very beginning, from my earliest moments of friendship and compassion after our first adventure at the beach to Jared coming to my rescue on the side of the highway in his great white steed, all the way to him taking his latest volleyball loss like a loving champion.

And as Jared and I enjoyed our last days on our first joint mission trip, I knew it would not be the last. We'd both spent our lives living up to the expectations we'd placed on ourselves for the benefit of others, not knowing we were never quite grasping our true callings in life. Now, we grasped those callings with two hands, charging toward them each and every day with renewed purpose.

Together.

Become a *Renewed Heartie!*

- **More personable encounters with me and my writing process**

- **Upcoming projects**

- **Giveaways**

- **And more!**

www.facebook.com/groups/renewedhearties

For a limited time, join the group and share a post with your favorite quote from *From Mourning to Dancing* and you'll be entered to win a $50 Amazon gift card!

Giveaway runs from April 2, 2025 - April 30, 2025.

ACKNOWLEDGMENTS

Thank you, GOD. I can't write these books well alone, but without You, I can't write them at all.

To my amazing early readers: Thank you, Orlando, Jim, Philip, MJ, Alyssa, and Allison. I'm so grateful to have such a faithful and committed team. You're not just people willing to give up your time to read for me, which you certainly do, but you are friends, confidants, and genuinely awesome, supportive human beings! You always manage to understand and appreciate the heart of these books in ways I couldn't even see myself. You are each incredibly invaluable, unwaveringly encouraging, and you all bring a little something different to the table each time. Without you all, this process fails.

Cara, thank you for sticking it out with me for so long and being a true cheerleader the whole way through.

Kirsta, thank you for your last minute input! I don't know if I've reminded you lately how much you mean to me, but it's a lot. If only we could be 17 again, with our midnight fast food, playing Mario on SNES, while waiting for the phone to ring. We sure had some wild times, lol.

Thank you, Brianna, for graciously letting me borrow your grandmother's name for this story.

And thank you, dear reader, for picking up this book!

LOVE YOU ALL & GOD BLESS — HEATHER

ABOUT THE AUTHOR

HEATHER CAMACHO'S mission is to tell stories of love and faith, dedicating her craft to sharing the testimonies, truths, and promises of the Word with readers worldwide.

A Midwesterner turned Texan, she resides on a small ranch in the southern coastal region with her husband, three kids, and their many animals.

When she isn't writing, reading, or homeschooling, she enjoys sewing clothes for her children, making quilts for her friends and spending time with her horses.

WWW.HEATHERCAMACHO.COM

facebook.com/HeatherCamachoAuthor

instagram.com/heather.author

threads.net/@heather.author

amazon.com/author/heathercamacho

goodreads.com/heathercamacho

tiktok.com/@heather.author

www.ingramcontent.com/pod-product-compliance
Lightning Source LLC
Chambersburg PA
CBHW030751310726
48969CB00005B/1365